IMPROPER ADVANCE

"Shall I put you in your place, madam?"
The earl's voice was husky and very close.

With gentle firmness, he cradled the
back of her head in his large palm, tipping it
to bring her face up toward his. Sloane
gasped silently at the desire burning in his
eyes and willed herself not to respond as he
lowered his head to cover her mouth with his.

She expected a harsh kiss, one meant to
prove mastery, but instead, his lips brushed
against hers gently, coaxing, teasing, and
chiding with devastating sweetness. In spite
of her determination to remain unmoved,
Sloane's response was instant and knowing—
and explosive.

UNWILLING HEART

Sharon Gillenwater

To Paula, who dared me to try; my son Justin, for all the times he patiently waited "just a minute"; my agent, Olga Wieser, for taking a chance on a rookie and not giving up; and especially my husband, Gene, for his love, advice, encouragement, and unwaivering belief that I'd succeed.

Book Margins, Inc.

A BMI Edition

Published by special arrangement with Dorchester Publishing

Printed in the United States of America.

UNWILLING HEART

1

"Confound it, Tearle. Open the door."

Tearle Louis Grayson, Earl of Beckford, cast a mildly amused glance at his irritated brother-in-law, Viscount Bailey Mathers. If Bailey had known the earl in his younger days, he would have realized the sparkling eyes and twitch of the lip meant mischief was in the making.

As it was, Bailey stood impatiently on the portico of the earl's country house, tapping his foot and glaring at him. "Why the devil don't you open the door?"

"Can't. It's locked." While his friend sputtered over this new information, the earl lifted the brass, lion head knocker and pounded on the door. The sound echoed through the massive honey-colored stone house to be met with momentary silence.

The earl turned away from the door, his gaze skimming past the four great Corinthian columns of the portico to study the surrounding grounds. He nodded his head in approval of the freshly mowed green grass and the brilliant sweeps of daisies, fragrant lavender, and red and white carnations blooming on this sunny June day of 1818. Beyond the expanse of grass, creamy violets with deep purple centers, pink and white snapdragons, and blue Johnny-jump-ups cast delicate strokes of color beside the paths which roamed among the elm, maple, and oak trees scattered around the house.

"Grimley always keeps the door locked if he is in the inner regions of the house. Has a fear of burglars, don't you see," he explained, looking back at his brother-in-law.

Bailey was just about to reply that no, he didn't see, but closed his mouth upon hearing an indistinguishable bellow come from somewhere inside the stone walls. He shot the earl a disbelieving look and muttered something about bedlam when the sound came again, more clearly this time.

"I'm coming, I'm coming! Give a man a chance to get there. Keep your hat on."

The lock clicked and the door swung open to reveal the elderly butler, tall and thin, his frown contradicted by the twinkle in his eyes at the sight of his lordship. He stepped aside, opening the double doors wide to allow the two gentlemen to enter.

"Welcome home, m'lord. You weren't expected until tomorrow." His gruff manner implied his lordship should have had the decency to wait until his scheduled arrival.

The earl stifled a chuckle. "Bailey was quite anxious to return. You know how it is with these new fathers-to-be."

"Can't say that I do, sir, having never been a father myself. I trust the last two months have treated you tolerably well, m'lord?"

"Tolerably, Grimley. We've covered a great deal of territory during the time. Paris and Venice were particularly pleasant, but it's good to be home on English soil again and back in Gloucestershire." He handed the man his tall felt hat and turned to stroll down the great hall. As always, his gaze rose to enjoy the sheer majesty of the high vaulted ceiling with its deep oval recess and wide border of elaborate floral plaster work. Although much of the mansion had been redecorated over the years, the great hall remained essentially as it had been built in 1675.

Grimley took the Viscount's hat as well and placed them in the proper closet before shuffling after his lordship. The earl stopped beside an ornate picture of his great-grandfather and turned to await the other two men.

"I'll tell Mrs. Honeycutt you have arrived, sir. She'll be in a dither having her dinner menu disturbed. Then I'll see to the airing of your rooms, m'lord, as that particular chore was to be done tomorrow."

"Thank you, Grimley, although you know Mrs. Honeycutt never gets ruffled, much less in a dither over something so minor as unscheduled dinner guests."

"As you say, sir." The elderly gentleman moved on down the hall, stopped midway, and turned around. "Lady Corine is in the drawing room, m'lord."

"Very good. No need to announce us, Grimley; we can make our arrival known to her ourselves."

"I thought as much, sir." The butler continued his journey past the drawing room toward the kitchen at the rear of the hall.

By now Bailey's mouth was hanging open. "My word, is he always like this?"

His lordship released his long-suppressed chuckle. "Has been for as long as I can remember. Now, by Jove, it really does feel like I've come home. He does an amazing transformation when we have a party. Becomes the most proper of butlers. At least he used to when we lived here as children. It will be interesting to see if he has changed over the years. Might liven things up if he greeted all our guests with the same lovable temperament."

At that moment, Grimley reached the door of the kitchen and boomed, "Mrs. Honeycutt, throw another potato in the pot. His lordship's home." His shout was followed by a screech of surprise and a clanging crash as a stack of pans hit the floor. Grimley stepped back and threw a glance down the hall, meeting his lordship's eye with such a gleam of satisfaction that the earl burst into laughter.

The drawing room door flew open, and a slender, pretty, young woman raced across the hall to throw herself into her husband's arms. After a long and passionate kiss, Bailey gently chided his bride. "Corine, darling, you mustn't tear around so. You might hurt yourself or the baby."

"Nonsense. We're in perfect health." She patted her slightly rounded stomach and pecked him on the cheek. "But thank you for worrying about me." Turning to her still-smiling brother, she said, "We didn't expect you until tomorrow or the next day. Oh, I'm so glad you didn't delay in London."

She held out her hands to the earl. He took them in his own much larger ones and obligingly kissed her cheek. Even to the most casual observer it was obvious they were kin. Both had curly locks that shimmered like a ripened wheat field blowing gently in the wind, but Lady Corine's eyes were a pale, clear blue where the earl's were a deep bluish-purple, the color of the first crocus in spring. The planes of Lord Beckford's face were more angular, but had they been as soft as his sister's, or had he not had a stern set to his jaw, he would have been proclaimed too beautiful for a man.

The earl released his sister and led the others into the drawing room. "Bailey made sure I finished my business in record time. He insisted we ride instead of taking the curricle, believing, however incorrectly, we could make better time on horseback. Can you imagine, dear sister? He actually questioned the speed of my bays as compared with that gray he calls a thoroughbred."

"Lou," she chided, using his boyhood nickname, "stop roasting my sweet husband.

I think it's nice of him to risk your sharp tongue simply to get home to me quicker." She gazed lovingly at her spouse for a moment, then continued. "I must say, Brother, you are in a rare good humor. The trip must have gone well for you. I can't remember when I've heard you laugh as you did a few minutes ago."

"Humph. It wasn't the trip," said Bailey. "He's been in a deuced temper the whole of these last two months. For some reason that uncivil man, who claims to be a butler, set his disposition up a notch or two."

Lady Corine laughed. "Even as a child, Lou was partial to Grimley, and the old man adored my brothers. He used to always be rescuing them from some mischief before father could find out. The scrapes those two could get into."

"You weren't so unscathed yourself, little sister. Don't let this lovely, delicate creature fool you, Bailey. She was a regular little hoyden in her childhood."

"Enough," said Corine, with a laugh. "Don't you even want to know where the children are?"

"The words were on my very next breath. What have you done with the little urchins, locked them in the wine cellar?"

"Of course not. They are in the garden with Mrs. Donovan. Come, we'll go find them."

"Ah, the marvelous Sloane Donovan. Your letters have certainly waxed eloquent about this worker of miracles you hired in my absence." The earl followed his sister and Bailey out the drawing room into the conservatory. The afternoon sunlight filled the room through the floor to ceiling windows, and the earl paused to sniff a pot full of bright red carnations.

He glanced around the room at the white wicker furniture and pots of greenery and flowers, sending his sister a beaming smile of appreciation for her decorating abilities. "Is she really all you claim her to be, Cory?"

"Yes, and more. She is an extraordinary woman, quite the opposite of that gargoyle, Miss Newbold. One week in the same house with her was enough. Why you ever kept her, I'll never know."

The earl looked sheepish. "I couldn't see myself interviewing governesses. I wouldn't know the first thing to look for."

"Obviously. I'm sure Newbold was on her best behavior when you were around, although even that was questionable. I simply made it a point to listen at the keyhole a few times. She was absolutely horrid to little Angela; no wonder the child was so quiet and withdrawn."

"Is she better now?" The earl's voice was grave; the customary frown returning to his forehead.

They reached the French doors leading to the back gardens. Lady Corine placed a gently restraining hand on her brother's arm as he opened the door. "Wait here a moment and see for yourself," she said quietly.

Giggles drifted to them on the late afternoon air. In a moment, two little figures raced across the grass. Jonny, age five, ran ahead of his little sister in a slightly lopsided footrace to cross the appointed finish line well ahead of the tiny girl.

''Slo', Angel can't win 'cause her legs are too short. Can you help her?''

Blond ringlets danced as the little girl jumped up and down in excitement. ''Yeth, Lo' help Angel. I want to win.''

Tearle eyed the child quizzically. ''She certainly appears more outgoing than when I last saw her.''

A soft feminine chuckle drew his attention to the woman crossing the grass to the youngsters. His sister had mentioned in her correspondence that Mrs. Donovan was four and twenty and a widow, but as he thought about it now, she had never mentioned her physical appearance.

She definitely did not fit the customary image of a governess or of any servant. The earl judged her to be about five foot six and of a weight which was distributed nicely over a very womanly figure. Her face was turned from him, but her light brown hair was piled on top of her head in a riot of loose curls. The curls were streaked with blond, no doubt bleached from the sun. The grace with which she moved spoke of gentle breeding and training. He noticed, too, that her dress was not typical of a governess, certainly not like the black mourning clothes Miss Newbold believed the proper attire. From every appearance, Mrs. Donovan could be a woman of the aristocracy, dressed in a simple, sprig muslin daydress of powder blue.

She laughed delightedly as the children ran to meet her, grabbed her hands, and pulled her along to the finish line, which would now be the starting point.

"You help Angel," Jonny commanded.

"Very well, both of you start, and if your sister needs some help, I'll lend a hand."

Jonny winked at her before dutifully taking his place beside Angela. At Mrs. Donovan's signal, they began the race with the little girl quickly lagging behind. The governess picked up her skirts to just above the ankles and ran after the children. Upon reaching Angela, she let go of her dress with one hand and grabbed the tot around the waist, swooping her off the ground, little legs still moving. Together, they sped behind Jonny until they overtook him just before the final mark and ran across the finish line one step ahead of him. All three collapsed on the ground in panting laughter.

Angela sat on Sloane's lap, studying the woman's drooping curls. With a smile lighting up her doe-like brown eyes, she reached up and swiftly pulled the remaining pins from the governess' hair. "I like it long," she said as the light brown and gold strands fell across Sloane's shoulders. "It'th bea-u-tiful."

"Thank you, Angel, but you know I should put it back up before dinner. A woman my age doesn't usually wear her hair down around her shoulders."

The earl deemed it time to greet the children and started across the lawn toward them. Sloane lifted her head, meeting his gaze directly and holding it with her luminous, wide, gray eyes. They sparkled from her laughter, yet something more intriguing lurked in their clear depths. He was drawn to the honesty and forthrightness he saw there. There would be no mincing of words from this woman, he deduced, nor was there one ounce of servility in her body. Her cheeks were softly flushed from the run and her slightly full, pink lips widened into a warm smile.

"Children, look who is here," she said quietly.

Jonny turned in the direction of her gaze and let out a whoop. "Papa! Papa!" Leaping to his feet, the little boy tore across the short distance between them to fling himself into his father's waiting arms. The earl hugged him tightly and tossed him in the air, catching him easily. "Again, Papa. Again." His lordship complied several more times until his son was laughing uncontrollably.

At last, he put the little boy on the ground and turned toward the governess and little Angela. To his surprise, Sloane was still sitting on the grass, although she had discreetly pulled her skirt down to cover her ankles. Angela sat on her lap, staring at the earl with a look of shy awe.

Sloane nodded her head to the earl in greeting before Angela said, "Papa ith bea-u-tiful," proudly emphasizing the newest addition to her vocabulary.

"Yes, he is, Angel, but men prefer to be called handsome instead of beautiful. He is also very tall, isn't he?" The little blond head nodded solemnly in agreement. "It might be a little scary to be lifted so high, or to be thrown up in the air like Jonny." Again the tot's head moved up and down. "Perhaps if your father knelt down to receive his hug, it might not be so frightening."

His lordship obediently knelt down on one knee, silently bemoaning the effect the grass would have on his cream-colored ribbed kerseymere pantaloons, but not an inkling of the thought showed on his face. Still the little girl hesitated.

"Hello, Angela," said the earl quietly.

She slipped her arm more tightly around Sloane's neck, looking uncertainly from her to the man kneeling in front of them.

"Angel, you'll make your papa sad if you don't give him a hug. I know it's been a long time since you've seen him, but he won't bite, I'm sure. You don't want to make him sad, do you?"

To the delight of the three year old and to Lady Corine's utter astonishment, the earl's face took on the look of a woebegone puppy. With a giggle, Angela climbed off Sloane's lap and trotted to his lordship's waiting arms.

Sloane glanced at Lady Corine to find her wiping tears from her cheeks. When she moved her gaze back to the scene in front of her, she found a certain mistiness evident in the earl's eyes also. Even Jonny watched his father and sister with something akin to astonishment before the spell was broken, and he became his usual rambunctious self.

"Uncle Bailey, can I have a ride on your shoulders?"

"Of course, nephew." Bailey swung the youngster up to his wide shoulders, ignoring the rather rumpled results to his dark brown morning coat.

Lord Beckford slowly stood, lifting Angela up with him. He noted Sloane had risen also. "Welcome to Beckford Hall, Mrs. Donovan. The children seem very fond of you and seem to be flourishing under your care. I'm grateful, madam."

"Thank you, my lord. I am happy here for it allows me to be near my family, and I find your children a joy."

He lifted a blond eyebrow. Although he was especially fond of his son and liked his rowdy ways, he had never heard a female declare the child to be a joy.

"If you will excuse me for a few minutes, my lord, I will gather up my pins and correct the havoc our little race has done to my hair."

Sloane stepped up beside the earl and his eyes slowly took in her appearance: the wind blew softly through her disheveled tresses, and the sunlight glinted off their highlights like spun gold; her eyes were of the palest gray possible before being called silver, with a darker gray ring around the pupil. He resisted the sudden urge to reach out and smooth her hair, wanting to feel the satin strands between his fingers. A brief uncertainty flickered in her eyes, momentarily replacing the serene confidence with which she had met his scrutiny.

His sudden smile would have disarmed the most worthy opponent. "Of course, Mrs. Donovan. Though we both know it was Angela that wreaked havoc with your hair. Take all the time you need before fetching the children. I'll enjoy the time with them, but I do need to change before dinner."

"Yes, my lord. Will you be dining with the children?"

It was his lordship's turn to look uncertain. As much as he cared for the youngsters, dining with them had never been a very pleasant affair. After the tiring journey, he wasn't sure he was up to a meal filled with childish ill manners and remonstrations from the adults.

Lady Corine spoke up, having removed all traces of the tears from her cheeks. "Do let us dine upstairs with the children, Lou. It's been my habit since you've been gone; I didn't want to eat alone in the dining room. I think you'll find their manners much improved, and Sloane will be there to keep an eye on them."

"It is settled then. Mrs. Donovan, take about half an hour to yourself, and then I'll send the children up to change for dinner." He looked down at the grass still clinging to Angela's dress. "I doubt Grimley would think too highly of grass sprinkling the Turkish rug." His glance shifted to a tuft of the green stuff still clinging to Sloane's gown.

She looked down at her skirt and brushed the offending blades from the material. Meeting this gaze with a rueful grin, she said, "Quite so, my lord. I shall see that we are all presentable."

Sloane took a few minutes to pick up her hairpins from the grass before following the others inside. She met Grimley upon reaching the door. She had soon discovered after her arrival at Beckford Hall that the butler was really a soft touch beneath his gruff and uncivil exterior. Therefore, she wasn't surprised when he patted her on the shoulder, but his words gave her pause.

"Don't know how you did it, Mrs. Donovan, but it's about time."

"Did what, Grimley?"

"Got his lordship to hug and hold that little girl. As far as I know, he's never once picked her up since she was born. Always kind, but never able to show her any affection. A pity to make the child suffer because of feelings for the mother."

Grimley left Sloane at the bottom of the stairs as he meandered to the library to see to his lordship. She stood there briefly, thoughtfully digesting this new information. Not knowing all the facts, she decided to reserve opinion until she knew more and went upstairs to change.

The evening meal progressed amiably for all concerned. Mrs. Honeycutt had indeed thrown another potato in the pot of hearty, vegetable-beef stew so there was plenty. Although the cook could work culinary magic with exotic sauces and rich foods when the necessity arose, she had long thought simple country fare to be the healthiest and promoted her cause whenever possible.

Still in the early months of her pregnancy, Lady Corine had quickly adapted to this form of eating and lightly scolded her brother and husband when they complained about the lack of variety. With the addition of heavy oat muffins, fresh fruit, and some of the finest cheeses to be offered, they capitulated gracefully.

The earl was pleased by the children's improved manners and by Sloane's gentle correction whenever they forgot themselves. The conversation was light, with the gentlemen relating some of the more merry encounters of their journey for the children's benefit. Lady Corine knew they would discuss the business which had taken them to the Continent later after the children were in bed, and had her own teasing comments for her husband and brother, her quick wit always at the ready.

But it was to Sloane that the earl found his eyes and thoughts secretly straying again and again. Dressed in a lavender silk dinner gown, her eyes grew darker. Her hair had been swept up into a simple knot at the back with short soft curls framing her face, displaying the sun-lightened blond streaks to advantage. On the whole, she was lovely, her ready smile lighting up her face and setting the imps to dancing in her eyes.

Somehow he was not surprised to learn she had traveled extensively, having spent almost a year on the Continent with her last employer. He was rather amazed, however, by her keen intellect and her obvious love of history. In his dealings with women, he found them generally to be shallow creatures only interested in trivial matters. He was proud his mother and sister were well-educated in addition to having a goodly amount of common sense.

His lordship had not lacked female companionship these last months, therefore he was mildly disconcerted by his strong attraction to the young woman whose silvery laugh rang out while Bailey recounted one of their more hilarious misadventures.

He made it a practice to never dally with his employees, knowing full well it only led to problems and the usual dismissal of the woman involved. He had seen too many unsuspecting young women turned out on the streets because of an indiscretion with their employer, finding themselves unable to obtain gainful work thereafter. He gave himself a stern reprimand and determined to keep his distance from this unwitting seductress.

The footman began to clear the table of the last of the dishes from the main portion of the meal. The diners relaxed in their chairs to await the removal of the cloth and the arrival of the first strawberries of the season delicately baked in a tart and slathered in cream. Jonny seized the opportunity to tell his father about his great butterfly chase.

In his exuberance, the child only exaggerated slightly, but gave a vivid description of his romp across the gardens, nonetheless. "It was my last chance to nab him, so I raised my net high and brought it swooping through the air just so." His arm stretched toward the ceiling before it swept down across the table and tipped over the full goblet in his path. He watched in dismay as the water crept slowly across the linen tablecloth in a journey destined to land in his father's fastidious lap. He lifted frightened eyes to the earl's scowling face. "Uh-oh."

Sloane rose quickly to stand behind Jonny's chair. Leaning over him, she plopped her napkin down in front of the slowly moving water. "It's a little like Waterloo, Jonny."

The little boy craned his neck around to look up at her in confusion. He looked back at the water, then to his father, who scooted his chair away from the table, putting himself well out of jeopardy. "Uncle Jon and Aunt Cory call Papa, Lou. It's short for Louis, but I think he likes his first name better." He stared thoughtfully at the wet table. "The water is going toward Papa's lap. Is that what you meant by watered-lou?"

All the adults, with the exception of the earl, laughed heartily. He managed to keep a stern face with the utmost difficulty.

"No, dear, that's not exactly what I meant," said Sloane, with a chuckle. She picked up the earl's napkin, casting him a mischievous look as she straightened back up.

Baggage, he thought. It's exactly what the minx meant. In spite of his determination to keep an sober countenance, he felt his lips twitch when he met her laughing eyes once again.

"The word is Waterloo, not watered-lou. Let's pretend the water is Napoleon's forces. My napkin," indicating the first one tossed down, "is the British forces under the Duke of Wellington. This end of the table shall be a place called Waterloo, where Wellington finally defeated the little general. Napoleon hurled his infantry and calvary against the stubborn wall of the British army for most of the day with neither side clearly winning. Late in the afternoon, the Prussian forces commanded by Marshal Blücher and General von Bülow came through the soggy corn fields."

She threw the earl's napkin down and began to soak up the remaining moisture. "When the French saw the Prussian army, about half of Napoleon's forces began to retreat. Soon the whole French army was transformed into a fleeing rabble."

Dramatically, she soaked up the last of the water and wrung the cloth out in a bowl which the footman brought her. "And Napoleon was kaput."

"I have never seen a more inventive history lesson, Mrs. Donovan," said the earl dryly. "You certainly have an active imagination." He waited until she sat down again, and smiled warmly as the footman rolled up the wet cloth. "And a very effective way of protecting your charge from a scolding. Jonny, do try to be a bit more subdued with the demonstrations next time, my boy."

His son grinned first at his father and then at his advocate. "Yes, sir. Jiminy, will you look at those tarts!" He promptly turned his attention to the dessert, trying to determine how to persuade Angela to give him her portion, too.

2

Sloane pulled the frilly, white nainsook nightgown over Angela's head and guided her tiny arms into the sleeves. "You had a nice evening with your papa, didn't you, dear?"

"Yeth, he wath nice. Never hug Angela before, juth Jonny."

"I'm sure he had a good reason, honey. You look so very much like your mother, it probably makes him miss her. Sometimes we hurt other people's feelings accidentally. I think your papa loves you very much, but just doesn't quite know how to handle you. You're not built to rough and tumble like Jonny. In your father's eyes, you probably seem very fragile because you're so tiny. Men tend to coddle lovely, blond ladies, you know."

Angela giggled and crawled up into bed. "Lo', I can't find 'Nelope."

"Did you look in your toy chest?"

"Wouldn't be there. 'Nelope never hideth there."

"Did you look under your bed?"

"Yeth."

Sloane smoothed a blond wisp from the child's eyes. "Do you remember when you had her last?"

The little face screwed up in a thoughtful frown. "Outthide. Before the race."

"And you didn't have her afterwards?"

"No. I wath with Papa."

"Very well. I'll go outside and look for her. You two settle down and play quietly. I shouldn't be long."

Sloane went down the servant's stairs and out into the gardens. She checked around the wicker table and chairs where they had taken tea, but found nothing. A sudden rumble of thunder drew her attention to the clouds overhead, and she increased the speed of her search. Just as the first drops of rain splattered on her silk gown, Sloane spied the doll under a rose bush. Grabbing the toy, she sped with unladylike haste toward the shelter of a large tree located halfway between her and the mansion.

With head bent down against the rain, Sloane reached the protection of the tree. Her kid slippers slid on the wet grass, causing her to sway precariously before two, strong, masculine hands reached out and pulled her to safety under the thick branches.

Very much aware of his lordship's hands resting about her waist, Sloane said a trifle breathlessly, "Thank you, my lord. I thought I would take a tumble for sure."

"It would be a shame to get so lovely a

dress muddy. Why are you running around
the gardens this time of evening with a storm
brewing? Do you have so many gowns,
madam, that you have no care if they are
ruined?''

She lifted her gaze to meet his, finding
those deep purple gems sparkling devilishly.
A sharp flash of lightning cut the air,
followed almost instantly by a deafening peal
of thunder. Startled, she jumped and found
herself being drawn gently closer to the earl.

''I didn't notice the storm until the rain
began to fall. I was preoccupied looking for
'Nelope, I mean Penelope.''

The earl gave her a tiny smile. ''One of
Angela's dolls, no doubt.''

''Oh, not just one of her dolls, my lord,
but her favorite, for this week at least. She
does change best friends rather often.''

''Typical woman, fickleness must be an
inborn trait.'' The words were said jokingly,
but Sloane detected a note of bitterness
underneath. The arms around her tightened
ever so slightly. ''Tell me, Mrs. Donovan, are
you always so impertinent with your employer? Waterloo, indeed.''

Sloane felt a gentle blush spread slowly
across her cheeks. She found it difficult to
think with his muscular body so close and his
breath blowing softly against her damp hair.
Since her husband's death, several men had
attempted to court her, some with honorable
intentions, others with not so honorable
ideas. Only a few, who eventually became
simply good friends, had ever gotten past the

first teatime or a ride about the countryside. No one, other than her beloved Casey, had ever set her heart to pounding with only a look—until now.

She dropped her eyes and took a shaky breath. "Forgive me, my lord. It was rather bold of me. The meal was so pleasant and lighthearted, I fear I got a little carried away."

"Shall I put you in your place, madam?" The earl's voice was husky and very close.

With gentle firmness, he cradled the back of her head in his large palm, tipping it to bring her face up toward his. Sloane gasped silently at the desire burning in his eyes and willed herself not to respond as he lowered his head to cover her mouth with his.

She expected a harsh kiss, one meant to prove mastery, but instead, his lips brushed against hers gently, coaxing, teasing, and chiding with devastating sweetness. In spite of her determination to remain unmoved, Sloane's response was instant and knowing— and explosive.

The earl's arms drew her close, forbidding escape. He deepened the kiss, encouraged by the graceful hand that slipped around his neck.

Sloane felt her iron will begin to melt, being forged into a new creation by the heat flowing in her veins. Her legs grew unsteady as he pressed her body against his hard frame. Her fingers slowly released their hold on the toy; her mind totally unaware as it slipped from her fingers.

The doll struck a rock when it fell to the ground, shattering the spell of their embrace just as effectively as the stone cracked the porcelain toy into a hundred pieces.

The earl released her, and Sloane stepped back, crouching to the ground in despair. "Oh, no. Look what I've done to poor Penelope. Angela will never forgive me. Whatever will I tell her? I can't say I was so busy making a fool of myself that I forgot about her and dropped it."

He knelt down beside her, surveying the damage with little concern. "Tell her you slipped on the grass and dropped the toy. You did slip and you did drop it."

"But it didn't happen like that. I'm no good at lies, not even half-truths. My face betrays me every time. Even Angel would know."

The earl stood, drawing her up in the circle of his arms. "Forget the doll for now. I'll help you explain." He tried to see her face, but she kept it down, away from his searching gaze. "Sloane, come to me tonight," he commanded softly.

Her heart turned over in her breast, but she grasped for sanity, trying to hide the effect of his words in lightness. Aiming her voice in the general direction of his perfectly tied cravat, she said with forced cheerfulness, "It would never do, my lord. As I've told you, I'm no good at lies or at keeping secrets. I would waltz down to breakfast in the morning, and Lady Corine would ask how I slept, and I would say that I slept very well.

And before I knew what I was about, I would
be prattling on about what pleasure I found
in your arms and how much more comfortable your massive bed is than my small one."

He chuckled and placed a light kiss upon
her forehead. "You're babbling, Mrs.
Donovan." Her mouth clamped shut. He
smiled again and traced the line of her cheek
in a feathery touch with the side of his
thumb. "You're right; you would find
pleasure in my arms."

He felt her body stiffen, and her countenance dropped farther as she turned her head
from him. She drew a shaky breath and
swallowed hard before she spoke.

"My lord, regardless of my inexcusable
behavior earlier this evening and even more
so now, I am not a loose woman. There has
been no man since my husband, and I don't
intend to fall into ill repute now. I made a
commitment to my convictions long ago, sir,
and though the temptation is great, I will not
go back on that commitment. Please forgive
me for giving you an entirely different, but
very wrong, impression of my character."

"Sloane, look at me." He sucked in his
breath sharply as her delicate face lifted
toward his. She had also been right about her
inability to hide her feelings. He was undone
by the conflict of emotions he saw on her ex-
pressive face. The remnants of her passion
warred with despair in her eyes, the softly
swollen lips gave evidence of his kiss while
her cheeks flushed hotly with embarrassment. Yet overriding all was such a vulner-

ability that the earl was compelled to protect her from harm, even if it meant protecting her from himself.

With tears glistening on her lashes, she said, "My lord, even though I am no green girl of seventeen, I am not adequately schooled in your ways to play the game."

He fought the impulse to cradle her in his arms, trying to understand this overwhelming urge to take care of her. He had never felt such a need before, and he didn't particularly like it. Indeed, all the other women of his acquaintance knew the game very well and played it with cunning and self-preservation. How could a woman of four and twenty, and a widow at that, be such an innocent? He removed his arms from about her and brought his hands gently to her shoulders, his gaze still locked with hers.

"Sloane, it is I who must apologize. I have behaved abominably. I assure you that I believe you to be a woman of the highest character. I cannot deny my attraction to you, but I do promise to try to curb my baser instincts in the future. As for this evening, I can only blame my behavior on the unusual good humor into which coming home has cast me, and perhaps on the moonlight."

To his relief, a tiny glimmer of amusement flickered in those cloudy, gray eyes. "There is no moonlight, sir."

"What? But I distinctly remember your lovely face glowing in the moonlight. Well, no matter. I'm certain there is moonlight somewhere, probably above the clouds, and it does have a tendency to put one in a romantic mood."

He peeked out beneath the branches to find the rain still pouring. Removing his dark blue superfine frock coat, he placed it carefully about her now-shivering shoulders. He was dismayed to find her face still downcast and her eyes troubled, though she clutched the jacket with trembling fingers and pulled it tightly.

"I am a deuced idiot, Mrs. Donovan. No doubt you will catch a chill in that flimsy gown, but my coat will keep you from getting a thorough drenching." The coat, which struck him at mid-thigh, fell below her knees.

"Now, madam," he said briskly, "since you are so fond of racing about my gardens, I would suggest you lift your skirt with one hand and hang onto my coat with the other. If you do not object, I will put my arm around you for security. No doubt my boots are steadier on this wet ground than your slippers."

She complied, and they ran down a path to the back door. Grimley opened the portal as if it were commonplace to see his master dashing through the rain with his arm around a governess. He nodded to them and shut the door, otherwise ignoring them. Still confused and embarrassed, Sloane avoided looking directly at him or his lordship.

"Mrs. Donovan," said the earl, "I brought Angela a new doll from France. I had thought to wait until tomorrow to give it to her, but under the circumstances, it would be better to give it to her now." He slipped the coat from her shoulders, pleased to find she had scarcely gotten damp. "If you can somehow explain what happened to 'Nelope, I will be along with the gift as soon as I have changed clothes."

Sloane glanced at him and looked away quickly. His soaked shirt and normally crisp, white dimity waistcoat were plastered to his frame, revealing the well-developed muscles and the strong arms which had been around her only moments before. Her pulse quickened and color invaded her cheeks, knowing he read her thoughts. She forced herself to meet his gaze, thankful, yet somehow hurt, that he had assumed a mask of indifference.

"Yes, of course, sir," she said, attempting a business like smile. "I shall tell her you have a gift. Perhaps it will ease her broken heart somewhat."

"My lord, what has happened to you?" Smythe, his lordship's valet, looked down at the wet, clinging buff breeches and mud-splattered white stockings with disgust.

"Hello, Smythe. Good to see you have arrived at last. I trust you managed the curricle and team with your normal ability?"

"Yes, my lord." Smythe looked Sloane over with barely concealed curiosity. "I assume, sir, you were caught in the rain and being gallant, offered the young lady your coat. Very commendable, my lord, but you must hurry up and change before you catch a chill."

"As you say, Smythe. It would be the

smart thing, since I am about to give in to the shivers. May I introduce Mrs. Donovan, the children's governess. Sloane, this is Smythe, the indisputable guardian of my wardrobe, and no doubt, my own welfare.''

The two employees exchanged brief greetings before Smythe ushered his lordship up to change, and Sloane hurried up to get the children into bed.

It had been almost a week since the incident in the garden. Angela had been quickly pacified with the new doll, poor Penelope instantly forgotten. The earl had avoided being alone with Sloane. In the presence of others, he treated her respectfully but with the cool authority befitting an employer.

Sloane found it impossible to forget those moments in the garden, yet she told herself she must. To a man like the earl, it was simply a passing dalliance; a challenge to put an impertinent governess in her place. But in her heart, she knew it had turned into something more. At unguarded moments, she would meet his lordship's gaze, occasionally finding a lingering desire evident there, but more often a look of puzzlement. He would search her face, seemingly to read her thoughts. More often than not, he would then turn abruptly and walk away.

Sloane pulled her spirited bay stallion to a halt at the top of a small knoll. It was her day off; the children left in the capable care of Bess, the young parlormaid. It had been her practice to ride early every Thursday morning, relishing her freedom and the fine horseflesh beneath her. She spoke softly to her mount, and the horse took off in a run across the meadow. They galloped up to the surrounding stone fence before she slowed him to a walk. Carefully inspecting the area of her intended jump, Sloane scouted the ground for any unexpected holes or tree limbs. When she found everything satisfactory, she turned Windsong around and galloped back across the grass and sweet clover.

The earl paused among the elm trees bordering the far side of the meadow. He had been up since dawn and was in the saddle shortly thereafter. He watched the young woman as she rode with abandon across his property. He knew the horse, for he had found the animal residing in his stables and had been advised it belonged to Mrs. Donovan. Even if he had not known the mount, he could not mistake the rider. Her deep blue-green riding habit set off her figure to perfection, and her happy laughter floated to him across the countryside.

He sat quietly watching as she removed the pert, black hat with its blue-green ostrich plume from her head and tied the ribbons so that it hung down her back. Reaching up, she pulled the pins from her hair and let it fall across her shoulders so it looked as carefree as the woman herself. Bending down, she stroked her horse's neck, talking to him. Instantly, the animal began to move, increasing his speed as he neared the rock fence.

The earl went rigid when he realized her

intention. "Sloane, no!" he yelled, kicking his horse to a full run. His fear turned to grudging appreciation as he watched her and her mount soar over the fence with plenty of room to spare. He took the jump also and reined in his glistening black stallion beside her.

Jumping to the ground, he strode swiftly to her side and grabbed her around the waist, pulling her from the horse's back. "Just what do you think you're doing, young woman?" he barked.

Planting her feet firmly on the ground, Sloane tipped her head to one side in a quizzical manner. She was tempted to give him a flippant answer, but further observation of his angry scowl warned her it would be unwise. His hands spanned her waist, but he looked for all the world as if he wished they were around her neck.

Laying a gloved hand lightly on his arm, she said quietly, "I'm doing just what I've done every Thursday morning for the last two months, riding and taking a jump of which I am quite capable."

"You have no business trying such a jump. Lady's saddles are made for moderate riding, not taking jumps which would challenge most men."

"My lord, if you must scold me, at least do it while we walk our animals. They should not be left standing."

He glanced down at his hands, suddenly aware of her closeness, and released her immediately. Taking up the reins, they walked through the grass keeping the thoroughbreds warm.

"You are right, of course, sir, that a lady's saddle is not made for such riding. But if you will notice, I am not using a sidesaddle this morning."

His lordship cast a look at the saddle and his frown deepened. "Do you always ride in so unseemly a fashion, Mrs. Donovan?"

Sloane couldn't resist a chuckle. "I didn't know you were such a prude, my lord. No, I do not always ride in this manner, only when I am alone, or wish to take the jumps. Lord Beckford, I have been riding since I was three years old. I'm not exactly a novice."

He stopped, turned sideways, and caught her arm to swing her around to face him. "How was I to know that, Sloane?" His gaze was piercing. "My word, you frightened me. I thought Corine was a daredevil, but you far surpass even her."

She turned back in their original direction, and he followed suit. He began to walk again, gently nudging her along, her arm still captive. "Tell me about yourself, Sloane Donovan. I would prefer no more disturbing surprises. By the way, why aren't you tending to the children?"

"Thursday is my day off, my lord." At his questioning expression, she continued. "I realize most governesses only have a day or two a month free, but I arranged with Lady Corine to take less salary and have more time off. It is better for the children and for me if we have a break from each other now and then.''

"You must have some other means of income or work amazing magic with what you earn from me." His gaze raced over her. Her blue-green riding habit with black military trim was made in the latest style, as were the half boots edged in blue-green and the tan York suede gloves. "I know of no other governess who could dress as you do even on a normal salary."

"Yes, I do. I have an income from my husband's estate. It is not large, but quite sufficient for my needs."

"Then why did you become a governess? Why do you not have a home of your own, instead of taking care of someone else's brats?"

"They aren't brats, nor do you believe they are." She stopped and sat down on a large boulder. He sat down beside her, and they released the reins, letting the horses roam and nibble at the grass.

"After Casey died, I couldn't bear being alone in our house. I moved back in with my parents, but it wasn't much better. Countess Landan has been a friend of my mother's since childhood, and she came for a visit. When I learned she was looking for a governess, I asked for the job. I love children but had none of my own, and I desperately needed something worthwhile to fill my time. She had a little girl, two years old, and a six-month-old baby boy. My time was happily occupied for the next four years." She smiled slightly, fondly remembering the countess' children, then shifted her gaze to watch the horses.

"Why did you leave her?"

"My family lives near here. I had come home for a brief visit and heard Lady Corine was interviewing for a governess." She looked up at him, meeting his steady gaze comfortably. "The Countess understood that I wanted to be near my family. York is such a distance away. My sisters had grown up while I was gone, and I felt as if I barely knew them any longer."

"You grew up near here?"

"Yes, although I was born near Bishop's Cleeve on my grandfather's estate. My grandfather is Baron Atherton." A look of recognition passed over his face. "I thought you might know him. He visits London often and is active in the House of Lords. My mother is his youngest daughter. She shares my love for riding and fell in love with grandpa's stable master."

"Your father?"

"Yes, Galen Kincade, the finest horse breeder in this part of the country. Grandpa was a bit put out to find his daughter in love with a commoner, but he's not nearly so crusty as he seems." Her smile spoke of her love for the elderly gentleman.

"In the end, he decided mother could only be happy with her Scotsman, so he gave the marriage his blessing, knowing mother had enough spunk to live through the scandal. He respected my father's ability with horses and helped him to get his own stables. It has proven a profitable investment for both of them."

"And was there a scandal?" He bent one leg and shifted his foot to rest upon the rock, draping his forearm across his knee.

"Oh, somewhat. Mostly just gossip, I suppose. Mother never cared too much for the frivolous life, so she wasn't too overset. We're buried deep enough in the country so it doesn't matter much. I'm sure things would have been different if they had been in London at the time. Mother had her comeout and one season. It was sufficient for her."

"What about you? Did you have a London season? I think not, for I'm certain I would have remembered you."

Her laugh brought a smile to his lips. "You flatter me, my lord. My comeout would have been the same year as your lady's, so I know you would not have noticed me. She was so beautiful; I'm sure you and everyone else only had eyes for her."

His face suddenly grew shuttered, and Sloane mentally kicked herself for her blunder. She hurried on, "But as for my comeout, no, I didn't have one. I followed my mother's example, you see, and fell in love with the head groom at my father's stables. I think he was so much like father, I couldn't help but fall in love with him. He was Irish, and the best horseman I've ever seen."

"What happened to him?" he asked quietly.

"He delivered some horses to Scotland. On the trip back, he caught a fever. He struggled home, but he was so very ill. The sickness settled in his lungs, and he died a few days later. He was only nine and twenty." Even now, it was hard to speak of his death without choking on the lump in her throat. She welcomed the arm that went around her and gratefully rested her head against the earl's shoulder.

"How old were you?" His voice was gentle, caring.

"Nineteen." She took a deep breath, regaining control, and sat up straight, but his arm remained around her. "My lord, I fear I may have erred the day you arrived home."

"How so?"

"By encouraging Angel to go to you. You see, I didn't know at the time that it was . . . difficult for you. She must remind you very much of your wife. I fear I pushed you into holding her, and inadvertently wounded you. In doing so, surely you were reminded of your wife and how much you miss her. I'm sorry if I brought up an old hurt."

He removed his arm from around her shoulders and stood suddenly, looking far off in the distance. When he turned toward her, his expression was unreadable. "There was no harm done, Mrs. Donovan. I have neglected the child shamefully the last three years. True, it was because she reminded me of her mother, but I assure you I am not languishing over a lost love." He called softly to the horses. When the animals came, he turned to Sloane, handing her Windsong's reins. "Why do you call him Windsong?"

"Because when we're racing, I feel free as the wind and it puts a song in my heart."

"Very poetic."

"And a lot of balderdash," she said, her eyes twinkling. "My father gave him to me when I moved back here. He had named him long before I ever acquired him. Now, I must go and change saddles. I'm to visit my parents, and my mother would faint if she saw me riding astride."

"I'm glad someone makes certain you behave properly," he said, with a chuckle. "Is your father's place on the way to Evesham? I haven't lived here since I was ten, so I'm still unfamiliar with my neighbors."

"No, they live about three miles west of Evesham on the way to Worcester."

"Then I shall accompany you anyway. The magistrate was just telling me day before yesterday of the increased robberies in the county. You really shouldn't be riding away from the estate by yourself."

"But, my lord, I've done so every week since I've been here, and I've come to no harm."

"Perhaps, but that practice will now change, Mrs. Donovan. You are not to ride alone. If I am not available to accompany you, you will take one of the grooms. I'm certain your father will escort you back to Beckford Hall."

"I do not wish to put you out, my lord, but if you are going in my direction, I would be pleased to have your company. I would like you to meet my family, if you can stop for a few moments. I know my father would be proud to show you his stock."

He helped her to mount, then swung agilely upon Trojan's back. Grinning devilishly, he inquired, "Would you like to race, Mrs. Donovan?"

Returning his grin, she said, "You're on, Lord Beckford." Whispering into Windsong's ear, the race began. The earl passed her about a hundred yards before the stables, adding insult to injury by leaping from the horse upon reaching the gate. When Sloane arrived a few seconds later, he was lounging lazily against the post as if he had been waiting for hours.

He pushed away from the post, walked to her side, and assisted in her dismount. "Perhaps I should have given you a greater head start, but I doubt if it would have helped. I always win," he stated matter-of-factly. He leaned forward slightly and whispered for her ears alone, "But you ran a good race, madam. One of the best." Suddenly he straightened, aware of the intimate appearance of the scene.

Surveying her dust-covered clothes, he said briskly, "We had best take my curricle to your father's, Mrs. Donovan. Be ready in half an hour." He turned to the stable master. "Tom, please prepare my team and vehicle." Without another word, he walked rapidly to the mansion.

Tom watched Sloane, who stood staring after the earl. "I think he likes you," he said, with a grin.

"He likes to give orders, you mean."

"Well, that, too, but most of the *ton* is the same." He stepped forward, towering over her. "Slo', we've been friends a long time, and I think I can speak my mind. Be careful of his lordship. He wants you, but he ain't the kind to marry even such a fine lady as yourself. Scuttlebutt has it that his wife cuckolded him. In fact, she was running off with her lover when she was killed. He ain't likely to trust no female after that. A man's pride can only take so much—especially one with as much pride as his lordship's got."

"Thank you, Tom. I think I've known where I stand with him from the very beginning. I assure you I don't intend to be added to his list of conquests."

Sloane hurried to the house to change, wishing she could be as confident as she had sounded to Tom. She wasn't at all sure she wouldn't wind up a part of the select group to have fallen prey to the earl's undeniable charm. She found she liked the man very much, too much for her own good.

3

Sloane watched in admiration as the earl expertly maneuvered his pair of bays down the winding road. His long, slim fingers held the ribbons gently, giving little evidence of the strength normally found in those elegant hands. Dressed in a coat of blue-gray superfine, a waistcoat of blue striped twill jean, and light gray pantaloons, one would be inclined to think he had spent the majority of the morning attending to his appearance, instead of the scant half hour it had taken before he had reappeared at the stables.

Sloane had arrived only a moment later, dressed in a deep rose, sprig muslin daydress with matching capote bonnet, her hair carefully tucked under the soft, puffed crown and stiff brim, giving no hint of her early morning ride.

With a comment of, "A vast improvement," the earl had handed her into the high curricle, waited a moment until the groom released the horses, and they were on their way.

"Your team is magnificent, my lord." She smiled her most beguiling smile when he glanced her way. "I don't suppose you would allow me a turn at the ribbons?"

"Your assumption is correct, madam, no matter how you try to charm me. You are well aware that a strong arm is needed for cattle such as these. At the moment all is peaceful, but should they take it in their heads to run, you would not be able to control them."

"Perhaps, but then you are here to help me, are you not?"

"Don't be coy, Mrs. Donovan. It doesn't suit. However, you may bestow that bewitching smile upon me whenever you want; on many other matters, I can be swayed." She laughed gaily at his own winsome smile, and the course for the day was set.

They dashed along at a fast clip, past plum orchards and fields of asparagus and strawberries nurtured to market perfection in the lush, fertile soil of the Vale of Evesham. Tiny lambs scampered about the meadows with their mothers, while the rams pranced about majestically near the fences made of flat, honey-colored Cotswold stone.

Stone cottages, heavy laden with climbing ivy and an occasional thatched roof, dotted the landscape, their gardens thick with the promise of an abundant harvest. For three of the four miles north of Beckford Hall to Evesham, the land to the east of the road belonged to the earl. His estate covered an even greater area to the south and east of the Hall.

It took about three quarters of an hour to cover the distance to Kincade Stables. Upon arriving, it appeared the whole compound was deserted, but a few minutes later, a groom hurried from the stables and took the reins. The earl hopped down and lifted Sloane from the curricle, past the brightly painted yellow wheels and highly polished black wood.

"Sloane, you're just in time." Seeing double, the earl shook his head. He looked again, still seeing two identical red-haired, freckle-faced boys peering around the corner of the stable. "Hurry up," they said in unison.

"Buttercup is about to foal."

"And we'll miss it if you don't come on."

"Run along, boys, we'll be there in a minute," answered Sloane. The heads disappeared around the building. "Oh, dear, I suppose that wasn't very polite of me. I should have introduced my brothers to you."

"Your brothers?"

"Yes, Hobie and Tobie. They're twins."

"I hadn't noticed." The earl chuckled dryly.

Impulsively, Sloane held out her hand. "Will you come?"

"Lead the way." He took her hand and followed as she hurried to the last stall of the stable. Just before reaching the straw-covered delivery room, he tucked her hand through the curve of his arm.

The two ten-year-olds sat perched on the side of the stall, while a tall, broad-shouldered man knelt beside the little mare. A pair of gray eyes, identical to Sloane's, lifted to greet the new arrivals.

"Glad you made it in time, lass."

"I am, too, Papa. Papa, this is the Earl of Beckford. My lord, may I introduce my father, Galen Kincade."

The two men exchanged pleasantries before Galen's attention was drawn back to the little mother. In a few moments, a wiggly, wet, little foal struggled to stand.

Sloane's hand pressed the earl's arm, and he covered her hand with his free one, squeezing gently. He turned his head from the new mother and baby, his attention drawn to Sloane's glowing face.

Tears misted her eyes as they always did when she saw the first struggles of a new life. "Isn't he beautiful," she said in hushed tones. "I never fail to be in awe."

The earl gazed in fascination as a tear slipped from her lash and rolled down her cheek, completely unnoticed. He had never known a woman who would watch an animal's birth, not even his mother or sister. He felt he had been granted a rare privilege in sharing the experience with this unusual woman.

He was unaware of Sloane's father watching him. Galen Kincade took notice of the warm regard with which the earl observed his daughter. The father's brows drew together slightly as the earl's expression softened, a look of tenderness passing over his countenance. Galen's gaze moved to his daughter's hand so firmly held against his lordship's arm.

At that moment, sensing his perusal, the earl looked across the stall. Glancing down at the hand which gently encompassed Sloane's, he felt like some young buck caught in an indiscretion by an irate father. With a calmness he did not feel, but which his years of experience provided, the earl gave Sloane's fingers a quick squeeze and released them.

Sloane smiled at him and then looked back at the mare. "Papa, she seems terribly tired. Has she had a difficult time?"

"Yes, it's been a long labor. She could use with some of your gentle consoling, Sloane. Your soft voice and gentle touch will calm her so she can sleep."

"Of course." Sloane pulled her hand from his lordship's arm. She took off her hat and hung it on a hook nearby. Taking a smock from another peg, she slipped it on and buttoned it. Obviously her father's, the shirt almost covered her gown. She crept softly into the stall and sat down on the hay beside the new mother. The horse lifted her head just enough to rest it in Sloane's lap.

"I'll come by after I've finished my business in Evesham, Mrs. Donovan. If you are ready to go at that time, I would be happy to drive you home."

Sloane stroked the animal's head and spoke softly as the earl had done. "Thank you, my lord, but I had intended to stay until after dinner. My sisters are coming over soon for a visit. I'm sure papa wouldn't mind giving me a ride."

Galen watched the exchange with interest. There was a special light in his daughter's eyes when she looked at the earl, an awareness which had been directed at only one other man. "My lord, if your business puts you this way around dinner-time, we would be honored if you would be our guest this evening. Libby lays a splendid table, and I know she would be pleased to have you."

"I would enjoy it, sir. I had thought my business might take awhile, so I am not expected at home this evening." Galen accompanied the earl from the stables while one of his men took care of the foal. "I shall endeavor to hurry matters and arrive at the appointed time and save you the inconvenience of having to drive your daughter back to Beckford Hall. I hope I can return soon enough to examine your stock. Mrs. Donovan has been abundant in her praise of your animals."

"She's a mite prejudiced, but we do raise fine horses," said Galen, with a proud smile.

Shortly after lunch, Sloane stood in front of the cottage with her father. Since she would be riding one of his horses later, she had changed into an old skirt and blouse and borrowed her sister's riding boots.

"You're sure everything is ready, Father? Tony has piled extra hay where I'm to fall?"

"Yes, lass. He made sure that corner of the paddock is extra soft. You're certain you want to go through with this, Sloane?"

"Of course, Papa. We cannot let Lady Wentwood buy this horse. She'll break her fragile neck, and then no one would purchase another animal from you."

"Here she comes now. Blast, she's got her no-account brother with her. Watch out for him, lass. He's a vulture. Downright offensive the way he's been flirting with Roseanne."

"I wondered why she shut herself in her room when she heard Lady Wentwood was coming."

Sloane took her father's arm and walked out with him to meet the elegant curricle as it came to a halt in front of the stables. Lady Wentwood was a raven-haired beauty whose charms had proven irresistible to any number of men. Married at eighteen to an elderly but very wealthy viscount, she had come into a considerable fortune upon his demise just two years later. Having remarried a dashing young major only a year after her first husband's death, she again found herself a widow after the Battle of Waterloo. Now seven and twenty, wealthy, and still a beauty, she preferred to play the merry widow, carrying out her affairs with little regard for the effect such liaisons had on others.

Sloane watched her discreetly. Lady Ebony Wentwood was everything Sloane was not. Her appearance and manner were polished to perfection. When speaking to any man, whether the groom or Galen, her voice was low and husky, somehow sensual yet refined. She was worldly, yet charming. Her lovely body conjured up only one word in Sloane's mind—ripe.

"Lady Wentwood, Lord Carlisle, may I present my oldest daughter, Mrs. Sloane Donovan. Sloane is an excellent rider, my lady, and has consented to put Firedancer through his paces for you. I am still of the belief that the animal is much too spirited for a lady to handle and would dissuade you from purchasing him."

"Yet, Mr. Kincade, you consent for your daughter to ride him? Are you inferring that she is a better horsewoman than I am?"

"With no disrespect intended, my lady, there is no one who could lay a finger to the way Sloane rides. She is simply the best there is. Otherwise, I would not let her near this animal. If you wish to prove me wrong, madam, you may take a turn with Firedancer, but remember, please, it is your neck I'm thinking about."

Lady Ebony coldly examined Sloane, taking in with some contempt the white smock shirt which had been tucked into a plain, full, gray skirt. It was the garb of a peasant, but she could not in any way call the woman wearing such despicable clothing a peasant. She glanced angrily at her brother, who was surveying Sloane with an entirely different attitude.

"Very well, Mr. Kincade, since you are so

worried about my neck, you may risk your daughter's. Even my own brother has spoken against this steed. We shall see if Mrs. Donovan is all you have made her out to be."

Sloane gave Lady Wentwood a confident smile and took the reins from the hand of her brother, Tony. He came around to boost her up onto the animal's back. "Don't go trying to prove anything, Slo'. Remember that we don't want her to buy Firedancer. Just put him through his paces, and when you come back, Hobie will let the chicken loose. When he goes up, just fall off. Just make sure you're near the hay," he whispered.

Sloane nodded, securely ensconced in the sidesaddle. She had been riding Firedancer every week for the past month, trying to get him accustomed to the sidesaddle and the lighter weight of a woman. The horse, sensing somehow that he was being put to the test, reared immediately, drawing a gasp from Lady Wentwood and a muffled curse from Lord Carlisle. It took all of her expertise, but Sloane continued to speak softly to the animal, handling the reins with calm authority to bring him under control.

Tony opened the gate, and she directed her mount through it, giving him just enough rein to allow for a canter across the damp grass.

In the momentary confusion, no one noticed the earl's arrival. He stood beside the fence, a deep scowl marring his attractive features. His eyes never left Sloane. His apprehension showed in his very stance, tense and poised to act if necessary.

"You needn't be overset, my lord. Galen would not let our daughter do anything he did not think she could handle."

Reluctantly, the earl broke his gaze away from Sloane and turned to the slim, delicate creature beside him. Sloane inherited her father's eyes and hair color, but her other features were definitely her mother's. Her hair was darker than Sloane's with red highlights, and her eyes were a golden green, but they held the same honesty and forthrightness as her daughter's.

"I'm certain you believe he would not, Mrs. Kincade. However, it is my inclination to believe that somehow his good judgment is lacking in this instance. That is no animal for a woman to handle, not even one so proficient as Mrs. Donovan."

"She has been riding Firedancer for over a month, Lord Beckford, and has come to no harm." Her voice had dropped low. "However, please continue to show your agitation, for we do not want Lady Wentwood to purchase the horse. There is no doubt she would not be able to handle him, but she is most insistent that her ability is equal to the task."

Lady Wentwood noticed the earl and moved to his side in a swaying gait. "My dear Tearle, I had no idea you were in our little part of the world. Have you come home to Beckford Hall at last?" Her husky voice was at its best, her smile her most seductive.

The earl forced a smile, regretting that he could not keep a more watchful eye on

Sloane. "We have indeed, Lady Ebony. My sister moved the children here some two months past, but I have only returned a week ago from the Continent. She has done amazingly well in restoring the old place." His eyes moved back to Sloane, who galloped across the meadow somewhat recklessly, to his way of thinking.

Lady Ebony saw the direction of his gaze, and the concern mirrored on his face. "I had no idea Lady Corine was here. We've but just returned from London ourselves. I must get over to visit soon."

"Yes, you must," the earl said absently. "I trust you are not thinking of buying that animal for yourself?"

"Well, I am considering it. He is magnificent, and I daresay I can ride as well as Mrs. Donovan."

Sloane slowed the animal and began a series of intricate maneuvers and small jumps. At the last gate, Firedancer balked, rearing and spinning around. Sloane hung on and brought him to a halt, still some distance from the spectators.

"I doubt it, Ebony. I've never seen a woman so accomplished on a horse's back. I wouldn't recommend purchasing the animal. She is barely able to control him, and I understand she has been training him for a month. He is much too spirited, in need of a firm hand."

"A man's hand, Tearle?"

"A strong man's hand."

Sloane spied the earl conversing with

Lady Ebony. The pang in her heart at the sight of them together caused her much consternation and, for a moment, she lost her concentration. She headed Firedancer back toward the stables at a trot, her mind occupied with the way Lady Ebony laid her hand possessively on Lord Beckford's arm. Somehow, she found it consoling that he seemed to pay little attention to the lovely woman by his side.

Suddenly, a quail flew from a tall clump of grass in their path. Firedancer shied away skittishly, then reared, higher and quicker than he had ever done before. Caught unaware, Sloane flew from the saddle and hit the ground in an ungraceful heap.

"Sloane!" The earl jerked his arm from Lady Ebony's grasp and raced across the damp ground, heedless of the damage being done to his highly polished Hessians. Galen ran toward his daughter also, but the younger man proved the faster and reached her first.

He knelt beside her as she pushed herself up on her elbows, fighting to regain her breath. "Sloane, where are you hurt?"

She was puzzled at how calm his words were when his face reflected such anger, and for a moment didn't answer.

"Sloane, talk to me. Where are you hurt?"

Her father arrived, and Sloane gave him a wobbly smile. "I'm all right. I just had to catch my breath." She was touched by her father's sigh of relief and didn't have the heart to tell him her leg ached dreadfully. Allowing the earl to help her sit up, she said, "Papa, you forgot to tell Firedancer the plot to our drama. He wasn't supposed to throw me until I reached the hay."

"You mean you planned to be thrown?" His lordship turned a scathing look from daughter to father.

"Don't blame father, Lord Beckford. It was my idea entirely, only it didn't go as planned. Firedancer wasn't supposed to be frightened by a quail but by a chicken, and it wasn't supposed to happen until I was beside the hay Tony piled up for me."

"I don't believe this. You've both taken leave of your senses."

"Sloane, lass, you truly aren't hurt?" asked her father, his face lined with concern. "His lordship is right, it was a rattlebrained thing for us to do."

"Balderdash. Of course, I'm all right. I just need to sit here for a minute. You'd better get back to Lady Ebony, Papa, and try to persuade her not to buy that horse."

"I'll go, but I don't think she'll need too much convincing. I caught a look at her face when I ran by, and I feared she would faint. Turned a bit peaked, she did."

"Humph. Ebony Wentwood never fainted once in her life," said the earl. "But hopefully your little drama has shown her how foolish it is for a woman to try to ride such an animal. Do go back to your customer, Mr. Kincade. I shall take care of Mrs. Donovan and assist her to the house." He did not add that he intended to give her a piece of his mind along the way and would probably administer the same verbal thrashing to her father shortly afterward.

With Galen's back to her, Sloane grimaced and slipped a handkerchief from the sleeve of her blouse. Chatting nonsensically, she tried to slide the wisp of cloth under her skirt to stop the warm trickle of blood oozing down her leg.

The earl shifted so his body was between Sloane and the others. "Let me see your leg, Mrs. Donovan."

"There is nothing wrong with my leg, my lord. I'm just a little shaken from my fall."

"Nonsense, woman. I saw you press your handkerchief against your leg. I am not such an idiot to believe the dark stain on your skirt is from the mud. Now let me see your wound, or I assure you, madam, I will personally pull up your skirt, probably much higher than necessary."

Sloane took quick note of his determined look and drew the skirt up to her knee to reveal a nasty bruise and small but bloody cut on the upper calf above her boot.

"I hit a rock when I fell. Please, don't tell papa. He feels badly enough already."

The earl took the cloth from her hand and made a pad, pressing it against the wound. "Hold this tightly against your leg, madam."

Removing his own crisp, white, linen handkerchief from his pocket, he formed it into a bandage and tied it around her leg over the pad securely but not so tight as to cut off the circulation. With a gentleness which startled her, he ran his fingers along her calf.

"I had not thought you to be so witless, Sloane. It is highly inconsiderate of you to blemish such a perfect limb. You are certain you have no other injuries?"

"None, my lord." She did not tell him her backside ached almost as much as her leg in fear he would deem it necessary to examine that part of her anatomy also. "I would be grateful, sir, if you could help me to my feet."

He pulled her up, steadying her when she gasped in pain. "I fear I will have to carry you, Sloane. You have a nasty lump on your leg, and it is obviously painful to walk."

"Oh, no, my lord," she cried softly, "you mustn't. If you carry me, Lady Ebony will buy the stallion for sure, certain that should she be thrown, you or some other gallant would come to her rescue. Pray, my lord, do not undo all we have accomplished this afternoon."

He stared at her for a moment, finally deciding she spoke only half in jest. "Minx! At least take my arm, you silly child, and let me bear as much of your weight as possible. I certainly do not wish to destroy your grand scheme."

"Thank you, sir. You are kind." She took a step, gripping his arm and mangling his coat sleeve in the process.

"This will never do, Sloane." He pulled his arm from her grip and slid it around her waist, offering her his other hand for support, too. By the time they reached the paddock gate, the knot in her calf had been worked out by the exercise, and Sloane was able to walk with hardly a limp. The earl moved his arm around so she could slip her hand through it. Walking past the corner of the stables, they found Lady Ebony seated beside her brother in the curricle.

"Mrs. Donovan," cried Baron Carlisle, "I do hope you were not seriously injured."

"Nothing but my pride, my lord. I dare-say I shan't be riding Firedancer anytime again soon."

"Nor shall my sister, madam. I believe she has been convinced to purchase one of your father's less spirited animals."

"Have you, Lady Wentwood?" asked Sloane.

"Yes. I have no desire to be thrown in such a manner, Mrs. Donovan, and since your expertise seems to be so widely known, I shall not question such an authority. By the way, Tearle, dear, how is it you are so well-acquainted with Mrs. Donovan's abilities when you've just returned to the district?"

The earl felt Sloane bristle at Lady Went-wood's innuendo, and pressed her hand against his side in subtle warning. "Mrs. Donovan is the children's governess, Ebony. I have seen her ride, and, being acquainted with her father, I know he taught her well."

"A governess? Then I am to assume there is no Mr. Donovan?" Her manner was so catty, the earl felt like asking her if she wanted a bowl of cream, but instead scowled at her crudity.

"I am a widow, Lady Wentwood."

Ebony looked pointedly at Sloane's hand tucked through the crook of his lordship's arm. She laughed deep in her throat and glanced knowingly at her brother. "One doesn't often keep such close company with a mere governess. Very convenient, wouldn't you say, Alan?"

Carlisle chuckled, then his smile became a smirk as the color flooded Sloane's face. "You certainly know how to pick your help, Beckford. You'll have to let me know which agency you used. I'd like to pick up a fancy little governess like her myself." He prodded the horses into motion, and the curricle left the grounds at a fast clip, accompanied by a lingering trill of feminine laughter.

Sloane looked from her father's flushed, angry face to the earl's grim one. "My apologies, Mrs. Donovan. I would not have had you subjected to such talk. However, you must face facts, madam. You are a very attractive young woman, and I am a single man. The greatest pastime of the *ton* is gossip. I fear you have not heard the last of Lady Wentwood's malicious tongue."

The color fled from her face, but Sloane raised her chin slightly. "My reputation is sound, my lord. I care deeply for your children and have no intention of leaving when Angel is overcoming her shyness. I am not one to back away from a challenge, sir."

His expression changed little, except perhaps to become a little more stern. His mouth set in a tight line and a tiny muscle clenched in his jaw. He stared after the curricle for a moment. When he turned his attention back to his companions, he found Galen walking toward the house, muttering muffled curses under his breath.

"There is something else you should know, Sloane. Ebony Wentwood has made up her mind I am to be her next husband. She is a foolish woman, but a very determined one. I have no intention of ever becoming legshackled again, but she does not seem to get the message. She views you as an adversary, an impediment to her goal. She will be vicious in her quest, although I have bluntly told her that under no circumstances will I ever marry again. Once afflicted with that sorry state was enough."

Distracted by the bitterness in his voice, Sloane asked softly, "Was it such an unhappy marriage, my lord?"

"Yes."

"But not all marriages are so, Lord Beckford. I was very happy, and you have but to look at Lady Corine and Lord Mathers to see their happiness."

"They have not been together long enough for the monotony to set in."

Sloane chuckled to hide her dismay. "I can hardly think life with Lady Corine would ever prove to be monotonous."

"Perhaps not, but I fear all women tend to grow unhappy with their wedded state,

just as men seem to do. It is not long before
the eye begins to wander and soon the feet
also."

Sloane felt compelled to touch his brow
and smooth away his hurt, for though he
tried to sound casual, his eyes reflected deep
pain. Instead, she gently pulled on his arm,
leading him toward the large stone cottage
with the thatched roof.

"Come, my lord," she said softly, "I will
show you proof love can be real and can
weather the storms. One has but to watch my
parents to see that not everyone's feet stray,
nor that all love grows sour."

As if to prove her point, they opened the
door to find her parents in an embrace. Instead of jumping apart in embarrassment,
they merely broke off the kiss and remained
standing in each other's arms.

Elizabeth Kincade grinned at her
daughter and the earl. "Come in, dear. I was
trying to smooth your father's rumpled
feathers, although I don't know why he let
someone like Lady Wentwood ruffle them in
the first place. Her opinions carry little
weight around here."

"I should go and change my clothes,"
said Sloane. "I'm afraid I muddied my
working things rather badly. Mama, here
comes the rest of the family. Will you handle
the introductions for Lord Beckford while I
change?"

The earl peered out the window at the
two approaching vehicles. Out of the corner
of his eye, he glimpsed Hobie and Tobie

racing across the yard, followed by Tony and another young man.

"Just how many of you are there?"

"I have seven brothers and sisters," laughed Sloane. "The one with Tony is Shawn. His twin sister, Dawn, and her family are in the first carriage. Her husband, Howard Crandall, is our local vicar, and they have a little baby girl six months old. Clarice and her husband, Michael, are in the second coach with their three children. Michael is Squire Denton's eldest son. My sister, Roseanne, is upstairs."

"Hiding from Carlisle, no doubt."

"Correct." Sloane's face grew tender. "She's the painter in the family." She led him across the room to a sunny corner where a beautiful oil painting stood almost completed. It was a scene from his estate, captured with great detail and accuracy. "I hope you do not mind. Lady Corine gave her permission to sketch the scene. The rest she has done from memory."

"She does indeed have a great talent. I shall have to speak with her about purchasing this piece. I have a fancy to hang it above the drawing room mantel and remove that morbid picture of grandfather." Always acutely aware of Sloane's change of mood, his lordship did not miss the brief sadness which passed over her face. "What is it, Mrs. Donovan?" he questioned softly.

"When you speak with Roseanne, please do so slowly. She had an inflammation of the ears when she was twelve which left her quite hard of hearing. She isn't totally deaf, but if we speak too rapidly, the words blur together. She says if we slow down our speech and pronounce our words distinctly, she can understand. I believe she lip-reads most of the time. She handles it well, yet she is understandably shy around someone she doesn't know. Please have patience with her, my lord."

"I shall. Now run along and change while I prepare myself for the onslaught."

"I'm not sure anyone can prepare for my mother's brood," said Sloane, with a laugh. "You see, we all eat together, with the exception of the tiniest babe. It makes for a fun, but occasionally rowdy mealtime."

Her assessment was correct. The meal started out reverently enough with the vicar offering the grace. It was apparent the blessing was an integral part of mealtime whether the clergyman was present or not, for even the youngest children sat quietly with folded hands until the prayer was over.

The conversation which followed was lively and intelligent. No gossip here but relevant issues of the day were discussed with enthusiasm, each viewpoint given equal time. Even Roseanne was not left out. Shawn sat on one side of her and Sloane on the other, each making an effort to keep her informed of what was being discussed and making certain she was given the opportunity to express her thoughts whenever she wanted.

Later, back in his own library, sipping his nightly brandy, the earl reflected on the day and the evening. He felt he had run the gamut of his emotions in one day. He couldn't remember when he had enjoyed a dinner so much, except perhaps before his marriage with his own family around his father's table.

Lady Wentwood's words rang in his ears. Blast that woman! Until he met Sloane, he had been tempted to play Ebony's little game; not to the extent of marrying her, but only to persuade her into a less permanent arrangement. But now, her loveliness did not move him. When he closed his eyes, it was a delicate face framed with sun-streaked, light brown hair and luminous gray eyes that he pictured.

He had avoided Sloane all week, but his desire for her had not lessened. Now, after spending so much time with her today, other unwanted feelings were coming into play. Feelings he did not want to think about. He set his glass on the marble-topped table and proceeded up to bed, seeking his rest. Rest did not come—only those thoughts he had tried to avoid.

4

Sloane halted at the landing of the great walnut barley-sugar twist staircase. The earl stood at the top of the stairs, conversing with Smythe. For an instant, she considered doing an about-face and racing back down the steps, but refrained, knowing such an action would only earn her a contemptuous remark from his lordship.

It had been over two weeks since she had seen the earl, other than for a glimpse or two as he went about his duties on the estate. He was dressed for Lady Wentwood's ball, and Sloane thought he couldn't be more handsome. His black frock coat fit his broad shoulders perfectly, setting off the white satin waistcoat to emphasize his slim waist. White silk stockings and black satin breeches hugged his powerful legs like a second skin.

Sloane's heart swelled with pride at his magnificence before crumbling into a dry, choking powder. Sloane was in love. From all indications, the earl was not.

It had been three weeks since they dined with her parents. Seemingly, his lordship had a pleasant time with her family and with her. On the way back to Beckford Hall, he had flirted with Sloane outrageously, leaving her at her door with a smile which promised much with its tenderness.

The following morning, however, Sloane found him cool and distant. He maintained this attitude until Corine and Bailey left for their own home three days later. When Sloane brought the children out to tell their aunt and uncle good-bye, Corine hugged the governess as well. It was obvious that her action irritated her brother.

"I shall miss you, Sloane," said Corine. "You became such a dear friend while Bailey was gone. I would have been terribly lonely without your companionship."

"Thank you, my lady. I have greatly enjoyed your friendship, also. You will take good care of yourself, won't you?"

"I have to. Bailey won't let me out of his sight and treats me as if I were made of eggshells. Please keep me posted on Angela's progress. I believe she will completely overcome her shyness."

"I'll be happy to let you know how she is doing. Have a pleasant journey, my lady." The children hugged their beloved aunt one more time before Tearle kissed her on the cheek and helped her into the carriage. Moments later, the coach disappeared down the lane. Without a word to Sloane or the children, the earl turned abruptly and strode away.

Afterwards, the earl's mood grew surly with everyone, but especially with Sloane. No longer did he drop in occasionally to take his dinner with her and the children in the nursery dining room. She learned from Grimley that his lordship dined alone in his study on the few evenings he was at home. In fact, all instructions from the earl or inquiries on her part were relayed by Grimley. Tearle Grayson made it clear he wanted nothing to do with her in any way other than as a governess for his children.

The earl glanced down at her, and Sloane quickly shifted her gaze to study the brush strokes on uncle so-and-so's portrait. When he started down the stairs, her eyes returned automatically to him.

His scowl disappeared and his gaze softened as it swept over her. "Do I meet with your approval, madam?" he asked, amusement evident in his voice.

"Yes, my lord." Sloane struggled to keep her voice even. To the earl's surprise, she stepped into a deep curtsy, not rising until he slipped his fingers beneath her bent arm and drew her up.

"Why do you humble yourself to me?" The words were spoken quietly, but his eyes narrowed dangerously when he lifted her chin with a crooked finger, forcing her to meet his gaze.

"I have come to realize my proper place

here. As a governess, I am little more than a servant, sir. A few weeks ago, I overstepped the limits of my position and thus earned your contempt. I do not wish for you to despise me, my lord." She broke off and turned to face the railing, aware she revealed too much of her feelings both by her words and her expression.

The earl placed a hand on either side of her, gripping the handrail convulsively. He held his rigid body away from her, knowing if he touched her, it would be his undoing.

"You may work for me, but you are not my servant," he hissed in her ear. "You will never be any man's servant, Sloane Donovan." He paused a moment, his breath warm on her cheek, sweeping through her soul like a caress. "Sloane, I don't despise you. I adore you," he whispered. And he was gone, racing down the stairs without a backward glance.

Stunned, Sloane stared with unseeing eyes across the high vaulted hall. The sound of the front door closing brought her attention to the floor below. Grimley walked by, his footsteps first tapping on the tile, then muffled on the rug, apparently unaware of her presence.

She moved on up the seemingly endless staircase, pausing briefly to peek in on the sleeping children. Once in the confines of her own bedroom, she sank down in a yellow, overstuffed chair by the window. Her thoughts spun around like a calliope, and she rested her head against the back of the chair, closing her eyes briefly.

"If you adore me, Tearle Grayson, why do you run off to be with her?" she whispered bitterly. *For a man determined not to marry again, you have a strange way of avoiding the woman trying to trap you,* she thought.

It occurred to her that possibly what the earl had in mind for the beautiful Ebony had nothing to do with marriage. Since Sloane would not be his mistress, perhaps he had decided to avail himself of Ebony's lovely and willing charms.

Sloane sat until long after the twilight became darkness. She searched her mind and her feelings, weighing the consequences of the two avenues open to her. Even as she considered the options, she knew there was only one course she could take. No matter how much she loved the earl, she could not turn her back on her family by becoming his lover. To do so would only bring shame upon her family and her late husband's good name.

She rose and lit a candle, changing for bed. "I suppose I should be happy you respect me enough not to push me, my lord," she whispered. But she wasn't happy; she was more miserable than she had been in a long, long time.

Knowing sleep would be late in coming, Sloane drew on a deep burgundy silk dressing gown and slippers and trod softly downstairs. She tiptoed past Smythe, who was dozing in a chair in the great hall near the library door, apparently awaiting his lordship's return.

She went into the library, closing the door quietly behind her. A single glass candlestick glowed on a sleek Hepplewhite inlay library table, and she lifted the light to read the titles along the lengthy shelves. At last, she found what she was looking for, a newly published work by Mary Wollstone-craft Shelley called *Frankenstein*. She placed the candle back on the table and turned to go.

"I thought you would have preferred something more along Miss Austen's line."

Sloane jumped, giving a startled gasp, and peered into the darkened corner of the room. In the dimness, she could just make out the earl's silhouette.

"I beg pardon for the intrusion, my lord. I did not know you had returned from the party."

The earl uncrossed his ankles and slowly stood. He crossed the room toward her, cautiously placing one foot in front of the other. His cravat was untied and hung loosely about his neck; his shirt was rumpled and open at his throat. He came to a halt in front of her, swaying precariously, but managed to right himself.

"My lord, you're foxed!"

He gave her a silly grin. "The esteemed Earl of Beckford is never foxed, m'lady. Only slightly into my cups, don't you see." With extreme care, he placed his empty glass and equally empty brandy bottle on the table.

Unfortunately, he leaned over a little too far. He would have toppled over if Sloane hadn't put her hands on his chest to stop his descent. Gritting her teeth with the effort, she pushed him upright, grabbing his arms to steady him as he nearly fell over backward.

Once he was standing straight again, she removed her hands and said, "Why didn't you stay at the ball?"

"Too many daughters and too many pushy mamas."

Sloane felt her lips twitch at the corners, but she managed to control her grin. "I would have thought Lady Ebony would keep all the competition away."

"She tried, but I outmaneuvered her a few times. Deuced woman is an octopus."

"An octopus?" Sloane couldn't stifle her giggle this time. Oh, but wouldn't she love for the sultry Ebony to overhear this conversation!

"Too many arms. Always hangin' onto me. Has to have more than two, at least six."

"But, my lord," Sloane said, laughing, "an octopus has eight legs."

"Not talking about legs. Talking about tenacles."

"You mean tentacles."

"That's what I said."

"Well, not quite, but I will concede that Lady Wentwood is very tenacious."

He looked at her thoughtfully before the silly grin crept across his face again. "Slo', I think you're quizzing me." He tapped her on the nose with his forefinger. "Or are you slowly quizzing me?" His face brightened, and he chuckled. "Maybe she's a squid."

Sloane laughed out loud, a sound most pleasing to the earl. He brought his hand up to run his fingers through her long, flowing hair. Her heartbeat switched to double-time at his caress, and she tried to think of something to say.

"I left because the only one I wanted to hold in my arms wasn't at the ball," he said softly.

Her heartbeat leaped to triple-time, but her voice was only a little breathless when she asked, "Was your lady ill?"

"No. She wasn't invited. Paltry sport of Ebony not to invite her. But I'll remedy that oversight. I'll dance with her now."

Before Sloane had a chance to wonder at his words, he swept her into his arms and began to waltz her around the room. *Frankenstein* went flying. The earl grabbed her free hand in his, while her other hand went reflexively to his shoulder. He gave her a roguish grin and began to sing a mildly bawdy song in a beautiful but loud baritone. The warmth of his hand caressed her back through the thin silk, momentarily vanquishing sound reasoning.

The library wasn't small, but it wasn't arranged for dancing either. One chair toppled over, then another. When they bumped into a table and an expensive silver pitcher crashed to the floor, Sloane decided enough was enough. She set her feet firmly on the rug and pulled her hand free from his grasp.

Placing three fingers against his lips, she

scolded, "My lord, you must be quiet and stop dancing around. You'll wake the children with all your noise." He stopped singing and kissed each of her fingers in turn. "Stop that," she snapped, jerking her hand away. He gave her such a hurt little boy look that she almost reached up to smooth away his unhappiness, but caught herself just in time.

"My dear lord, we must get you to bed."

"With you?" he asked hopefully.

"Of course not. Now come along. Surely with all your racket, you woke Smythe." She slid his arm across her shoulders and guided the reluctant earl toward the door. He came to a jerky halt a few steps away from the portal.

"Am I really dear to you?" His voice was silky smooth, all traces of foolishness having vanished.

I wish I could only tell you how much, her heart cried. She set her jaw and then said, "Of course, my lord. You've been very endearing to all of us these past few weeks." The earl flinched as her barb hit its mark.

Sloane opened the door to find Smythe awaiting them. He slipped the earl's other arm around his shoulders and helped Sloane guide the now docile man up the great staircase. When they arrived at the earl's bedroom, the valet left them in the hall on the pretense of turning down the bedding.

His arm still across her shoulders, the earl swung around to face Sloane, resting his free hand on the wall near her head. She hugged the wall with her back to keep a small distance between them.

"Will you tuck me in?" he asked, his lips brushing her forehead.

"No, I'll save that chore for Smythe." She was annoyed at the weakness of her voice.

"Then I shall have to settle for a good-night kiss instead."

"I think not, my lord."

"I shall sing again if you don't."

"You wouldn't."

One blond eyebrow raised expressively. "Do you challenge me, Mrs. Donovan?" he asked softly.

She let her gaze roam over his beloved face for a moment, unaware of the yearning so evident on her own countenance. Sloane could read the daring sparkle in his eye and decided he just might do it. Besides, she did so want to kiss him and feel his arms around her if only for a moment.

"I think not this time, my lord," she said softly, putting her hands around his neck.

The earl smiled tenderly, holding her gaze with his, and ran a fingertip along the side of her jaw and across her bottom lip. Sliding his hand around to the nape of her neck, his gaze dropped to her lips. Her soft hair curled around his fingers as he lowered his head until only a breath separated them.

"Not ever," he whispered, his mouth still hovering above hers, waiting for her to come to him.

Sloane hesitated for a heartbeat, then stretched a fraction of an inch to meet his kiss, delighting in the gentle firmness of his touch. He teased her lips with his tongue, and she opened her mouth, granting him a small victory in this battle of wills.

His hand dropped down from the wall to her waist, pulling her fully against him, while his other hand roamed slowly over her back. He deepened the kiss, and Sloane felt his control begin to waver, much like her own. Fighting an inner struggle, she gave a little push against his chest.

Reluctantly, he raised his head and eased his hold but did not completely set her free. The earl took a deep breath and released it slowly before speaking.

"Can you honestly tell me you prefer spending the night with the monster rather than with me?"

"No, but it is not a matter of preference." Sloane looked up into his eyes, her gray ones tinged with regret. "There is really only one choice I can make, my lord. I cannot bring shame upon my family."

"I see."

She watched him closely, hoping he might understand. His face revealed nothing, so she decided to change the subject.

"You've led us a merry chase this night, sir. You aren't nearly as tipsy as you would have us believe."

He chuckled. "I never said I was foxed. You were the one who arrived at such a brilliant conclusion."

She smiled in return. "I must go back down and retrieve the monster."

He didn't move, but studied her face in the faint light of the hall sconce. "I'll not give up, Sloane. I've tried to stay away from you, but it has only made me such a grouch that no one wants to be near me. You will be mine, Sloane Donovan. You'll find I can't resist a challenge, and you're a very delightful and desirable one."

"You know I can't be what you want me to be."

"We'll see, sweetheart." He kissed her on the cheek and leaned back so she could scurry down the hall to her own room.

Sloane shut the door behind her, forgetting her intention of returning to the library. In a daze, she slipped off her dressing gown and shoes, dropping them in a heap beside her bed. She crawled under the covers, the memory of his words and touch as real as if he were still with her.

She spent the night tossing and turning, alternately muttering Gaelic curses at her love's arrogance and stubbornness and muffling her sobs in the pillow when the longing and loneliness overwhelmed her. She couldn't decide which was worse—having him ignore her completely, or knowing he would charmingly hound her in a quest she could not let him win.

The next day Sloane sat in the warm afternoon sunshine, the click of her flying knitting needles blending with the faint singing of the birds in the background. She was vaguely aware of Angela's chatter as she played with her dolls at Sloane's feet. She had learned to knit at her Scottish grandmother's knee and had often been thankful of the ability to do something productive when her mind was otherwise occupied.

She slept little the night before, as evidenced by the dark smudges beneath her eyes. Her heart waged a war with her conscience all night long with no clear victor. Still brooding over the earl's behavior, she absently recalled that she hadn't seen or heard from Jonny in quite a while.

"Slo', look at me. Look how high I can climb."

Apprehensive, Sloane looked up at the large tree in front of her; her gaze climbing higher and higher until she spied Jonny some twenty feet above the ground.

"That's quite an accomplishment, dear, but you'd better come down a little lower. The wind is picking up." She was amazed at how calm her voice sounded when she was shaking like the leaves blowing in the breeze.

"All right," Jonny answered grudgingly, "but you're my witness. You saw how high I climbed."

"Yes, Jonny. Now come on down, please." Sloane stood up, clutching her knitting as if it were the branches while Jonny made his descent. Suddenly, he lost his footing and was left hanging by his hands, his legs dangling several inches above the next branch.

"Slo' help!"

"Dear God, don't let him fall," she

whispered frantically, throwing the knitting to the ground in her flight to the tree. "I'm coming, Jonny. Curl your legs up and hold onto the branch with your feet, too." Over her shoulder she called, "Go get your father, Angel. Hurry!"

The tot stared at her for a brief moment before running across the garden toward the house, shrieking at the top of her lungs.

Shakily, Sloane began her climb up the tree, fighting down the bile which rose higher in her throat with each ascending limb. She tried to distract herself from her fear by calling encouraging words to Jonny.

She reached the branch just below the child and established herself firmly on its wide span. Holding onto the tree for security, she put her free arm around his waist and gave him instructions.

"Now, dear, I've got you. Let go with your feet and slowly swing them down." He did as he was told. "Good boy. You're only a few inches above the next limb. Let your hands go; I'll hold you until you can get your feet on the next branch." He complied, turning slightly to hold onto the tree trunk once his feet were safely planted. They worked their way down the tree with Sloane helping him through the rough spots until they were about eight feet above the ground.

"You can jump to me now, Jonny," said the earl, standing below them.

Jonny flashed his father a grin and released Sloane's hand, catapulting himself away from the tree through the air to his father's waiting arms.

The earl caught him easily. After giving him a bear-hug, he released him and set him on the ground. "Are you all right, son?"

"I'm fine, Papa. It was a little scary when I was up so high, but Sloane helped me down to where it wasn't so spooky." He frowned up at his father. "I don't think Slo's doing so good. She looks green."

The earl straightened and called to Sloane, "You can come down now, Mrs. Donovan. Jonny is safe. Jump if you want; I'll catch you, too." No response. The earl stepped closer to the tree so he could see her face. Sloane stood with her arms locked firmly around the trunk, her eyes squeezed shut. She was definitely green.

"Can you get her down, Papa?"

The earl did not miss the worried concern in his son's voice. "Of course, son. I believe Mrs. Donovan is afraid of heights. It's a very common malady. You take your sister into the kitchen and tell Mrs. Honeycutt you may have a treat. Ask her to please brew up a strong pot of tea and send Grimley out to me."

Jonny shot a worried glance up at Sloane before looking at his father. The earl calmly removed his brown frock coat and red and cream striped waistcoat, throwing them casually across the lawn chair. Jonny gave a satisfied nod, fully confident that if anyone could get his favorite governess out of the tree, his father could. He grabbed his sister's hand and led her toward the house.

The earl climbed swiftly until he reached the limb on which Sloane stood frozen. He was thankful it was thick and sturdy. He carefully forced his arm between her and the wood, edging it around her waist, and tried to pry her away from the tree. She whimpered and clung to the bark fiercely. The earl stopped pulling and gently pressed his body against her.

"Sloane, it's all right. I won't let you fall. Do you feel my arm around you? Do you feel my strength?"

Eyes still tightly shut, her nod was so imperceptible he would have missed it if he had not felt her hair brush against his chin.

"Let me help you down, sweetheart. Let me be your strength. I know you're afraid, but I'll get you down. Do you trust me?"

"Yes." Her voice was barely a whisper.

"That's my girl. Now, I want you to open your eyes, but don't look down." He glanced down to see Grimley arrive below them, panting from his run. "Sloane, Grimley is just below us. I'm going to lower you down to him." He felt her stiffen. "We're really not that high. Let go of the tree and take hold of my hand." When she hesitated, he whispered, "Trust me sweetheart. I would never let you be hurt."

She forced first one hand and then the other away from the tree to grab onto him. She opened her eyes and fixed her gaze on the leaves in front of her.

"That's my girl. Now, I'm holding your hand tightly. Do you feel secure?" Another brief nod. "Very good. I'm going to nudge your feet off the limb, Sloane, and lower you to the ground. Grimley is, there and he will catch you."

"Tearle, I can't," she whispered frantically.

He held her close for a moment, resting his face in her fragrant hair, and savored the sound of his name in her soft voice. "You must, Sloane, or we'll be up here all night, and I, for one, don't relish the idea of sharing the tree with the owls."

She tried to give him a weak smile, but failed. At the same time, he gently pushed her feet from the tree. She moaned with terror as he carefully and slowly lowered her to the ground into Grimley's waiting arms. The old man held her up as her knees buckled and gratefully surrendered his place to the earl when he dropped from the tree.

He swept her up in his arms, cradling her like a child. "You're safe, now. Just try to breathe deeply. I'll take you inside."

Her arms were curled against his chest, her fingers clasped tightly into a fist. He carried her into the library and placed her on a couch. When she tried to sit up, he gently pushed her back down.

"You will stay there until I give you permission to sit up, Mrs. Donovan. You are still quite green. Close your eyes and rest a moment."

Bess, the parlormaid, rushed in with a

small basin of cool water and a cloth, setting them on a table beside the couch. "Do you want me to stay with her, my lord?" she asked, dipping the cloth into the water. She squeezed out the piece of flannel and placed it on Sloane's forehead.

"No. I will stay with her, Bess. Thank you."

The young maid curtsied and left the room, leaving the door open behind her. The earl picked up the cloth, waving it gently in the air before wiping Sloane's face. He slipped his fingers beneath her neck, unfastening the top several buttons of her white cambric daydress. He massaged her neck for a moment then pulled the fabric away from her throat. He dipped the cloth in the water again, wringing it until it was only damp, and washed her throat.

He folded the cloth and laid it across her forehead and eyes just as Grimley arrived with the pot of tea. "Thank you, Grimley," he said, not looking up. "That will be all for now." The butler inclined his head and left the room, shutting the door behind him.

Sloane picked up the cloth and handed it back to the earl. "I feel better." The earl took her hand and pulled her up slightly, fluffing pillows behind her back so that she still reclined. Noting her wince, he turned her hand palm up and grimaced at the bloody, scraped skin.

"You've harmed yourself, my dear." He took both her hands and washed them in the basin as a mother would care for a child's

wound, moving Sloane deeply by his gentleness. "You will need some of Mrs. Honeycutt's salve for your hands." He dried them
on a soft piece of linen and rang the bell for the
butler. When Grimley appeared, he requested the ointment and bandages.

"Do you feel like having a cup of tea?"

"Yes, thank you."

"Have you always been terrified of
heights?" the earl asked, adding a generous
amount of cream and a teaspoon of sugar to
her cup of tea. He handed it to her, his fingers
lingering as she took it. Her hands still
trembled slightly, but she managed to keep
from spilling the tea.

She took a sip and settled the cup and
saucer on her lap. "I was a regular hoyden in
my childhood, roughing it with my brothers,
getting into all sorts of mischief. I wasn't
afraid of anything until my tenth birthday.
Tony dared me to climb the big elm tree at
the back of the house. I climbed almost to the
top. On the way back down, I fell and broke
my arm."

"And you've been frightened of heights
ever since?"

"Yes. I don't think it was so much the
terrible pain of the broken arm as it was the
horrible feeling of falling. Of seeing the
ground coming up at me and knowing there
was nothing I could do, nothing to grab onto.
I had nightmares for years about climbing a
great cliff and falling over the edge."

The earl smiled a little. "I think we've all
had those kind of dreams. I usually wound up

on the floor."

"I never did. I'd never land . . . just keep on falling until I would wake myself up screaming." She couldn't stop a shudder, but took a deep breath and forced herself to relax. "But I outgrew them." She wondered if the dream would return tonight.

He watched her closely and as he so often did, seemed to read her thoughts. "If the nightmare returns, I'll be here." He stared at his cup for a moment, then raised his gaze to hers, startling her with its intensity. "Why did you try to rescue Jonny? Why didn't you call for me?"

"I wasn't sure where you were. He was dangling in midair and I just couldn't take the chance he would fall. I didn't know if I could get him down; I only knew I had to try."

"Even though you were terrified," he mused.

She could no longer meet his penetrating gaze and looked down at her lap. When he spoke again, the ragged edge in his voice brought her head up abruptly.

"Thank you, Sloane." He set the teacup back on the tray, rattling it slightly. "Are you finished with your tea?" He cleared his throat as she handed him the nearly empty cup. Grimley returned with the ointment and bandages. The earl applied a liberal amount of the cream to her hands before wrapping them in the cloth strips.

"You may remove the bandages in the morning. I think you'll find the salve works wonders. Now, my dear, you will go up and rest until dinner. No, don't try to walk. I'll carry you." She started to protest, but he stopped her with a look. "Please, Sloane, it will make me feel better."

For the first time that afternoon, she smiled. "I think it would make me feel better, too, my lord." He swept her up in his arms once again, and she snuggled against his neck, her hand resting on his shoulder. He carried her up the stairs and placed her gently upon the bed.

"Try to sleep. I'll send Bess up to check on you before dinner. If you want to have a tray brought up, you need only ask."

"Thank you, Lord Beckford," she said sleepily when he pulled off her slippers and drew a soft blanket over her.

"I prefer it when you call me, Tearle, sweetheart," he said softly, brushing a curl from her cheek.

She smiled faintly, whispered his name, and closed her eyes, deciding that charming hounding was a definite improvement over being ignored.

5

"I don't think Uncle Jonathan's ever going to get here," moaned Jonny. He turned away from the nursery window, dropping from his knees to slouch on the dark blue brocade window seat.

Sloane smiled at the unhappy little boy, her eyes twinkling at the smudge left by his nose on the windowpane. "Don't you know that a watched pot never boils? If you find something to occupy your time, he'll be here before you know it. Actually, I don't believe he is expected until afternoon. There will be plenty of time for you two to attend church with me as usual."

Jonny's grimace made Sloane smile again. "Now, my dear, you can sit still for that long. The vicar's not so long-winded. Come here, Angel, and let me help you with your dress. Then, you can put your shoes on."

The little girl moved to stand in front of Sloane's chair, putting her French doll on the bed beside them. Sloane pulled the sheer pink organdy dress over her head and down over the rose pink calico slip. "I watch the people in church," Angela announced solemnly. "Jimmy flirt'th with Molly right under her papa'th noth."

Jonny jumped up to kneel on the window seat again and laughed. "That's because the Squire's most always asleep. His wife had to poke him in the ribs last week 'cause he started to snore. Hey, there's a carriage coming up the lane. He's here! Come on, Angel!"

He bolted off his perch, grabbing his sister's arm on the way to the door, and pulled her along with him. They dashed through the portal before Sloane could stop them.

"Jonny, bring your sister back here; she's not fully dressed." Sloane jumped up to follow, tripping over one of Angela's shoes. A quick glance around the room failed to produce the mate. "Oh, bother. She must have kicked it under the bed."

Crouching down on all fours, Sloane lifted the edge of the bedspread to peer beneath the mahogany bedframe. She spied the shoe, stretching her arm to its full length before her fingers closed around it. The heavy spread drooped over the side of the mattress, brushing against her hair, loosening several hairpins in the process. She scrambled to her feet and gave a few of the pins a quick push with her free hand as she raced toward the door.

The children's excited cries drifted up

the stairway, indicating that they were well ahead of her. Sloane dashed down the stairs, heedless of etiquette, in a valiant effort to catch up with the children before their father saw them. Unhappily, her mad race was in vain.

Swerving around the last turn in the staircase, she gained a clear view of the front entrance. The doors were flung wide open, and the children made a beeline for the front steps. Angela slipped a little in her stocking feet, but Jonny helped her to right herself. Both the earl and his brother stood in the portico and turned to watch the youngsters' charging arrival.

Tearle cast a quick glance at the children before turning his eyes to the woman plummeting down the stairs. Suddenly, Sloane realized she was under scrutiny and slowed her pace.

The earl's hungry gaze did not leave her. Three or four stray tendrils fell across the nape of her neck, and a larger strand of honeyed silk curled down her cheek just in front of her ear. Her face was flushed, and her bosom heaved beneath the light jonquil dress of sprig muslin.

His eyes followed the curve of her gown up the very respectable high neckline to the lace edging at her throat, all the while having some very unrespectable thoughts about kissing the soft skin it covered. For the briefest of moments, he entertained the insane fantasy of sweeping her up in his arms and marching back up those same stairs, leaving his brother and children to their own devices.

It was his brother, however, who brought him back soundly to reality. "My, my," Jonathan said softly, "and to think all those old toplofty matrons would have us believe it uncomely for a woman to race about. You've improved the scenery around here, Louie, my boy. Vastly improved the scenery." At that point, Jonathan was smothered with the exuberant hugs of the children, which he returned with laughing affection.

Sloane thought her heart would pound right out of her chest as the earl devoured her with his gaze. It wasn't just the desire reflected in his unusually open expression; it was more the tenderness spreading across his face at the sight of her that struck the harmonizing note in her heart's song.

Then, his brother said something and the soft countenance hardened. "You will be teaching my daughter to be a regular hoyden, Mrs. Donovan, if you continue to carry on like one. A bit more decorum would be in order, I think."

Embarrassed, slightly flustered by his sudden change, and feeling another heavy twist of hair slip from its pin, Sloane stammered, "I . . . I'm . . . forgive me, my lord. It was just what I was trying to prevent, sir. In her excitement, Angel left without letting me button her up completely."

The earl glanced scathingly down at the slippers that dangled in Sloane's hand. His mouth tightened as he turned toward the little girl happily holding onto her uncle's coattail, the thin ribbon sash of her dress hanging to the ground.

"Angela, come here." Disapproval and anger were evident in his quietly controlled tone. Angela's eyes grew wide as saucers, and her lower lip quivered as she tried to hide behind their guest. "Angela, obey me," the earl said impatiently.

"Please, my lord," pleaded Sloane softly, "don't frighten her." Her voice dropped to a whisper, "She has not quite conquered her fear of you. Please, remember that she is still just a small, shy girl." She raised her voice just above a whisper. "The blame for her disarray should rest upon my shoulders, my lord."

The earl looked down at Sloane's earnest face, his gaze dropping to her soft pink lips, and the memory of the last time he kissed her popped absurdly into his mind. He shook his head, certain he was going mad as a weaver.

Turning back to the cowering child, he studied her for a moment before saying kindly, "Angela, please come over so Mrs. Donovan can button you up. I know you were excited to see Uncle Jonathan, and I'm not angry with you."

The little girl stared at him an instant longer before taking a hesitant step toward Sloane. The governess immediately knelt down and held out her arms. Angela hurled herself across the open space to the security of Sloane's embrace.

After a long hug, Sloane directed her to

turn around and made quick work of fastening up the three tiny buttons at the low square neck of her gown and tying the sash into a pert bow. When she picked up the shoes, the earl leaned over and lifted his daughter in his arms.

"Hold your foot still so Mrs. Donovan can put your slipper on," he commanded quietly. Angela looked up at the earl and cautiously slid an arm across his shoulder.

Sloane rose and held the child's foot in one hand while she pushed the slipper on with the other. When she had quickly shod both feet, his lordship gave the child a kiss on the cheek and placed her on the floor.

"Go rescue your uncle, Angel. Jonny is already monopolizing him." The little girl scurried off as he turned again to Sloane, blocking Jonathan's view of her. A smile twitched the corner of his mouth as she tried to straighten her appearance.

"Do you have any idea how badly I want to kiss you right now?" he murmured. Her hand paused, then continued fastening up a curl. "I came within a hair's breadth of tossing sanity to the wind and hauling you right back up that staircase." Her gaze flew to his, and he chuckled. "Ah, I see you could tell. You are utterly delightful in *deshabille*, sweetheart, but I would prefer to be the only man to see you in such a fetching state."

Sloane felt the hot color rush to her face. "Angela's shoe was under the bed, and the spread fell on my head when I got down on the floor to pull it out."

"I would have loved to have been privy to that scene." The earl laughed softly and absently tucked a golden streaked wisp of hair behind her ear. "Kindly disregard my earlier comments about decorum, Sloane. Life would be morosely dull around here if you became a gargoyle."

Without realizing what she was doing, Sloane pressed her cheek against the hand that lingered there. "Gargoyle, my lord?" she asked dreamily.

His thumb caressed her chin as his fingers cradled her jaw. "Cory's pet name for your predecessor." Suddenly, the earl was reminded of his brother's presence and dropped his hand, straightening quickly. Sloane's face grew even hotter when she remembered where they were. Hastily, she tucked the wayward strands of hair under any available pin and regained some sense of order, both to her appearance and her emotions.

At that moment, the tolling of the church bells began to echo across the vale. The earl smiled down at her. "Let me introduce you before you go." He stepped aside to face his brother, who by now was watching them with keen interest.

"Mrs. Donovan, may I make known to you my brother, Lord Jonathan Grayson. Jonathan, Mrs. Sloane Donovan, the children's governess."

Sloane dropped a shallow curtsy. "I am pleased to meet you, Lord Grayson. As you can see, the children have greatly looked forward to your visit."

Jonathan's dark brown eyes crinkled with laughter. "I really hadn't noticed, Mrs. Donovan." He paused a moment and then smiled, an expression that no doubt would have caused a flightly woman to swoon in adoration at his feet. "I must say that your manner is a bit unorthodox, but you seem to be working miracles in this household. I daresay if I'd had as lovely a creature for my governess, I'd still be wearing short coats."

"Jonathan, quit trying to put Mrs. Donovan to the blush," the earl cut in coolly. "Madam, you'll be late for church if you don't leave now."

Sloane was relieved to shift her gaze away from Jonathan's open appraisal. "I needn't go, my lord, if you want me to take care of the children. I fear they are much too excited to listen to the vicar's sermon today."

"I agree," the earl replied, watching Jonny chase Angela around the curricle standing in the drive. "You go ahead. I think we can keep these urchins occupied for the few hours you are gone. Please hurry home, though. I'm sure I'll be more than happy to have you take them off my hands." As an afterthought, he said, "Give my regards to your brother-in-law, the vicar," and cast a meaningful look at his brother.

Jonathan acknowledged his message with a slight nod of his head, the morning sun catching a glint of red in his chestnut brown hair. "I think I have something to occupy the children, Mrs. Donovan."

He turned and stepped back to the curricle, retrieving a large box from behind the seat. A wiggly puppy stuck his black and white head and front paws over the edge and barked excitedly.

"A puppy! You brought us a puppy. Please, Papa, may we keep him? He's a real stunner, ain't he Sloane?"

"Isn't he, Jonny, and yes, he is indeed a pretty little bundle of curls," laughed Sloane.

The earl raised one eyebrow at his brother, who answered his unspoken question a little defensively. "Well, we had a dog when we were their age. Thought it would be good company for them. He's a cocker spaniel, so he won't get too big. You remember how much fun we had with old Pudge, don't you?"

The earl's countenance softened as he looked out over the park-like gardens. Memories of childhood romps across those lovely grounds with their English sheepdog flooded his mind. "Yes, I remember."

"Very well, you may keep the dog, children, but you must always treat him kindly. I do not care for animals in the house, so he will have a special place in the kennel where he can be cared for properly. As long as he is with you, he may have free run of the grounds, providing he doesn't start digging up the shrubbery. When he is not with you, I expect him to be confined to the kennel. Under no circumstances is he to be allowed in the house. Do I make myself clear?" He addressed his son in particular, since he already had a collection of turtles and birds in the nursery playroom.

Both children nodded excitedly. "Yes, Papa, we'll be good to him and keep him out of the house," cried Jonny. "Uncle Jon, does he have a name?"

"Yes, he does. I decided such a fancy fellow could only be called by one name—Beau. After all, he does look like he is dressed in evening clothes. See how his black back and legs look like a coat, and his white belly and chin look like a white satin waist-coat and cravat?"

Jonny nodded, then frowned. "Why Beau, Uncle?"

"He's named after Beau Brummell, Jonny."

"Oh, yes, I've heard of him. He was the first star of fashion."

The earl chuckled. "Among other things. Go get your bonnet, Sloane. I'll have the phaeton brought around for you."

"Thank you, my lord. Good morning, gentlemen." Sloane turned and walked quickly, but gracefully up the stairs.

Jonathan handed Beau to the children. "Take him for a run, imps. He's been cooped up a deucedly long time." He watched them race across the grass after the springing puppy before turning to his brother.

"Where did you find that enchanting bit of womanhood?"

"I didn't; Cory did. She hired her while I was on the Continent. The children adore her."

"I might say the same thing about you," said Jonathan, as they strolled across the grounds to sit in wicker chairs clustered beneath the shade of several oak trees.

The earl hesitated before answering. "I am fond of her. She has been raised a lady, but certainly not in the same mold as most we run across. Yesterday, she climbed up in the old oak to help Jonny down when he lost his footing."

"You're quizzing me."

"Upon my honor, I'm not. She climbed up—a process I didn't see, unfortunately—and maneuvered Jonny down far enough so he could jump to me when I arrived on the scene. That's when the trouble started."

"Trouble?"

"It seems our heroine is terrified of heights. Once Jonny was down, she couldn't move. I had to climb up after her."

"Cozy. I'd have kept her up there a while," Jonathan said, with a wicked gleam in his eye.

The earl grinned. "Well, I will admit she does wear the most tantalizing lavender perfume, but I had a devil of a time persuading her to hug me instead of the tree trunk."

"She probably couldn't tell the difference," whooped his brother.

The earl smiled lazily, his eyes twinkling, but did not bother to respond.

Grimley shuffled up to the table with refreshments, a bright smile lighting his wrinkled face. Jonathan jumped up from his seat and offered the old man his hand. The butler hastily put down the tray and shook the young lord's hand.

" 'Tis good to see you again, Lord Grayson. You were just a gangly lad when I saw you last, but you've grown into a fine looking gentleman."

"Thank you, Grimley. I'm happy you approve and glad to say you haven't changed a bit. Do you still keep Mrs. Honeycutt hopping?"

"Not as high as I used to. She's getting a bit old to scare too often. Wouldn't want the old gel to keel over with the vapors, m'lord."

"No, Grimley, we wouldn't want that." Jonathan laughed as the butler poured both gentlemen a glass of Madeira. After being reassured there was nothing more the gentlemen needed, the old man bowed and left them to their conversation.

"Atherton is her grandfather. Her parents live on the other side of Evesham. Do you remember Kincade Stables?"

"No, but then I haven't been here in about ten years." He looked around at the grounds and manor in a slow appraisal. "The old place looks as good as it ever did, better in fact. I'm glad you moved back here, Tearle. I think it suits you." His eyes narrowed as he watched his brother glance casually toward the front door.

Sloane hurried between the portico's Corinthian columns and down the steps, taking the groom's offered hand, and stepped lightly into the waiting phaeton. Tearle watched the vehicle move down the drive with an air of studied indifference.

"Widow?"

"Yes. Her husband died several years ago."

Jonathan frowned. "If she's Atherton's granddaughter, why is she working as a governess? He's pretty plush in the pocket."

"She does have a monthly pension of some kind which allowed her to negotiate more freedom than most in her position and obviously provides for her wardrobe. However, she likes children, and after her husband's death needed something to do with her time. Her father was Atherton's stable master and although her mother taught her how to be a lady, she doesn't have too great a liking for the *ton*."

"Pity. She'd break more than a few young hearts; probably have a whole retinue of bucks at her beck and call."

The earl smiled. "Feeling like an old man after eight seasons, eh? How are things in town?"

"Winding down. Most everybody has escaped the heat and gone to the country. Andrew and George went to Brighton. Ted's gone up to Yorkshire to his father's place, and Rodney decided to give Bath a whirl. Glad to be away from them for a while, and away from all the paragons this season produced."

"Nothing caught your fancy, eh?"

"None I cared to follow to Brighton. I flirted with Amy Amhearst for a while, but decided she's just like the rest of them.

Doesn't have an original thought in that pretty head of hers; but I'll admit it's a very pretty head. Almost enough to forget she's a pea-brain."

The earl looked grim. "Take some advice, little brother. Beauty's not enough; in fact, it can be a detriment. Actually, marriage can be a detriment, but I think you should find a wife. I don't plan on marrying again, so you should raise a passel of children, with at least one or two sons in the brood. God forbid that anything should ever happen to Jonny, but I'd hate to see the title go to cousin Egbert or his repulsive brats."

"Lord, yes, he'd squander everything away in a fortnight." Jonathan held his glass up to the light, apparently admiring the clear white wine, while he surreptitiously watched his brother over the rim. As hard as Linette's death had been for Tearle, he knew his marriage had been even harder.

Knowledge of his sister-in-law's adulterous ways had been brought home to him on his last visit before her death. Without any encouragement on his part, she had come to him in the middle of the night very obviously intent upon seduction. He had practically thrown her out of his room two minutes after she came in. As far as he knew, Tearle never found out about her visit, and he prayed he never would.

Before that, he had often wondered what had dried his brother up, what had changed him from a quick-witted, easygoing man into a hard-shelled cynic. It had taken only those brief moments to show him that a man must look beneath the beauty and fancy trappings of a lady to see if there was indeed a gentle and kind woman beneath.

"Well, I'll keep my eyes open. Perhaps I'll run across some irresistible child in next season's crop. I'm not quite ready to throw the handkerchief. Haven't sampled all the sweet bits of muslin I'd like yet."

"What has getting married got to do with that? There's no need to forego a little pleasure on the side just because you've got a ring on your finger."

Jonathan shifted in his chair and looked at the earl closely. "There was a time when you thought otherwise."

"I was as green as grass and incredibly stupid. You needn't look for fidelity in marriage, Jon, because you won't find it. Loyalty and trust are a rare commodity, and love is nonexistent. No, my boy, you'd better resign yourself to finding some plain little miss who's compatible and then be willing to find your passion someplace else when you get bored—or when she does."

Jonathan sat quietly contemplating his brother for a long time. Finally, he rose and set his glass on the table. "I think I'll change and go for a ride. Will you join me?"

"Certainly," the earl said with a shrug.

They had only gone a few steps when Jonathan said, "I hope you're wrong, Tearle. If that's all there is to look forward to in marriage, why bother?"

"Exactly," said the earl curtly, his tight

lips and closed expression declaring that the discussion had ended.

Midmorning, several days later, the earl paused in the second floor gallery, stepping into the shadows to avoid being seen by the couple in the great hall below. Although he could not ascertain what was being said, it was obvious his brother had put on his most charming expression and manner.

The younger lord made some witty comment, and Sloane's tinkle of laughter floated up the great arch to reach Tearle's ears. She quietly replied, emphasizing her comment with a wave of her hand.

Unexpectedly, Jonathan caught Sloane's hand and brought the palm up to his lips. Anger singed the earl as his brother's lips lingered overlong on that smooth skin. His anger was only somewhat abated by Sloane's reaction. The straightening of her back, hot flush of the cheeks, and her quick departure indicated she had not welcomed the younger man's attentions.

The earl sprang quickly down the stairs, snapping crisply to his brother as they met in the hall, "I want a word with you in my study, and close the door behind you."

Jonathan followed him through the library into the smaller sunlit room, annoyed at his brother's commanding attitude. Unlike many of his colleagues, Jonathan's father had bestowed upon him a more than generous allowance and investments. He would never be dependent upon his brother's good graces for his livelihood and resented it when Tearle directed his air of authority toward him.

"Don't treat me like an errant child, Tearle. What's got you so high in the boughs?"

"Quit trifling with Mrs. Donovan. She's no light skirt," he said, conveniently forgetting that was exactly what he had been trying to make of her for several weeks. "She's not a candidate for a summer dalliance."

"What makes you so sure a summer dalliance is all I'm after?"

The earl stared hard at his brother before turning toward the window and dropping his hands on the sill. "She's a good woman, Jon. Leave her alone."

Although Jonathan had only been flirting with the governess to pass the time, he wasn't quite ready to capitulate to his sibling's will. And, he had to admit, he was curious about his brother's defense of the lady's virtue. Tearle was barely able to restrain his anger; the tension between them grew tight like a bowstring. If he didn't know better, he'd be inclined to think that his woman-hardened brother was jealous. Not a speck of his humor showed on his face, but Jonathan grinned inside.

"I suppose I could, but she's such a charming little thing, it'll be hard. Actually, I was thinking of seeing if she wanted to take a little trip. I hear Paris is rather nice since law and order have been restored."

The earl whirled about, his scowl so deep his eyebrows practically met. "Don't you dare insult her by mentioning such a thing. If you want to remain as my guest, you will keep that charm of yours to yourself, not to mention your hands!''

"My, but aren't we touchy where Sloane is concerned."

The earl took a deep breath, obviously making an effort to calm down. "I'd do the same if it were any of the women in my employ. As the lord here, it's my duty to protect them from rogues like you.''

"I wonder," murmured Jonathan, then he grinned. "You mean I have to take my devilishly handsome person over to the inn if I want to . . . uh . . . slake my thirst?''

"Precisely." The earl still looked grim.

"Very well, to keep our friendship from dying a certain death, I shall treat Sloane . . . er . . . Mrs. Donovan with the utmost courtesy and respect. Such a waste; just when she was beginning to come around.''

The earl forced a smile. "I think that's stretching it a bit.''

They were interrupted by a knock at the door. When the earl granted entrance, Grimley came in. "You have visitors, m'lord." The old man rolled his eyes heavenward and gave an exasperated sigh. "Lady Ebony Wentwood and Lord Alan Carlisle are waiting in the drawing room, sir." At the lift of the earl's eyebrow, he continued, "They are wearing their riding clothes. Good thing you don't have to change.

Shall I tell Mrs. Honeycutt we'll have guests for luncheon?"

"Yes, you might as well, Grimley. After a ride, it will be too near mealtime to send them away." As the butler turned and shuffled down the hall toward the kitchen, the earl stepped through the door and called softly, "No screams today if you please, Grimley. Break the news to Mrs. Honeycutt gently."

The man never broke his turtle-like pace, but nodded his head in agreement. "As you wish, m'lord."

When the gentlemen entered the drawing room, Lord Carlisle and Lady Ebony stood by the window watching the grooms lead their horses back and forth in the lane beside the house. As usual, Lady Ebony was stunning in a bright red riding dress. A matching hat trimmed with black embroidery and tassels set off her shiny ebony curls to perfection. Her alabaster skin glowed with the slightest touch of pink as she extolled her horse's fine points to her brother.

"Good morning, Lady Ebony, Carlisle. Good of you to drop by. You're looking as lovely as ever this morning, m'lady."

Lady Ebony turned her dark brown eyes toward the earl and ran her gaze over him slowly. "Thank you for the compliment, Tearle, darling." She held out her hand so he might kiss it. "I might add that you are looking as wickedly handsome and fit as ever."

He kissed her hand obligingly, knowing he lifted his head much too quickly for her satisfaction. "What brings you over to Beckford Hall today?"

"I simply had to show you my new horse, Mercury. He's not as spirited as the one I almost bought, but swifter, I think. I had hoped we might go for a ride. He prances so prettily, you see." She smiled that enticing smile, and the earl silently acknowledged the horse matched his mistress; she knew how to prance very prettily, too.

"Of course. In fact, I was just heading out. Jonathan, will you join us?"

Jonathan paused in his conversation with Carlisle about a recent boxing match they had both attended. "Sorry, I can't this morning. I'm promised to the Squire for luncheon, so I must be leaving shortly. I should be back soon afterwards; perhaps I can spend some time with you then."

"I'll look forward to seeing you, Jonathan, if his lordship hasn't sent me on my way." Ebony hooked her arm through the earl's as they walked to the front entry. "I'll have to be very sweet so you'll let me stay. I have so looked forward to spending the day with you. Life was terribly dull in London after you left, darling."

The earl glanced at Brian, the new footman, who had hastily taken his place by the front door. Although the youngster stood rigidly at attention, his ears were on the twitch. His lordship slipped his arm from beneath Lady Ebony's.

"I'll stroll on down to the stables and pick up Trojan. I need to stretch my legs a bit before I ride. I'll meet you out front in just a few minutes."

"I can hardly bear to wait," pouted Lady Ebony in her sultry voice.

The earl watched the footman as he handed Carlisle his hat and crop with confident ease. When he handed Lady Ebony her crop, however, the lad's face flushed beet red and his hand shook. The boy glanced in embarrassment at the earl and barely controlled his astonishment when the earl winked at him.

Tearle walked quickly toward the stables, deciding a day with Ebony would provide a welcome diversion. Perhaps he would flirt with her a bit just to throw Jonathan off the track. It just wouldn't do to have him think he was over-concerned about Sloane. He frowned, wondering why it seemed so important to keep his infatuation with Sloane a secret from Jon. There had been few secrets between them over the years, none of which had concerned interest in a new ladylove.

The earl drew up short as he neared the stable. Sloane and Tom, the stable master, were outside, talking as they walked Trojan in the paddock. He would not have eavesdropped except for the mention of his name.

"How's Lord Beckford treatin' you?" Tom asked, his concern obvious as he watched Sloane's face closely.

Sloane sighed. "Oh, he's been very kind

and considerate since Lord Grayson came, but I don't think he is particularly noted for his restraint. Soon, I fear, it will be as before. I am merely an amusement for him, a country oddity, a challenge since I won't give in to him."

Tom dropped his arm comfortably around her shoulders. Their friendship was such an old one that Sloane thought no more of the gesture than if it had been one of her brothers walking with her.

The earl, however, interpreted the scene very differently. He was so shocked by the sudden piercing stab of jealousy that he didn't hear Sloane quietly inquire about Tom's own pursuit of the parlormaid, Bess, nor Tom's proud reply that she had accepted his offer of marriage.

"Oh, Tom," Sloane cried, flinging her arms around him enthusiastically, "that makes me so happy."

"Ah, me too, lass," he laughed, squeezing her shoulders affectionately. "We'll be married right away, as soon as his lordship gives his permission, o' course."

The earl stomped into the paddock, snatching the reins from Tom's fingers. Sloane jumped back, and Tom dropped his arm from her shoulders. "Get back to work, both of you."

"But today is my day off, my lord," Sloane said in confusion. "I had planned to visit my parents."

"You'll be going no where today, madam. I have need of your services. Lady Ebony and

Lord Carlisle have come for a visit. I will want the children presented to them at tea-time and your presence is essential to their good behavior. Now, get on with your duties —immediately." He swung up on the horse, glaring down at Sloane when she hesitated, a determined, angry look slowly spreading across her face.

"It is unfair to require me to work today, my lord. I am to go with my family on an outing, and it would be inconsiderate to ask them to change their plans. Surely, Bess can handle the children as well as I."

"Immediately, Mrs. Donovan—and wipe that rebellious look off your pretty face and hold your saucy tongue, or you'll be looking for another position."

"Yes, my lord," Sloane said hotly, spinning on her heel and stalking off toward the house.

The earl swung his horse around, meeting Tom's astounded gaze with such wrath that the large man cringed inside. "You shall never have my permission to marry her—never!" He spun Trojan around so quickly, the horse reared in protest, but his strong hands quickly controlled the animal, directing him to go around to the front of the house.

Tom whistled silently, pulling off his cap to scratch his head, and stared after the earl.

"Glory, what got into 'im, do ye reckon?" asked one of the stable boys, stepping cautiously around the corner of the building.

Tom shook his head and frowned. "If I

didn't know better, I'd say he was jealous."
He pulled on his cap and continued to shake
his head, muttering under his breath as he
walked in the direction of the servant's
entrance to tell Bess what had happened.

6

The earl pulled out Ebony's chair after their luncheon and offered her his arm. They had ridden for some time, thus Jonathan returned from his visit to the squire before they had completed the meal.

"I'm going to show Lady Ebony some of the things I collected on my last trip to the Continent. Do you want to join us?" he asked, directing his gaze at the other two gentlemen.

"We'll join you in a little while," said Jonathan. "Carlisle has challenged me to a game of billiards, and you know I can't pass up that opportunity."

The earl smiled, although if one were to look closely, it would be apparent that it was only for show. "You'd better watch him, Carlisle. He's grown very proficient in the last year or so. Whipped me soundly just last evening."

"In that case, I shall go easy with my bets," replied his guest.

The four left the dining room together

but the earl and Lady Ebony turned toward the library while the other men went across the hall to the billiard room.

"I love the tapestries, Tearle. They lend such magnificence to the hall. Did you purchase them on your trip?"

"Yes, in Brussels. They are sixteenth century Belgian. I much prefer them here instead of all those pictures of my various ancestors. I have relegated those items to the staircase and the gallery upstairs where they belong."

They walked into the library where Ebony spied an ornate gold filigree paper box on one of the walnut tables. "Oh, this looks interesting. Did it belong to Marie Antoinette?"

"No, supposedly it belonged to Napoleon, but it is difficult to be certain of these things. I'm sure half the trinkets in France are said to have been his. According to the lady who gave it to me, the little general filled it with the stationery used for his most intimate correspondence."

"Mmm, sounds delightfully scandalous." Ebony cocked her head and smiled coyly. "A gift from a female admirer, I assume. Should I be jealous of her, Tearle?"

"I see no reason to be, Ebony, since the lady in question is an elderly friend of my mother's." Although tempted, he refrained from adding that he didn't give a whit whether she was jealous or not.

"You've lowered and enlarged the windows," Ebony said enthusiastically as they strolled through the library. "I think that's just what Papa should do. It brings the outdoors in, so to speak. He has moved the main rooms down to the ground floor as you have done, but the lower windows make all the difference. I shall have him come over. When he sees how wonderfully light everything is, I'm sure he'll want to do the same." She paused thoughtfully, pursing her lips prettily. "But, how did that affect the basement windows? Aren't they too close to the bottom of these now?"

"No, I had them made smaller. I knew it would make the basement too dark for the servants to live and work, so we built on the new kitchen at the back and added the servants wing out to the side. Now, we just use the basement for storage and as a wine cellar. It works rather well, I think."

"I suppose the servants like their new rooms and being above ground. I never thought about it before, but I guess it would get dreadfully gloomy below stairs in the winter."

"I confess I hadn't thought of it before the remodeling either. Mrs. Honeycutt kept exclaiming about how wonderful it was to see the sunshine while she worked." They stopped in front of one of the large windows, looking out over a circular bed of tall yellow hollyhocks. "She and Grimley have taken to sending the other servants outside for a bit on sunny days. I must say they aren't as pale as usual, and appear to be healthier."

"But how do they get their work done if

they are gadding about outside?"

"Oh, they make certain they have something productive to occupy their time. I'm not all that lenient." He rolled his neck from side to side in an effort to stretch out the stiffness.

"Darling, you've been so tense all day. Why don't you sit down and let me rub your neck and shoulders. You'll be getting a migraine if you don't relax."

He let her lead him around to the red velvet settee and started to sit down.

"Wait, darling. Do take off your coat so I can reach your neck and shoulders better. I'll do my best not to mess up your beautiful neckcloth." Her body brushed provocatively against his as she helped him shrug out of his jacket.

He gazed down at her with a lazy sensuality that lit a responding spark in her eye. "I don't think I'd mind if you messed it up, Ebony; if it were for the right reason."

She laughed her husky laugh and ran a finger lightly along his chin. "Later, darling. Now, we must help your poor neck."

"In that case, let's go in here where it's quieter." The earl guided her into his study, giving the door a shove behind him. He walked across the room to a dark blue, brocade couch, not noticing that the door was still slightly ajar. The earl sat down and Ebony moved around behind the couch.

"Lean your head against the cushion. I can reach your neck and shoulders just fine."

The earl closed his eyes and let Ebony's

sure, strong fingers knead the knots in his muscles. His head had been hurting most of the morning, since he'd seen Sloane at the stables, in fact. At the mere thought of her, he tensed.

"Relax, darling," whispered Ebony, close to his ear. "Don't think about whatever upset you. You must put it out of your mind so my magic can work."

She began to hum softly, and the earl remembered that she had a lovely voice. He concentrated on listening to the melodious tones and forced himself to relax. A few minutes later, his muscles moved pliantly beneath her fingers, and the pounding in his head began to fade.

He felt her fingers carefully untie his cravat and pull it from beneath his collar. She unfastened the first several buttons of his shirt, and slid her fingers beneath the material to stroke his chest as her lips touched the side of his neck. He found himself wishing that the long curl draped across his shoulder was honey brown instead of sable.

Blast that woman! he thought viciously. Must she haunt me even when she cares for another? I don't need her. I've just gone too long without a woman, and lovely, willing, passionate Ebony will suit me just fine.

"Shall I help you to relax completely, darling?" she whispered against his ear, her teeth nibbling at his earlobe.

"You can't do it from there, Ebony."

"It would be difficult." She laughed

softly, coming around the end of the couch.

The earl took her hand and pulled her down onto his lap, bringing her palm to his lips. "You do have magic in your hands, Ebony. My head feels much better."

"I have many hidden talents, my lord."

He moved his gaze over her slowly. "I wouldn't say hidden, m'lady."

"Thank you, darling, but there is so much more I want to share with you." Sitting on his lap, her face was a little higher than his. Lowering her head, she said, "Let me show you the rest of my magic, Tearle. Let me show you how wonderful we can be together."

Sloane tiptoed out of the nursery and very carefully shut the door. Jonny was busy drawing in the sitting room located next to the children's bedroom. He looked up when she came in and smiled at her.

"I'm getting better, Slo'. Uncle Jonathan showed me some tricks about cemetery, and it makes the coach look better."

Puzzled, Sloane stepped up behind him and looked over his shoulder at his drawing. "Yes, it does look better, but the word is symmetry, which means balance."

Sloane sat down in a comfortable chair to read while Jonny kept busy. Five minutes later, the book lay in her lap, her mind rehashing the earl's earlier angry outburst. She couldn't fathom why he was so angry. She could think of nothing she had done wrong, except to confide in Tom. Even if the earl overheard them, her comment had not deserved that kind of reaction.

Suddenly, Jonny dropped his pencil and looked up at Sloane, a horrified expression on his face. "Oh, no. I forgot to take Beau back to the kennels!"

Sloane sat up straighter. "I thought you were going to ask Brian to do it."

"I was but then I got to watching some baby birds with Angela and forgot. Do you want me to go try to find him?"

"No," she replied sharply, "I'll go. You might forget what you went out to do." At his brokenhearted expression and bowed head, Sloane felt a stab of regret at having spoken in such a manner. She quickly moved to his side and bent over to give him a hug. "I'm sorry I spoke unkindly, dear. Please pay me no mind. I'm just a bit irritable today."

"That's 'cause Papa wouldn't let you have your day off. I don't know why we have to meet Lady Ebony anyway. I already know I don't like her." He looked up sadly at Sloane. "Slo', do you think she's going to be our new mama?"

"I don't think so, dear, but then your father doesn't tell me what his plans are. I wouldn't worry about it too much. She's just a guest, and he wants to show off his lovely children. You stay here and I'll go look for Beau. Promise me you'll stay put?"

"Yes, ma'am. I wouldn't want to run into Papa. He'd want to know what I was doing roaming around the house, and then I'd have to tell him about Beau, and then he really would be in a pelter."

"I won't be too long, hopefully. Be very quiet so Angela doesn't wake up."

Sloane hurried down the back stairs and outside, calling to the puppy softly. She searched around the garden and near the trees where the children had been playing, yet there was no sign of the pet. She noticed the outer doors to the conservatory had been left open so the breeze could blow through and decided to investigate.

A quick look around the room revealed a couple of tipped over plants and muddy foot-prints leading through the inner doorway to the great hall. Sloane sped through the portal and down the hall, calling softly. Both doors to the library were open, so she extended the search there. Her sharp eyes caught a glimpse of a little, quivering black nub of a tail as Beau pushed the study door open just enough to wiggle through.

"Oh, no," she moaned, "he'll get mud all over the Turkish rug." Sloane hurried across the library as fast as she could without making too much noise. "Beau, come here, you naughty—"

She gasped, standing like a statue with her hand still gripping the doorknob. Ebony was sitting on the earl's lap, her black hair flowing across her white shoulders, and his lips pressed against the swell of her breast in a very intimate fashion.

At Sloane's startled cry, the earl lifted his head and appraised her coolly, his fingers automatically adjusting Ebony's riding dress

to a less revealing position. "Have you taken
to entering without knocking, Mrs. Donovan?" he asked in a deadly cold voice.

Sloane was speechless as she stared at
them—Ebony perched possessively upon his
lap, and the earl staring back at the governess as if she were something to be flicked
aside in irritation. She had not thought it
could hurt so much to see him in another
woman's arms.

As always, her face mirrored her
emotions, and the earl frowned slightly as he
studied her reaction. This time when he
spoke, his voice held a trace of warmth. "Is
there a problem? Were you searching for me,
perhaps?"

At that moment, Beau's sharp bark
attracted their attention. Sloane moved like a
sleepwalker toward the puppy. When he saw
she was coming after him, Beau crouched
down and slithered across the floor to her,
sensing trouble.

"No . . . I . . . I was after Beau. He got—"
She cleared her throat, fighting back the
tears that demanded release. "He got in
through the conservatory. Forgive me,
m'lord." She paused, her gaze meeting
Ebony's triumphant one. Sloane straightened, and nodded at the woman with more
coolness than she felt. "Your pardon, Lady
Wentwood." Picking up the animal, Sloane
retreated through the door, closing it
properly behind her.

Ebony turned to Tearle with a smug
smile. "Now, darling, where were we?"

Suddenly, the earl was irritated with the woman in his arms. He had been embarrassed by Sloane's entrance, and her obviously pain-filled reaction to the scene left him confused. He thought gratingly that if he heard one more "darling" he might just dump the curvaceous bundle warming his thighs on the floor.

"Get up, Ebony. This is much too public a place for lovemaking."

"Shall we go upstairs, Tearle?" she asked as he helped her to her feet.

"No, I don't carry on my amorous affairs in front of my children, Ebony. I don't know what possessed me to allow things to go as far as they did."

"You were obviously overcome with the passion of the moment, darling." The earl had his back to her so she didn't see him wince at her endearment. She began buttoning up the front of her dress while the earl straightened his shirt and moved over to a small mirror to retie his neckcloth. "You don't suppose she'll talk to the other servants, do you? I would hate for our little, um, moment of pleasure, to get around to our friends."

The earl looked over his shoulder and said mockingly, "Are you worried about being compromised, Ebony? Don't be ridiculous. You won't catch me with that old snare. Everyone in the *ton* knows your liaisons are too numerous to mention."

He stepped to the end of the room and opened the door to the library. "I'm going out for a breath of air, Ebony. Why don't you stay here for a while and arrange your hair. No one will disturb you as long as the door is closed."

"If you'll only wait a few minutes, I'll go with you."

"No, thank you, that isn't necessary. I won't be gone long."

Tearle moved swiftly down the hall and out the side door in the direction of the kennels, only to arrive in time to see Brian coming out of Beau's cage.

"I see you got the pup back where he belongs. Did you happen to see which way Mrs. Donovan went? I need to talk to her."

"She went toward the rose garden, m'lord." The young man started to add that she looked terribly upset at having let the puppy get in the house, but the earl's terse thanks and quick departure halted those thoughts before they became words.

Thinking she was alone in the garden, Sloane sank down on a stone bench and gave in to quiet sobs, hiding her face in her hands. After a few minutes, she heard someone sit down beside her and raised blurry eyes to find Lord Carlisle watching her.

"My dear Mrs. Donovan," he said kindly, "whatever has happened to upset you so?" He pulled a crisp white handkerchief from his pocket and attempted to gently dry her eyes.

Sloane turned her head away, struggling to calm herself. She felt him press the handkerchief in her hand.

"Please, my dear, if you won't let me dry your eyes, do so yourself. There is nothing quite so distressing as a woman's tears. If I'd known I'd find a watering pot here in the garden, I might have let Grayson beat me in another game." He waited patiently as she wiped her eyes and cheeks and finally blew her nose. "There, now, that's better. I saw you run from the house. I suppose Beckford cut you up royally over something the pup did."

"It doesn't matter, m'lord."

"Ah, there you are wrong. I think it matters very much. I don't think Beckford realizes what a prize he has in you." He picked up her hand and began to stroke the back of it with his thumb. "I would treat you with great care and the tenderness deserved by one of such beauty. Why don't you come with me, Mrs. Donovan. I'll show you how a Carlisle takes care of rare treasures."

Sloane pulled her hand from his. "Are you proposing marriage, Lord Carlisle?"

The gentleman was somewhat taken aback. "Well, uh, no, Mrs. Donovan. Marriage wasn't exactly what I had in mind."

"Oh? Just what did you have in mind, m'lord?"

Carlisle regained his aplomb. "Well, I have a lovely home leased at Brighton for the summer. I thought you might like to spend a little time there with me. The sea air is wonderful this time of year, of course." He moved a little closer and traced his finger lightly around her ear. "I am known as a very tender and consummate lover, my dear. It would prove to be a very pleasurable interlude for both of us."

"I'm not interested in interludes, m'lord," said Sloane, standing abruptly. "I have only given myself to one man, Lord Carlisle, and that man was my husband. If I ever choose to share a man's bed again, it will be a marriage bed, and I will be very much in love.

"Now, if you will please excuse me, I must return to the house right away. Angela is probably already awake from her nap and in need of being held for a while."

"I apologize for misjudging you. I will accompany you to the door, madam." He stood and walked along beside her until they reached a small copse of trees some distance from the servant's entrance. Suddenly, he chuckled and took Sloane's arm firmly.

"My lord, release me this instant."

"Not likely, my dove. You see, I am in need of being held for a while myself. Your little speech was done very nicely, but 'tis nothing more than a Banbury tale. A woman of your fire couldn't go without a man for long."

She struggled against him, but while not a very large man, he was strong. He dragged her into the small grove, hiding them from view of the house. "I shan't take all from you now. I just want to give you a little taste of my passion for you. I'm sure you'll find it to your liking, sweeting." She pounded his chest with her fists as he pulled her toward him.

"Ah, yes, do struggle, dove. It makes it so much more exciting to show you who's the master."

"Let me go! You have no right to do this."

He grabbed her left hand and pulled it around behind her back, pinning it there while he used his other hand to capture her right fist and jerk it around behind her back, too.

"Don't be stupid, woman. Do you think you're so high and mighty that only Beckford can taste of your charms? Ah, you have the act down well, my girl. Most anyone would believe you are truly offended, but not I. I'm sure he has dipped at the cup more than once. A man would have to have more constraint than his lordship to live in the same house with you and not possess that lovely body.

"As to rights, I have privileges same as him, simply because of who I am. You are here to serve us." He held both her wrists in one hand and grabbed her hair with the other.

Sloane pulled against him until the tears sprang to her eyes. Carlisle stared down at her and swore softly. "You're too beautiful. I can't wait. I must have you now. Submit. Don't make me force you."

"No," Sloane cried, praying someone would hear, but sick with the knowledge that all of the servants were busy in other areas of the estate.

His mouth came down hard on hers, crushing, bruising, intent upon inflicting pain. He continued until she grew weak from need of air, then he raised his head in triumph.

He released her hair and began to finger the high neck of her sky blue gown. "Shall we see what's beneath this lovely dress, my dove? How do you afford such pretty things on a governess' salary?" He chuckled, an evil glint in his eye. "You must please Beckford well. Will you share with me as willingly, or must I tear it from you?"

"No," whispered Sloane, shaking her head as hot tears trickled down her cheeks.

"Release her, Carlisle." The earl's voice was cold and piercing, like a razor-sharp blade.

Carlisle jumped back, releasing her, and tripped over a tree root. Catching himself, he straightened and looked his host in the eye. What he saw there made him momentarily regret his attraction to the tempting young governess.

"Have you taken to rape?" The earl glanced at Sloane, who had slumped against the trunk of a tree, her hands hiding her face.

"Of course not, er, that is, I thought she'd be willing enough. Figured you wouldn't mind sharing her, since I'm a guest and all. Guess I was mistaken."

"You were very mistaken." The earl's face was white with rage. "In the first place, she is not mine to share. In the second place, it is very obvious she did not welcome your attentions. Others may run their houses dif-

ferently, Carlisle, but here none of the
women are forced to submit to anyone. If you
wish to remain the afternoon, keep your lust
in check. Now get out of my sight before I do
something we will both regret."

"Yes, m'lord. Dreadfully sorry about the
misunderstanding." With a frightened look,
he made a hasty retreat.

Tearle watched Carlisle until he disappeared in the house, then he stepped back
into the circle of trees, gathering Sloane in
his arms.

"It's all right, sweetheart. He won't
bother you again. I'm so sorry. I never
thought he'd be so bold, or I never would
have allowed him here. Did he hurt you,
sweet?"

Sloane lifted her face from where she
had buried it against his chest. At the sight of
her cut and swollen lips, he swore harshly,
his face contorting with pain and anger. "I
should have called him out, or at least
planted him a facer."

Sloane stiffened and pulled away. The
tears were spent, the fear gone. Now, all she
felt was shame and anger. "Why, m'lord? Because he insulted a mere governess whom he
thought a trollop, another man's mistress?"
She laughed bitterly. "You'd be laughed out
of the *ton*, m'lord. Besides, he can't be
blamed totally for his actions."

"You don't mean you encouraged him? I
can't believe that."

"Of course I didn't. I meant it just

doesn't signify because I'm a governess. As he said, those in service are expected to give without question, to serve the grand lords and ladies of the *ton*, regardless of the request or heedless of the personal cost or shame. It's long past time that the *ton* and others like you learned that we're people, too. We have feelings, self-respect, and pride just like anybody else. Just because a person works doesn't mean she is an inferior being."

"Surely, you can't believe I think that way?"

"Can't I? The only difference between you and . . . and Carlisle is that you've tried gentle seduction where he tried force. You both want the same thing, Lord Beckford, but you can't have it. I won't be a rich man's plaything! I won't!" With this angry declaration, Sloane broke away from the earl and flew to the servant's entrance.

Jonathan had met Carlisle on his way to the house and correctly guessed what had been going on. He arrived on the scene in time to hear Sloane's impassioned speech. He watched his brother curl up his fist and pound a nearby tree, but waited briefly before stepping into Tearle's line of vision. "You know, for two seemingly intelligent people, you both are acting like dimwits." At his brother's questioning scowl, he continued blithely, "It is as plain as the nose on your face that you two are in love, but neither one of you will admit it."

"Rot! I told you before there is no such

thing as love, and Sloane has made it very clear she wants nothing to do with me."

Jonathan shook his head. "Of course, she doesn't want to be your mistress. As you said, she's too fine a woman."

"She wants to marry Tom. It's him she cares about, not me. She is enthralled with masters of the stable, and doesn't give one whit for an earl."

"Such a shame her priorities are so backward." Jonathan paused thoughtfully, all teasing vanishing. "Tearle, she's not in love with Tom. She's running from you."

"She wouldn't marry a man just because she wanted to get away from me. All she has to do is leave here to accomplish that."

"Does she? You're besotted with her, my boy, and my guess is that you would follow her wherever she went. No, Tearle, she's terrified of being hurt. She's afraid you'll use her until you're tired of her, and she'll do anything to prevent it. Even if it means marrying a man she doesn't love."

Tearle shook his head wearily. "You've been reading too many novels, Jon. I don't want to discuss it any further. She'll not marry Tom, because I won't give them my permission."

Jonathan finally lost his temper. "And, just because you, the mighty Earl of Beckford, proclaim it, you think they'll stop? Of all the arrogant, idiotic notions. How in the name of heaven did I ever get such a mutton-head for a brother?" With this outburst, he turned on his heel and headed for the conservatory, leaving his brother seething behind him.

7

Sloane pressed the cold cloth to her lips one last time. She looked at her swollen eyes in the mirror and shook her head. Although she had applied the cold compress to her eyelids as well, it was still obvious she had been crying.

Thankfully, Jonny had fallen asleep before she returned upstairs, curled up in the comfortable chair where she often read to him.

Sloane was certain she had never been so angry in her entire life, but what bothered her even more was that the bulk of her wrath wasn't directed at Carlisle. He was an arrogant, deceitful coxcomb to be sure, but he would be leaving at the end of the day, and she wouldn't have to fend him off anymore.

No, her anger was directed at the earl—for his tender compassion in the garden, for his forceful defense of her honor and the pain on his face when he saw her cut lips, for holding her so gently that she wanted to cling to his strength forever. She railed at him for all the nights she had tossed and turned, longing to be in his arms, and because she found it harder each day to hold true to the principles of a lifetime.

"You're a stupid fool, Sloane Donovan, for loving a man who'll never give the kind of commitment you need." Staring at herself in the mirror, she straightened her shoulders. "Remember who you are. You are Lord Atherton's granddaughter and of the honorable line of Kincade. You aren't some thin-blooded little miss who has to bow and scrape before your master. You can leave anytime you choose."

But she wouldn't leave, and she knew it. Sloane told herself she must stay because of the children, but she was quite aware they weren't the only things holding her at Beckford Hall.

This frustration only fueled her anger so that by the time the children were dressed to go down at teatime, she was ready to wage war if the need arose. She wouldn't be undone by Ebony's superior glances nor Lord Carlisle's snide tongue, and if the high and mighty Earl of Beckford tried to put her down, she had a few choice remarks of her own to make.

Sloane was just combing Angela's last ringlet into place when a knock sounded at the door. At the command to enter, Bess stepped inside and shut the door.

"His lordship is ready for the children, Mrs. Donovan. He said you weren't feelin' well earlier, and that I should bring the children down if you weren't up to it." The maid glanced at Sloane's puffy lip and eyes and looked away quickly.

"I'm fine, now, Bess, but thank you. Beau bumped my chin with his head and made me bite my lip. It hurt so badly, I'm afraid I cried like a baby, but other than being a little swollen and sore, it isn't too great a bother." Sloane had turned away from the others on the pretense of putting the brush on the vanity. She was afraid this time Jonny would see through her tale. He had been sleepy enough earlier to not notice she was lying when she explained what had happened, but this time he was bright-eyed and extremely alert.

"It is my place to supervise the children, and I'm happy to do it. Don't they look just wonderful?"

"Yes, mum, they do." Bess beamed at the youngsters dressed in their finery, not a hair out of place. "Your father will be proud to show you off."

Jonny squirmed and scuffed the rug with his toe. "I'd rather stay up here."

"Well, I wouldn't," said Angela. "I want to meet Lady Ebony. Her lookth pretty."

"She is pretty, Angela, but remember, dear, what's on the outside isn't as important as what's on the inside."

"I don't think her inthide would look very pretty. Doth it look like a rabbit'th inthide?"

Sloane shook her head and laughed. "I

doubt it. Where did you see a rabbit's insides?''

"The kitchen boy was cleaning one for dinner a few days ago," cut in Johnny. "We watched him. I thought it was great, but Angela felt a little sick."

"I don't blame her. What I meant, Angel, was that even a person who isn't a beauty to look at can still be a lovely person if they are kind and loving to others. Outward beauty fades, but a kind heart never gets wrinkles. Now, come, your father is waiting.''

Moments later, the trio entered the drawing room. The earl lounged negligently against the mantel as Lady Ebony proficiently poured the tea. Both Jonathan and Carlisle rose when Sloane entered the room. Jonathan's smile and encouraging wink acknowledged her bravery for jumping into the lion's den. Carlisle appeared uncomfortable and avoided looking at her directly.

The earl strolled across the room to meet them, his dark, penetrating gaze compelling Sloane to look at him. He swiftly appraised her lip and lifted his gaze to her eyes, his frown deepening as he noted the telltale signs of her tears. Anger flared in those crocus blue orbs, but his eyes narrowed when he sensed that her own anger was simmering just beneath the surface.

The earl made the introductions of his children and guests. Jonny pleased his father with his gentlemanly bow, but no more so than Angela's somewhat awkward curtsy.

After the introductions, the children perched on the chairs indicated by their father.

Jonny absently swung his foot back and forth until he glanced at Sloane. At her speaking look and the sharp shake of her head, he stopped the movement. Chancing a look at his father, he breathed a sigh of relief to see the earl smile.

Lady Ebony noted that smile, too, and decided to try a new tactic on the earl. "You have lovely children, Tearle. Your lucky young gentleman favors his father, and, of course, Angela is the mirror image of Linette. You'll have more than your share of offers in a few years, and plenty of mamas hanging out for your son, too."

"I don't want to even think about it," Tearle said, with a short laugh. "There'll be plenty of time to think of such things years from now."

"Oh, I wouldn't put off such important matters too long, darling. Children are so precious, we must always be on the lookout for their future and well-being. I do so regret not having any of my own, but then, of course, I'm not ready to stick my spoon in the wall, so perhaps I'll have that joy yet."

"Somehow, I can't picture you with a passel of brats hanging on your knee, Ebony," said the earl.

"Well, I wouldn't want a whole houseful, nor would I want them constantly hanging on my knee, but I'm sure there must be great satisfaction in spending time with one's own child, even if only for a few hours a day."

A few minutes a day is more like it, thought Sloane. She felt the earl's gaze on her as she sat beside the children. Looking at him quickly, she met his twinkling eyes. The amused twitch at the corner of his mouth told her he had once again used his uncanny ability to read her mind. That he could almost make her laugh in spite of herself only rekindled her frustration.

The conversation continued for some time with the discussion often directed at the children. Lady Ebony seemed to go out of her way to include them in the talk, and appeared to have a genuine interest in their hesitant replies.

Sloane and her charges had almost decided the afternoon would never end when Grimley knocked on the drawing room door.

"I beg your pardon, m'lord, but the architect is here. I showed him into your study as you asked."

"Very good, Grimley. Lady Ebony, Carlisle, please excuse me for just a few moments. Since the man was supposed to have arrived yesterday, I really should go meet him and find out about the delay."

"I'll come, too, Tearle. I'm anxious to hear what he thinks of your heating idea," said Jonathan.

"We won't be too long. Children, finish your cake and make your bows to our guests soon before you have an attack of the fidgets."

Since Jonny had just picked up another apple fritter, it took several minutes for them to finish.

"Well, Mrs. Donovan," said Lady Ebony, "you seem to have recovered from your little shock of this afternoon. I do hope you won't mention the, uh, situation to anyone else. It would only cause people to talk, and I'm sure you wouldn't want to cause any slurs against the earl. He is such a gentleman."

"I have no intention of speaking of either of this afternoon's incidents, Lady Ebony."

"Either?" The lady looked confused.

Carlisle spoke for the first time, and Sloane was startled by the undisguised malice on his face. "I ran into Mrs. Donovan in the garden, Ebony, but she wasn't in the mood for company. I even proposed a little excursion but she is very reluctant to leave such a lucrative position."

Ebony laughed, tilting her head up just a fraction, in effect, striking a pose. "How that must have rankled, Alan dear, to be refused by one in her position."

"My position has nothing to do with it. Even if I were the toast of the town, I wouldn't go anywhere with you." Sloane shot Carlisle a look of pure loathing. "Come, children, make your bows."

Jonny bowed quickly, aware of the tension building in the room. Even to his five-year-old mind, it was obvious that Sloane thought Carlisle was kin to something that crawled out of a hole.

Angela stood to the side of Lady Ebony, innocently unaware of the undercurrents flowing between the adults. She watched the lady with great intensity.

"Well, what is it you want, child?" asked Ebony. "Out with it and don't grow tiresome."

"I wath juth lookin' for wrinkleth."

"Wrinkles?"

"Yeth. 'Lo thaid people who are pretty on the outthide get wrinkleth when they grow old, but you muth not be too old. You don't have much."

"Oh, don't be ridiculous. Make your curtsy and be on your way, you irritating little girl."

Poor Angela hastily attempted her curtsy, but caught her foot on the hem of her gown and stumbled. She caught herself by grabbing Lady Ebony's arm, but knocked over the lady's cup of tea in doing so. The cup fell into her lap, drenching the beautiful red riding habit.

Ebony pushed Angela aside and jerked her arm free from the child's frightened grasp. "You naughty brat. Just look what you've done to my new dress. You wicked, wicked child."

Before Sloane could even imagine what the woman had in mind, Lady Ebony slapped Angela on the cheek. Angela let out an injured howl, and Sloane jumped to her feet. Just as she reached for the little girl, the study door flew open.

Lady Ebony realized the enormity of her

transgression in a split-second glimpse of the earl's face. Seasoned in covering up her errors, Ebony snatched Angela from Sloane's fingers and pulled the screaming child into her arms. She held her firmly against her shoulder and crooned words of comfort.

Sloane stood where she was, her fingers clenched in almost uncontrollable rage. "You horrible, evil—"

"What's going on here? What's wrong with Angela?"

"Poor Angela accidentally spilled tea on my dress, and this creature slapped her. I know governesses sometimes resort to brutality, but this is inexcusable." Ebony spoke quickly, stroking the child's back, holding the sobbing little girl to her with unseen force.

"She's pulled the wool over your eyes, Beckford. A regular tyrant to embarrass and hit a child like that in front of company." Carlisle assumed a look of concern, shaking his head sadly. "Such a shame, such a shame."

The earl stared at Sloane, taking in her flushed, angry face, the combatant's stance, and her clenched hands. The anger he had been nursing all afternoon burst inside him like a cannon blast, exploding into an undeniable rage.

"You will leave this house immediately, Mrs. Donovan. I will not allow anyone to be cruel to my children. To slap her over a spilt cup of tea is despicable."

"You can't possibly think that I hit her!

How dare you?"

"Your actions speak for themselves, Mrs. Donovan. You are dismissed. I want you out of this house within the hour."

Sloane stormed out of the room, slamming the door practically off its hinges.

The earl turned to the parlormaid who hovered wide-eyed in the corner. "Bess, take the children upstairs. You will assume their care until I find someone else."

She picked up the weeping child and nodded for Jonny to follow. Angela rested her little face on Bess's shoulder, the red imprint of a hand glaring up at the earl.

" 'Lo, 'Lo," she cried softly.

Jonny's face took on a militant expression, and he faced his father squarely. "Papa."

"Go with Bess, Jon."

"Papa, I need to talk to you."

"Not now, Jonny."

The little boy hesitated a minute, but in the face of his parent's fierce expression, his bravado wavered. He made one last gallant attempt. "Papa?"

"Not now, Jonathan. Go upstairs."

"Yes, sir," he said, hanging his head, and beating a hasty retreat.

The earl sighed and turned back to his guests. "I'm very sorry about this. I'll have the footman show you to a guest room, Ebony. You can wait there while one of the maids sees about your habit. Perhaps they can get the stain out somehow."

"It is of little consequence, darling, but I am a bit sticky. I do need to wash up."

The earl snapped a terse command to the footman, then headed for his study when Ebony left the room. Jonathan was standing near the study door and caught his brother's eye as he passed by.

"Idiot."

The earl slammed the door behind him, causing a nearby painting, a serene country landscape by Constable, to shift precariously on the wall. He poured a large measure of brandy in the snifter and threw it down his throat.

Sloane was waiting in the nursery when Bess brought the children up. Taking Angela in her trembling arms, she sat down in the rocking chair and gently rocked the child. After several minutes of quiet assurances, Angela's sobs became hiccups. Every few minutes, a shudder wracked her small body. Gradually, the rocking motion and Sloane's soft lullaby eased the girl into a less than restful sleep.

After putting her to bed, Sloane once again sat down in the rocker and pulled Jonny onto her lap.

"I tried to tell Papa you didn't hit Angela, but he wouldn't listen. I let you down, Slo'. I'm sorry."

"No, Jonny, you didn't let me down. Your father is so angry right now, he can't think straight. It wouldn't have mattered if you had been able to tell him. I'm not sure he would have believed you."

"I don't tell lies, Slo'." He stared up at her indignantly.

"I know, but your father might think you were just trying to stand up for me." She rubbed her hand up and down his back. "I just don't understand it. I can't imagine how he could believe I would hit either of you."

"Lady Wentwood was a pretty good actress."

"Yes, unfortunately, she was. Well, my dear, I must leave you for now. Your father has ordered me to go, and I must obey him. It will serve no purpose to cross him."

"You can't leave, Slo'. What will Angela and I do without you?" He snuggled against her, his little hands clinging to her possessively.

"You'll have to learn to like the person your father finds to take my place. You'll be kind to her, won't you?"

Jonny started to cry. "You can't leave us, Slo'. You can't. Angel will quit talking, and I'll be so sad I'll hurt inside all the time, just like now."

"Oh, Jonny, please don't cry. You must be strong for my sake." Sloane's grip tightened, and she leaned her cheek against his blond curls. "I don't want to go, but I must. I hurt inside, too, so please don't make it any harder for me."

"I hate Papa! I hate him!"

"No, dear. You mustn't hate him. What

he has done is wrong, but he doesn't know it. He thinks he is doing the right thing."

"And, when he finds out it wasn't really you, he'll ask you to come back, won't he?"

"I don't know."

"You would come back, wouldn't you?" Jonny raised his head, his earnest little face begging with all his heart.

Sloane hesitated and decided in her present condition she couldn't even attempt to shadow the truth. "I don't know, Jonny. As much as I love you and Angela, I'm not sure I could work for your father anymore. We seem to be at cross purposes a lot lately. However, even if I don't come back, you may certainly come to see me. I'll be staying with my parents. I don't think I'll seek a new position anytime soon." She tried to wipe away his tears with her fingertips.

"Now, hop down and feed your pets. Bess will stay with you. I must go change."

Jonny hugged her tightly. "You'll always be my best friend, Slo'. Always."

Tears pricked her eyes, the sadness of her loss clouding her anger. "You'll be mine, too. Always."

Jonny climbed down and halfheartedly began feeding his turtles. Sloane went into her bedroom and pulled her portmanteau off the top shelf of her wardrobe. She began pulling clothes out of the wardrobe, throwing them into the case, heedless of the growing wrinkled mess. Half-blinded by the tears that slipped from her eyes, she had absolutely no idea which garments she crammed into the bag.

On the floor below, Jonathan and Carlisle glared at each other across the library. Neither man had said a word since Lady Ebony and the earl left the room.

In the study, the earl stared across the garden at the giant oak. Under the oak, he had kissed Sloane that first evening. Later, she had climbed the tree, in spite of her terror, to rescue Jonny. The wind caught a branch and waved it gently, like a long finger wagging at him in reproach. Memories flooded his mind—her sweet face turned up to his in the twilight; her gentle, loving way of getting Angela to talk; her patience with Jonny; and, yes, her courage, however impetuous it sometimes appeared to be. The earl tossed the glass carelessly on a small table.

"Jon's right; I am an idiot." He pulled the bell rope and the outer door was opened instantly by Grimley. "Have Jonny brought to me at once. Also, send word to Lady Ebony that I would like to see her in the library in ten minutes. I don't care if her dress is wringing wet, I want her there."

"Yes, m'lord." The butler shut the door, but not before he allowed the earl to see his wide grin.

Moments later, Jonny bolted into the room. "Yes, Papa?"

The earl looked sternly at his son. "Jonathan, I'm going to ask you a question, and I want you to think carefully before you answer. I believe you have always been honest with me, and I demand nothing less. You will answer truthfully, even if it is painful to do so. Do I make myself clear?"

"Yes, sir." Jonny nodded his head and watched his father with wide-eyed caution.

"Did Mrs. Donovan slap Angela?"

"No sir!"

"Who did?"

"Lady Wentwood."

The earl didn't realize he was holding his breath until it rushed out. "Please explain what happened."

"Lady Wentwood got mad because Angela was staring at her."

"That's when she slapped her?"

"No, she was just crotchety then."

The earl frowned, a bit puzzled. "Why was Angela staring at her?"

"She was lookin' for wrinkles." Jonny grinned.

"Wrinkles?"

"It's kind of hard to explain. Anyway, Lady Wentwood got mad and told Angela to go away. When she tried to curtsy, she tripped on her skirt and knocked over the tea-cup. That's when the old hag slapped her. She must of known you'd be mad, 'cause when she saw you coming through the door she grabbed Angela and blamed Slo'."

"Thank you, son. You may go back upstairs now."

Jonny started from the room but paused

beside the door. "Papa, you aren't really going to send Slo' away, are you?"

"I shall ask her to stay, Jonny, but I have done her a great wrong." The earl shook his head gravely. "I don't know if she will remain. Please don't mention our conversation to anyone, at least not until I have been able to explain to Mrs. Donovan myself. Is she still here?"

"Yes, sir. I heard her crashing around in her bedroom just before I came down."

"Crashing around?"

"You know, slamming drawers and stuff." He looked keenly at his father and hesitated. "I think maybe she was crying. I heard her sniffing a lot." He grew nervous at the grim look on his father's face. "But I guess women do that a lot anyway. I heard Bess crying this morning."

"It's acceptable for women to weep, Jonny. It's part of their nature. Now, run along. I'll talk with you some more later."

Jonny sped out of the room and ran into Brian, the footman. They both tottered for a moment before Brian got his footing and set Jonny straight. "Now, Master Jonny, what's the hurry?"

"Papa's going to ask Slo' to stay," Jonny said in a loud stage whisper.

"Jonathan, mind your P's and Q's. I realize you are bursting with the news, but you must refrain from telling anyone else, especially Mrs. Donovan." The earl stood in the doorway, a scowl marking his features.

"Yes, Papa. I promise I won't say anything else, and Brian won't either. Will you, Brian?"

"Of course not, m'lord. I knows when to keep my yapper shut."

"Run along, Jonny." The earl waited until the youngster raced up the stairs out of hearing. "Brian, was Lady Wentwood given the message?"

"Yes, m'lord, and I told the maid to hurry up with the riding habit. It's still a mite damp, I gather."

"That's of no consequence. Have our guests' horses brought around immediately."

"Yes, sir!"

The earl turned sharply on his heel and walked into the library, ignoring the two men sitting there. A short time later, Lady Wentwood joined them.

"Really, Tearle, couldn't you have waited a few more minutes. My clothes are practically dripping."

"You are fortunate, madam, that I don't have you stripped down to your shift and horsewhipped." He turned to face her, ignoring her gasp. Lady Wentwood started to speak, but stopped as she perceived his murderous look.

"You and your odious brother will leave immediately. If either of you ever sets foot on this estate again, I'll have you thrown off. I always questioned your character, but now I see that you are even more contemptible than I ever imagined. Your heart is black, Ebony. Hard and dark and cruel. I pray that you never have children. I doubt they would live to adulthood.''

"How dare you speak to me this way!
How dare you upbraid me in front of the
others!''

"Don't tell me you are embarrassed?
What you are feeling can be nothing
compared to the humiliation and shame you
heaped upon Mrs. Donovan's head. It is
nothing compared to the pain and suffering
you have caused my daughter. You cruel,
evil, malicious witch! Get out!'' The earl took
a step toward her but stopped himself from
going any further. He knew if he got close
enough, he would shake her until her head
rattled.

"I say, I can't have you calling my sister
such things.'' Carlisle made a cautious step
toward the earl.

"Get out! Or, so help me, I'll have you
tied on your horses like a sack of wheat and
paraded through the village.''

Carlisle took his sputtering sister's arm,
dragged her from the house, and threw her
up on her waiting horse. Those inside the
mansion could hear her screaming at him
until they reached the end of the drive.

The earl breathed a heavy sigh and ran
his fingers through his blond curls. Spying
Brian hovering just a few feet down the hall,
he beckoned him with a jerk of his head.

"Go up and tell Mrs. Donovan I want to
speak with her. Tell her to come down to the
study immediately.''

"Yes, m'lord.'' He raced up the stairs two

at a time, but returned a few moments later at what could only be called a reluctant pace.

"Did you speak with her?" asked the scowling earl.

"Yes, m'lord." Brian's face grew flushed. "I told her exactly what you said."

"Is she coming down?"

The footman shifted uneasily, stretching his neck against his rough starched collar. "Well, no m'lord, not exactly."

"Explain."

"Well, m'lord, she said since she didn't work for you no more she didn't have to do what you told her to." His face turned crimson, a glaring contrast to his carrot-topped head.

"Is there more?"

"Well, yes, m'lord, though I don't really think I should be the one to say it."

"Out with it, man."

"Well, uh, she said, uh, that you was an arrogant, stuffed shirted tyrant, and that she wouldn't talk to you if Prinny himself commanded it."

"Whew," said Jonathan, barely controlling his laughter, "I guess she's got you pegged."

The earl shot him an irritated glance and headed for the stairs.

"Uh, excuse me, m'lord," said Brian, wishing the floor would open up and swallow him, "she's not up there anymore. She was headin' for the stables."

The earl stopped with a foot on the first

step. He turned around slowly, a resigned look of dejection gradually spreading across his face. "You may go, Brian."

Jonathan stepped into the great hall. "Now, what's wrong?"

"She's gone to the stables. Running to Tom for comfort, no doubt. In all probability, he'll come storming in here and plant me a facer. Then he'll quit and I'll be out a stable master as well as the best governess a man could ask for."

"Beggin' your pardon, m'lord," Grimley cut in. "I know Tom is fond of Mrs. Donovan, but I hardly think he cares enough to risk Newgate, or even enough to quit his job."

"Of course, he does. If he wants to marry her, he'll certainly want to take her away from an arrogant, stuffed shirted tyrant."

"Well, now, m'lord, I can see where that would be true; if he wanted to marry her, that is. But it's not Mrs. Donovan Tom wants to marry."

"What?"

"He's in love with Bess, not Mrs. Donovan." The elderly butler's tone and expression implied this fact was known to all.

A lightning grin flashed across the earl's face. He sped down the hall toward the back of the house. "Grimley, you just earned a raise."

"Thank you, m'lord," said the old man, without a trace of enthusiasm, and ran a gloved finger across a small table to check for dust.

"Hey, Lou," called Jonathan.

"What?" The earl looked back over his shoulder, minutely slowing his pace.

"I think I like a woman with spunk. Any more where she came from?"

"As a matter of fact, there are," said the earl, disappearing through the doorway.

8

The earl loped down the path, arriving at the stables just as the groom finished saddling Windsong. "Mrs. Donovan, I would like a word with you."

"I have nothing to say to you."

"Oh, but undoubtedly you do, and I definitely have something to say to you." The earl stepped closer as the groom boosted Sloane up to the saddle. His lordship's hands closed around her waist and lifted her clear of the animal, holding her in mid-air.

"Put me down!"

"Not until you agree to come with me."

"I have no intention of going anywhere with you." She squirmed, pushing against his hands in an attempt to free herself. "Let me go, you brute. Haven't you humiliated me enough for one day?"

The earl drew her so close she could feel his hot breath against her ear. "Please, Sloane, hear me out." His rough whisper stopped her struggles, and she glanced up to meet his pleading eyes. He set her feet on the ground and slowly turned her towards him. "Will you walk with me, Mrs. Donovan?" he asked, his voice carefully controlled.

"Yes, my lord." She refused to take his offered arm and walked briskly ahead of him toward the vast expanse of garden. When they were clear of any listening ears, she turned to look at him. "Have you thought of further spiteful words to taunt me with, Lord Beckford? You were quite thorough earlier, I believe."

"I wish I could take back every word I said to you, Sloane. I made a grave mistake, a foolish, stupid, angry mistake."

"How could you even think for a minute that I would hit Angela? How could you?"

"I don't know. I was angry with you because you lumped me in the same mold as Carlisle and because . . . well, because you were going to marry Tom."

"What? We aren't going to marry."

"I know that, now, but I overheard you talking this morning and misunderstood. When I stepped into the library and saw you standing there so full of fury, I guess I thought you had taken your hatred of me out on Angela."

"I never said I hated you," she said, her voice trembling.

"Not precisely, but when you categorized me with someone like Carlisle, what else could I think? Now, after what I have done to you, the shame and humiliation—I can hardly bear thinking of it. Perhaps someday, when I have made amends and time has healed your hurt, you will find it in your kind heart to forgive me, but for now, I will not even presume to ask it of you. However, I must ask you to stay for the children's sake. They need you desperately."

What about you? her heart cried. She turned away quickly so he wouldn't see the question on her face. She ached with the need to be in his arms, to hear him say he loved her. She could forgive him anything if he only loved her. He was jealous of Tom. That was something, wasn't it? Yes, it was something, but it wasn't enough. A man could be jealous of his possessions, of his mistress.

He gripped her shoulders, his fingers kneading gently. "I sent Ebony and Carlisle away and left orders that they are never to set foot on this property again. I have hurt you terribly. I can never erase the pain I caused you, but I must beg you to stay. I fear I will lose Angela again if you are not here with her. Will you stay?"

Sloane didn't know what to do. She didn't want to leave, but she knew if she stayed she would only be hurt again. It suddenly struck her that he was begging; this proud, arrogant lord was actually begging her to stay—for the sake of his children.

When she didn't answer, his fingers tightened. "Please, sweetheart?"

Sloane's heart leaped to her throat. Did he have any idea how much longing and tenderness crept into those two simple words? She could not bring herself to leave, even though it might be foolish to stay. To turn her back on a chance of happiness with the man she loved, no matter how slim that chance, would be even greater folly. Already the pain of the afternoon had been eased, first by his apology and now by his unconscious expression of need. Somehow, she had to teach him that loving was worth the cost. But, I'll never be your whore, Tearle Grayson, she thought furiously. I'll only be a wife.

She shrugged off his hands and turned to face him. "I will stay because the children need me," she said quietly. Just as you do, she added silently.

"Thank you, Sloane. Will you go tell them the good news? I'll go by the stables and have Windsong put away for the evening."

Sloane nodded and walked quietly in the direction of the mansion. The earl watched her go, then stared at the late afternoon sun, hanging low and red in the sky. "I'll earn your forgiveness somehow, my love." He drew in his breath sharply, telling himself that the murmured endearment was nothing more than sentimental fribble. As he strolled toward the stables, his heart told him he was a liar.

Passing through the stables, he came face to face with Tom. Drawing to a halt, he studied the man's angry glare. "Mrs. Donovan will be staying here at Beckford, Tom, so her horse can be put away. By the way, may I be the first to wish you happy in your marriage to Bess." At Tom's gasp and swift change of expression, the earl chuckled.

"Yes, my good man, you have my blessing to marry the wench. We'll have a wedding feast here on the lawns for you. Invite anyone you wish; just give Mrs. Honeycutt an idea of how many to expect."

"Why, thank you, m'lord. That's mighty kind of you, Lord Beckford."

"Nonsense. 'Tis the least I can do. Now, go on up to the house and tell your beloved. Let me know if you need any help in procuring a license. You might make sure Mrs. Donovan hears the news. I didn't think it fair to tell her before I mentioned it to you."

"Aye, my lord, I will. Thank you again, sir."

Later that evening, Sloane was putting the children to bed when the earl stepped quietly into the room. Jonny grinned at him and hopped out of bed to give him a hug. Angela took one look at his lordship and buried her face in the pillow.

As the earl sat down on the bed beside the little girl, Sloane started to leave. He stroked Angela's back and didn't look up but said quietly, "Please stay, Mrs. Donovan."

She complied and retreated to a chair in the corner of the room. Jonny, realizing that his father's concern was for Angela, climbed up in Sloane's lap without a word.

"Angela," said the earl, "your papa made a very bad mistake this afternoon. I have learned a lesson from this incident, and I hope you and Jonny will, too. Do you know what I learned?"

Angela shook her golden curls, turning

her face to rest her cheek on the cool cloth, but avoided looking at her father.

"I once again learned how very wrong it is to accuse someone of doing something bad before I know all the facts. Mrs. Donovan and I had a disagreement earlier in the day, and since I was already angry with her, I didn't stop to think things through clearly. I let my anger take hold and color over clear thinking. In other words, when I saw you had been hurt, and Lady Wentwood accused Sloane of hitting you, I didn't stop to think how silly that was. Come here, pet."

Angela allowed the earl to pick her up and cradle her in his arms, although she did not come eagerly. "Angel, I'm very sorry you were hurt this afternoon. I know spilling Lady Wentwood's tea was an accident, and I'm not angry with you."

"Lady Wentwood ith mean."

"Yes, she is, and I told her as much. She won't ever bother you again, pet. I told her not to come back here. I'm glad to see your face is all better. Does it still hurt?"

"A little bit." She looked up at him with wide, searching eyes. "You wath mean, too. You wath mean to 'Lo."

"Yes, I was, and I'm very, very sorry for the things I said and the way I acted. I know it hurt you almost as much as being slapped, but I hope you understand that at the time, I thought I was doing the right thing."

"I gueth tho, but it made me hurt here." She placed her hand on her heart.

The earl hugged her tightly, his chin resting on her little blond head. His gaze reached out to Sloane over the yellow curls. "I know, pet, it made me hurt there, too." He laid her down on the bed, stood, and pulled the blanket up to her chin. "Now, you two urchins go right to sleep. We've all had a bad day, but tomorrow will be a better one."

Jonny gave his father another hug before climbing into bed. As the earl pulled open the door, Angela spoke his name.

"Yes, pet?"

"I love you, Papa."

The earl was hit broadside by her words. His face grew pale from the enormity of emotion flooding his soul at that moment. For the first time in the child's life, he said simply, "I love you, too, Angel." Without looking at anyone else, he left the room.

The following days were chaotic ones at Beckford Hall. The earl was caught up in his remodeling plans, spending hours going over the architect's drawings or conferring with the esteemed gentleman about an elaborate heating system the earl had in mind for the great hall. Once, as they were standing in the massive, high-ceilinged room, discussing the possibility of building ducts to bring the hot air in from the adjoining rooms, Sloane and the children strolled by.

Sloane looked over at his lordship to find him staring at her behind the architect's back. He smiled warmly, his eyes lighting up with happiness. He might as well have spoken out loud; his look said it plainly enough—I'm glad you're here.

Sloane felt ridiculously happy for the rest of the afternoon and even more so when she returned to her bed chamber after dinner. On the table beside her bed sat a perfect white rose in a silver bud vase. She thought the earl might have sent it up to her, but then dismissed the idea as being silly. More likely, Jonny brought it up. It wouldn't be the first time he had picked her a bouquet of flowers. But then again, he had never brought a single rose and certainly never one as perfectly formed.

The roses began to arrive daily. They would appear in her chambers every morning after the maid had been in to straighten up. When Sloane questioned the young girl she was told that Grimley had given her the roses with the instructions to place them on her bedside table. Later in the day, she found him in the library.

"Grimley, have you decided to pay court to me?" she asked, with a twinkle in her eye.

"Well, now, Mrs. Donovan, if I were about forty years younger—" he paused and chuckled, "even twenty years younger, I'd consider that a definite possibility. But seeing as I'm too old a critter for the likes of you, I must admit I have not."

"Will you explain the roses?"

"Well, they grow on bushes out in the garden, mum. George and Huntley do right well by his lordship's flowers. The roses are their pride and joy. They're especially pretty this year with all the sun. Might have something to do with the little canals George dug to water them."

Sloane grinned up at the old man affectionately. "I know how roses grow, my friend. I'm speaking about the roses that magically appear on my nightstand each day. The ones so beautifully cradled in the silver vases."

"Appear magically, eh? Well, I've known a few folk who swear there are still fairies running about, but I don't believe in them myself."

"Grimley."

"Well, his lordship did say I wasn't supposed to tell, but I can't have you thinking I'm about to ask for your hand, now can I?"

"No, I think not."

He took her arm and guided her over to a secluded corner. Sloane grinned at him since there was no one near enough to possibly overhear them.

"His lordship picks those roses himself, every morning before the dew dries up. He says they're best when the dew is still on 'em. He's real picky about which one he cuts each day. Says it has to be the most perfect one he can find, though mind you, he doesn't spend hours looking." The old butler grinned. "Me thinks he's besotted, but of course, 'tis not my place to say so."

"Oh, Grimley, do you really think he

cares?"

He studied her thoughtfully for a very long moment. "Aye, mum, he cares, but there's no telling what kind of relationship he has in mind, if you know what I mean."

"I'm afraid I do, but I won't be his, uh, companion."

"Good girl, stick to your guns. If a man gets desperate enough, he'll start thinking about marriage, even one as dead set against it as his lordship."

"He was hurt very badly, wasn't he, Grimley?"

"Aye, he was, but 'tis not for me to talk about. If he wants you to know about the witch he married, he'll tell you."

"Of course, Grimley. I must be going. There's no telling where the children have gotten off to."

Later in the day, she discovered workmen in her bedroom taking measurements and much commotion going on in the room next door. She stuck her head in the doorway to find the earl and several men bustling about.

"If I'm not out of line, may I ask what you are doing?" she asked.

The earl drew her aside, out of the workmen's way. "We're building you a water-closet and a bathroom."

Sloane stared at him with her mouth open. "My own personal water-closet?" she whispered.

"Yes. There will be one for the children

in the room on the other side of the nursery. These new inventions are wonderful. They actually work."

"And, a private bathroom?"

"Yes, there will be a tub installed right over there. It'll even have hot and cold running water. Smithfield had some help on the plans from Wyatville and they've contrived a system that will bring water up to the second floor. They're building the water tower and conduit over on the ridge right now."

"My own bathtub?" she asked, still whispering.

"Yes," he whispered back. "I started to have a ten foot plunge bath built, but they are *de trop* these days. Pity, then there would be room for two." He grinned when her gaze shot up to his. "Well, you never know, you might need someone to scrub your back." He frowned down at her. "I just realized you don't have a personal maid. How do you scrub your back anyway?"

"I . . . I manage just fine, thank you. What do you mean a personal maid? Whoever heard of a governess with a maid? Whoever heard of a governess with a bathtub for that matter?" She suddenly clamped her mouth shut, realizing she had forgotten to whisper, and that the workmen were looking at them curiously.

The earl chuckled and steered her from the room. "Do you want gold-leaf and cherubs?"

"What?"

"On the tub. I prefer plain porcelain myself, but we could add gold-leaf and cherubs if you wanted. Yes, I think cherubs with harps would be perfect."

"Hardly." She glanced up at him as they strolled into the nursery. "Are you building these modern conveniences near your chambers, too?"

"Just the water-closet and a shower bath."

Sloane decided a change of subject was needed. "How is the heating system coming?"

"Well, at the rate the workmen are going, they'll be finished by the first snowfall," he said unhappily. "They keep saying they'll finish sooner, but there seems to be a setback every day. I am convinced, however, that by putting the ducts in we will pull warmer air in from the drawing room and dining room. With its vaulted ceiling, the hall is dreadfully cold and drafty in winter. I think we'll see a difference this year."

Sloane halted in front of the doll shelves, and the earl stopped just behind her. He was so close her hair brushed against his coat as she tipped her head to look at the upper row of toys. She quickly concluded that as long as he was near she would stay warm this winter if not a single ember burned in any of the fire-places. Longing swept through her, and she knew he ached to touch her as much as she ached for his touch.

Tearle took a deep breath to steady himself, only to be assailed by the sweet, soft fragrance of lavender. A ray of sunlight glimmered across a golden streak in her hair, catching his eye and drawing it down to the delicate pink curve of her cheek, and he fell prey to its gentle seduction.

Without speaking, he leaned over and kissed her lightly on her rosy skin, sensing her silent gasp more than hearing it. Moving his lips to her temple, the earl breathed deeply of the scent that belonged to her alone and lifted his right hand in a sweeping caress along her upper arm. A tiny smile touched the corners of his mouth when he felt her tremble beneath his touch.

"I'd better go back down to the children," she said unsteadily. Sloane grabbed the doll she had come to fetch and, easing past him, raced from the room, feeling the earl's burning gaze all the way down the hall.

Before Sloane even climbed out of bed early the next morning, a soft tap sounded on the door. A young maid opened the door and peered in. "Excuse me, mum, but 'is lordship said I was to come up and 'elp ye."

"Come in; Annie, isn't it?"

"Yes, mum."

"What are you supposed to help me do, Annie?" Sloane scooted her pillow against the headboard and sat up against it as Annie closed the door.

"Oh, anythin' that ye need, mum. I'm to

be yer lady's maid, and to 'elp out with the children," Annie said proudly, standing straight with her hands clasped in front of her. "Anythin' ye need me to do, mum."

"Oh, dear."

"Is there a problem, mum?"

"Well, I don't quite know how to tell you this, Annie, but I don't think I need a lady's maid. I've never had one, you see, and I'm not sure what I'd do with you."

"Oh, I could 'elp ye dress, mum, and keep yer clothes clean and pressed, and do yer 'air, mum. I knows ye always look right nice, but it might make things easier for ye and all, and I'm good with 'air, mum."

"Would it make your job easier, Annie, if you were to be my maid?"

"Well, yes, mum, it would. It would be a step up for me, a step up from scrubbin' and such." She hesitated, adding shyly, "And it would mean a raise in wages, mum."

Sloane frowned slightly before deciding she could not turn the girl away. "Very well, I shall welcome your services, but you must be patient with me. I'm used to doing things for myself, so please don't think I'm snubbing you if I do something you feel you should be taking care of."

"Oh, I won't, mum. Now, I'll just bring ye up some 'ot water for a bath."

In a short while, the hip bath was filled, and Sloane nervously unbuttoned her gown. Not normally missish, she discovered she was very uncomfortable bathing in front of a perfect stranger. "It'll certainly be easier for you when the new tub is installed. At least then you won't have to carry all the water up from downstairs. That is a terrible chore." Sloane fingered the buttons, wishing the girl would leave.

"Would ye like me to leave ye alone, mum?"

"Yes, Annie, if you don't mind. I don't really think I'll need you."

"Do ye want me to wash your back before I go?"

"No, thank you, Annie," said Sloane, beginning to chuckle. She managed to contain her laughter until the puzzled girl left the room.

The bath, marble washbasin, and water-closet were completed in what Sloane was sure was record time. Except for that one day when the earl had behaved so outlandishly, he had been polite to the extreme when the workmen were about. He and Jonathan often took their dinner in the nursery dining room with Sloane and the children, complaining that there was too much mess downstairs from the construction of the heating system.

Their presence was always welcome, and often, in unguarded moments, Sloane would look up to find the earl watching her. She could almost feel his caress, and had to make a supreme effort to concentrate on the ongoing conversation to hide the effect he was having on her.

The roses kept coming every day, along

with other additions to her room—a thick
Turkish rug appeared on the floor, leaving
Sloane wondering how all the furniture was
removed and put back without her knowing
it; fine leather-bound issues of the latest
novels found their way to her nightstand; and
the curtains and coverlet were replaced by
light, billowy China silk in the palest
robin's-egg blue. The final addition to the
room was a floor length mirror ornately
decorated in gold leaf. Sloane laughed out
loud when she first saw it; tiny cherubs with
harps decorated the top arch of the golden
frame.

True to his word, as well as attending
Tom and Bess's wedding, the earl threw a
feast on their behalf. Not only was there a
lavish array of food, but he hired musicians
to play for dancing after the meal. The
summer day was perfect for eating outside
under the trees and for dancing away the
afternoon and most of the evening. Tom was
well-liked and respected throughout the area,
so the guest list was not a small one.

The earl played the amiable host, sharing
his smooth dancing skills with every lady
from the Squire's wife down to the lowest
scullery maid. But by the time Tom and Bess
left for their newly built cottage (a wedding
gift from the earl), and the wedding guests
headed for home, there was no doubt in
anyone's mind that his favorite partner was
the lovely Sloane Donovan.

Long after the candles were snuffed

across the quiet vale, husbands and wives, maids, footmen, and grooms could be heard whispering about how the earl danced every waltz with the governess, and how, during the whole of the last dance, they spoke nary a word but just twirled about the carpet of grass as if they were the only two people in England.

9

A few days after the wedding, Jonathan and the earl walked their horses at a comfortable pace along the road west of Evesham. The earl had casually mentioned riding out to Kincade Stables after their business was completed in the town. Although they made the trip on the pretense of showing Jonathan the immaculate stables and fine horses, Jonathan wasn't fooled in the least. Sloane was visiting her parents, and Jonathan was well aware that the earl intended to ride back to Beckford Hall with her.

"I have a bone to pick with you, Tearle."

"What now?"

"Quite some time ago you mentioned something about Sloane having a sister, but you have yet to introduce me to her. Is she as pretty as Sloane?" Jonathan smiled, looking hopeful.

"Yes, but she's several years younger."

"Not an infant, I hope."

"No, hardly that. She's somewhere

around seventeen or eighteen, I believe." The earl looked troubled and glanced around the green countryside. "I don't know if I should introduce you. I'm not sure she could handle a flirtation, Jon."

"Why not? Even country bumpkins know how to flirt."

"True, most country misses do, but Roseanne is, well, special."

"In what way? Is she over-shy? I find it hard to believe that anyone in Sloane's family would be retiring."

The earl looked back at his brother, his expression serious. "Roseanne is almost deaf, so it's difficult for her to get along if there are many people about."

"I see; that's why she didn't come to Tom's wedding." Jon's brow creased thoughtfully as he flicked a fly from his horse's neck. "How about in a smaller group? Can she understand at all?"

"Yes, if you speak a bit slower than usual and look directly at her. I believe she reads lips mostly. An illness in late childhood damaged her ears, so she talks normally. She's a very sweet and talented girl. Paints like a dream—you've seen the estate scene on the drawing room chimney piece."

"She did that?" Jon's face lit up. "She is extremely talented."

Jonathan was quiet for sometime, his eyes on the road ahead. He was something of an artist himself, though his drawings tended to be pen and ink sketches, and truly admired Roseanne's painting. He was anxious to see

other things she had done. And, he had to
admit, if she was anything like Sloane, he
knew he would find her enthralling.

"I would like to meet her, Tearle," he
said, looking at his brother with a somber
face. "I can be kind when I put my mind to
it."

The earl grinned at his brother. "I know
you can, youngster," he said and kicked his
horse to a gallop.

Sloane was in the drawing room with her
parents and Roseanne when the gentlemen
arrived. The butler, Crayton, showed them
into the room and returned shortly with tea.

Jonathan had met Sloane's parents at the
wedding and watched carefully as Sloane
touched Roseanne on the arm to get her
attention. Jonathan was spellbound; the
young woman's angelic beauty made him
breathless. From the top of her vivid red hair
all the way down her slender body, she was
delicate   perfection.   Her   clear   ivory
complexion reminded him of a pitcher of
fresh cream, and the soft color lighting her
cheekbones was like that of a fresh peach
ready to pick. A bit nervously, she lifted
bright green eyes to meet his dark brown
ones, and he almost swayed from the impact.

He took her fragile hand in his and
bowed low, kissing it respectfully. Forgetting
that he kept her hand in his, he lifted his head
and looked directly at her, speaking slowly
and distinctly as Sloane had done. "I am very
pleased to make your acquaintance, Miss
Kincade. I have greatly admired your

painting, the one hanging at Beckford Hall. I would very much like the honor of seeing more of your work.''

"Thank you, Lord Grayson." Roseanne smiled shyly and gently tugged her hand from his. "I would be happy to show them to you. Perhaps after tea?"

"Yes, of course." He returned her smile with a warm one, almost laughing out loud in bemusement. No woman had ever made his heart pound so violently, not even five years ago when he worked up the courage to ask that season's Incomparable to stand up with him. He forced himself not to stare and was rather pleased that he managed to carry on a somewhat respectable conversation.

After what seemed an eternity, the earl and Galen departed for the stables. Jonathan promised to join them there later after Roseanne showed him her studio.

She led him to a bright, sunny room at the back of the house. A half-finished landscape sat on an easel and several other landscapes lined the room between the windows. Stacks of finished pictures sat on the floor, leaning against the wall.

Jonathan studied the pictures hanging on the wall, then thumbed through a couple of stacks sitting on the floor. "How long have you been painting?" He raised his head to look at her, and when he saw her questioning look, he realized he had not spoken so she could understand. "I'm sorry," he said, growing a little flushed.

Roseanne dropped her gaze down to her

clasped hands in embarrassment. Jonathan stepped quickly across the room and took both her hands in his, waiting patiently until she at last looked up at him.

"Miss Kincade, please don't be embarrassed. I was so lost in your work that I forgot to look at you. I tend to forget a lot of things when I'm looking at paintings." He smiled whimsically. "Although, I can't fathom how I'd be that absentminded. When it comes down to it, I'd much rather look at you."

"Please don't tease me, Lord Grayson." Roseanne made a feeble attempt to move away, but he held her hands captive. She looked back at him uncertainly, and a little fearfully.

"I'm not teasing you, little one, and I promise you there is nothing to be afraid of. I will never knowingly hurt you, and if I unknowingly do, then you must tell me. You must be patient with me, reminding me if I forget to talk so you can understand."

"You speak as if you mean for us to be friends, my lord."

"I do, if you will but give me the chance. Indeed, Miss Kincade, perhaps we will become more than friends."

"I . . . I think not, my lord." Again, she tried to pull away, and again, he held firm, shifting both her hands to one of his. She turned her face aside, and he very gently turned it back to him with his fingertip.

"Have you never had a man pay court to you?"

"No, my lord, and I'm not foolish enough to think that you would do so, at least not in earnest."

"Then you should be so foolish, little one."

Her gaze flew to his, reading the truth of his statement. "Miss Kincade—" He waited until her eyes focused on his lips before continuing. "I did not mean to speak so openly, but I do not want you to be afraid of me. I want us to get to know each other, but it's important that you realize I won't just be flirting with you." He grinned. "Although, I expect when I have my feet back on the ground, I'll manage to flirt with you a bit."

She smiled uncertainly. "I don't know how to handle this."

"Nor do I, little one. No one has quite affected me this way before."

She shook her head. "No, please don't say that. You know there can be nothing between us. I can never marry."

"Why not?"

"Surely, that is obvious. No man would want me . . . like I am."

"You are wrong, Roseanne." His gaze burned into hers with such intensity that her legs began to shake. "You have blown me out of the water." He lifted her hands and pressed them to his chest, flattening her sensitive palms over the thundering beat of his heart. "Believe me, my dear, that is not the heartbeat of an unmoved man." He grinned wryly. "Now, I shall let you show me your father's stables before I forget myself completely and scare the wits out of you."

Roseanne stared up at him in wonder as he took her arm and steered her out the door and down to the stables.

In the drawing room, Libby Kincade put her embroidery down on her lap and studied her daughter. Sloane looked up from her knitting.

"What is it, Mama?"

"I think you should move back here."

"Whatever for?" The knitting needles paused in the middle of a stitch. "I'm content at Beckford Hall."

"Yes, I suppose you are," her mother said dryly, "and I'm sure his lordship is thrilled."

"Mother, it's not like you to beat around the bush. What are you trying to say?"

"The whole village, in fact, probably the whole county, is talking about you and Lord Beckford. Everyone has heard about your bathtub, your personal maid, the lovely new rug and curtains, and especially about the roses everyday. If anyone had a doubt in his head about the two of you, it was dashed at Tom's wedding. Your adoration of each other was so blatant that it stirred up the gossip mills to full power."

Sloane threw her knitting down on the green silk couch and jumped to her feet. "I thought you didn't give a hang about gossip. You didn't mind the talk a bit when you married Papa."

"No, I didn't, because I wasn't doing anything wrong."

"Neither am I!"

"Aren't you? Lord Beckford's dislike of marriage is widely known, Sloane; therefore, it is logical to conclude that he will only indulge his fancy for you by having an affair. He has showered you with presents over this last month, and openly danced every waltz with you at the wedding."

"Mother, I am not a green girl just out of the schoolroom. I can dance with whomever I want, as many times as I want."

"Not when the man is your employer. Sloane, I want the truth. Are you sharing Lord Beckford's bed?"

"Mama, how can you think such a thing?" Sloane's voice broke with emotion.

Libby walked slowly to her daughter's side and gently gripped her shoulder. "Because you love him, and whether he will admit it or not, he loves you. That makes for a very overpowering combination."

"Oh, Mama." Sloane put her arms around her mother and buried her head against her shoulder. "I haven't shared his bed, and I won't. I could not shame you nor Casey's memory by doing so."

"Then why do you stay, child?"

"Because I can't seem to make myself go." Sloane lifted her head and eased out of her mother's embrace. "He is showering me with gifts to try to earn my forgiveness; at least that is the main reason, I'm certain."

"For the incident with Lady Wentwood?"

"Yes, ma'am. And, really, other than the roses and Annie, who helps the children more than me, nothing has been of a personal nature. All of the improvements, the bath, the curtains, everything, go with the manor." She drew a shaky breath. "I stay in the hope that he will truly learn to love me and will be willing to marry me."

"Oh, Sloane, I fear that is an impossible dream."

"I know, but when I lost Casey, I never thought I could care for anyone as deeply again. Now, I do, and I can't just walk away from him. I have to do everything I can, within respectability, of course, to teach him what true love really is. Besides, I really can't bear to leave the children. They are already like my own."

"Sloane, are you strong enough to stand the gossip? It can hurt cruelly." Libby Kincade unconsciously twisted her hands, remembering the stings and barbs hurled against her when she first married.

"I don't care what people say, as long as I know I'm not doing anything immoral."

"Gossip aside, can you bear the pain if he does not come around and ask you to marry him? I don't like to see you hurt, dear."

"I will have to bear the consequences, whatever they turn out to be, but I can not leave now. Mama, he has been nothing but kind to me since Lady Wentwood's visit. He has not attempted, uh, seduction at all since then."

"But he did before?"

"Well, yes, he did, a couple of times."
Sloane grinned at her mother. "He kissed me
the first night we met."

"The first night? Oh, dear, he's a worse
rake than I thought." Her mother laughed in
spite of her worry. "I had always heard what
a cross-tempered fellow he was. Your Aunt
Matilda said he went around with a perpetual
scowl on his face when he was in town, but he
has always been perfectly charming here. I
suppose the country air agrees with him—
and possibly my daughter's company."

"I hope so, Mama. I hope so." Sloane
picked up her knitting and dropped it back in
the bag. "I really should go now."

The twins, Hobie and Tobie, burst into
the room. "Lord Beckford says you should be
leaving soon," said Hobie.

"Says you'll miss your dinner if you
don't go now, but I think he doesn't want you
to be out after dark," said Tobie.

"Really? What makes you think that,
dear?" Sloane ruffled his red hair. "Does he
think the bogeyman will get me?"

"Not the bogeyman," Tobie said in disgust, "there's no such thing."

Hobie chimed in. "He told Papa it was
too—"

"—dangerous. Highwaymen. He doesn't
think you could outrun 'em," said Tobie.

"But Papa said different. He almost
wagered you could."

"That's when the earl got the crotchets."
Tobie grinned at his twin. "He said you'd

probably do fine unless a chicken ran in front of you, then you'd—"

"—fall on your pretty rump."

"Rump? He said rump?" asked Libby, her eyes wide.

The boys' grins widened, and they nodded their heads sagely.

"Enough of such talk, boys. You're not at the stables, now."

Sloane smiled impishly at her mother and whispered in her ear, "Well, at least he said it was pretty."

"Sloane Donovan, you're as bad as your father." Libby tried to hide her smile, but gave up, chuckling as she followed her children out the door.

Sloane soon learned that she did care what people said about her. As she rode through Evesham with her escorts, the villagers were quite open with their talk. Most kept their comments low or hidden behind their hands, but a few of the more outspoken let their opinions drift on the breeze to reach the trio's ears.

"Just look at 'er, now. Flauntin' 'erself like she was somethin' special," said the baker's wife to her companion as they walked along the dusty street. "Just wait until 'e gets tired a playin' with 'er. Then, who'll she find to buy 'er fancy things?"

By the time they passed the village, Sloane's face burned and tears stung her eyes.

Jonathan glanced at his brother's furious

face then shifted his gaze to watch a tear trickle down Sloane's cheek. "I think I'll ride on ahead," he said quietly. He touched his heels to his horse's flanks and moments later disappeared around a bend in the road.

"I shall question each servant personally. When I find out who has been spreading these rumors, they will be dismissed immediately." Trojan pranced nervously, sensing his master's ill-temper.

Sloane averted her face and quickly wiped her cheek, swallowing hard to stifle the remaining tears. "All servants talk, my lord, but those at Beckford Hall are good people. I doubt if any of them spread the things we heard today. You know how tales grow twisted as they are repeated. I fear we have left ourselves open to gossip."

"What I choose to do in my own home is of no concern to anyone else."

"How wonderful it would be if that were true, but you know 'tis not. You know as well as I that gossip is prime entertainment, whether the participants are in the *ton* or in the village." Sloane took a deep breath and looked him straight in the eye. "My lord, you have been very kind to me this last month, and I am fully aware of the reason you have been so generous, but the gifts must stop. I do appreciate the improvements to my room, but you must do no more."

"And the roses?" His face softened, his expression growing tender and wistful.

Sloane dropped her gaze and flushed becomingly. "I have enjoyed the roses most of all, my lord," she said softly, "but they, too, must stop. Perhaps the remodeling might not have caused such a stir, but the bathtub, the maid, and the roses; well, one only has to have a small imagination to jump to the wrong conclusion."

The horses had relaxed as the tension eased between their riders, so they moved down the lane at a very slow walk. Tearle reached across the small distance separating them to gently caress her cheek with his fingertip.

"My beautiful Sloane, it seems I cannot right my wrong. I have only caused you more pain."

"I have long forgiven you for that regrettable day, my lord."

"What? Undoubtedly, you have taken a spiteful delight in letting me stew in my own remorse."

Sloane chanced a cautious peek at him under her lashes. The relief in his eyes overshadowed the trace of irritation in his expression. She sent him a beguiling smile, raising her head to look fully at him.

"Not really; I just enjoyed the flowers and the other things."

The earl threw back his head and laughed long and hard. He thought for a moment his heart would take wings and fly. All was not lost; she had forgiven him. His laughter subsided and he smiled at her, his eyes twinkling with devilment.

"Tell me, Mrs. Donovan, do you enjoy your tub?"

"Yes, I do, but I think putting it in the corner of my room would have been sufficient."

"Sufficient, perhaps, but not luxurious."

"My lord, a governess does not expect luxury."

"Of course not, but it simply matches all the other bathrooms, except mine. If I had not added the room for you, it would have thrown off the whole floor plan, and because I ordered several tubs all the same size, I was given a better price." He laughed at Sloane's frown. "There, I have completely destroyed the fantasy that you are being pampered. It's too bad our critics conveniently forget all the other remodeling that has been done."

Sloane's frown faded into a tiny smile. Floor plan or not, no other governess would have been treated to a fresh rose each day, cut by the master's own hand. Curiosity got the better of her.

"What's different about your tub?"

"It's square. Twelve feet square to be exact."

"Twelve feet?" she asked, shaking her head in wonder. "You could practically swim in it."

"Not quite, it's not deep enough. However, it is more than adequate for several to bathe in ample luxury."

"Several?" Her eyes grew wide.

"Four or five, although five might prove a little crowded. Don't be so shocked, Mrs. Donovan. Such things are done, although I must admit, it would be a new experience for

me. Not that I plan such an adventure anytime soon. However, I'm prepared in the
event I grow so depraved.''

Speechless, Sloane stared at him for a
few seconds before she caught the teasing
glint in his eyes and the twitch at the corner
of his lip.

''Heaven have mercy, I'm out riding with
a madman.'' With a saucy grin, she kicked
Windsong to a canter, laughing in the
growing twilight as the earl caught up with
her in the lane leading to Beckford Hall.

As they approached the stables, the earl
said, ''Sloane, my parents are coming for a
visit at the end of next week. Jon and I will go
to London on Monday. We will not return
until my parents have arrived. Their visit will
put an end to the wagging tongues. Surely,
my neighbors don't think I'm so wretched as
to flaunt my mistress before my mother,
much less to have them sharing my home.''
Not that it would bother Mum one whit, he
added to himself. I think she would like you
no matter what place you held in my life.

On Sunday morning, Sloane was
surprised to find the earl waiting for her and
the children when they came downstairs to
leave for church.

''I have ordered the coach brought
around, Mrs. Donovan, since I decided to
accompany you and the children to church
this morning.''

''You're going to church, Papa?'' asked
Jonny, his eyes wide.

''I thought I would, son, if that is agreeable with you," the earl replied dryly. "Do you think the roof will fall in?"

"No, I don't think so." Jonny frowned. "Does this mean I'll have to go to church when I'm the earl?"

"That will be up to you, Jon. It is not a requirement for an earl to attend church, at least not one of man's requirements. However, it certainly can't do any harm, and who knows, it might do some good. Now, run along and get in the carriage like a good fellow."

Jonny and Angela scampered across the portico and down the steps while the earl and Sloane followed behind.

"Are you trying to stop your decline into depravity, my lord?" Sloane grinned, her light gray eyes twinkling up at him.

"I'm certain the good vicar would like to think so, madam. I do hope he doesn't change his sermon just for my benefit." He smiled down at her, slowing his stride and taking her arm as they descended the portico steps. "Actually, since I'm leaving for town in the morning, I found I wanted to be with you." He steadied her when she tripped slightly. "Also, it can't hurt for our neighbors to see me attending worship with you and the children. Just don't let me start snoring, I beg you."

"Howard's sermons are seldom dull, my lord. I'm not sure anyone could fall asleep with his booming oration." She accepted his hand up into the coach, wondering if he truly snored when he slept. It was such an endearing and intimate thought, somehow, that she smiled slightly as she settled herself in the squabs. She glanced at him as he leaned back in the seat across from her.

"Occasionally, Mrs. Donovan, only occasionally. A poke in the ribs usually solves the problem." He laughed softly as color flooded her face, but the spark that flared in his purple-blue eyes set her pulse to racing.

They caused quite a stir when they walked into church. Except for the times the children attended service, the hereditary pew of the Earl of Beckford had been empty for over ten years. The old stone building fairly hummed with low conversations until the vicar took his place.

From the very first bars of the opening hymn, it was apparent Tearle Louis Grayson, the roguish Earl of Beckford, was no stranger to the music of the church. His beautiful baritone voice endowed the song with rich warmth and feeling. Although Sloane had a more than adequate voice, she didn't even try to sing. Instead, she let the deep, resonant tones surround her, wrapping her in the beauty of the music and the words. She closed her eyes, not daring to look at him, knowing all the love in her heart would come shining through.

As they sat down at the end of the song, Jonny set the hymnal on his lap, but when he wiggled in the pew a few minutes later, it slid down his legs toward the floor. Both the earl and Sloane grabbed it, their fingers touching across the cool leather binding. The earl's

fingertips closed over hers for an instant,
then he pulled the song book from her hand,
straightened, and placed it in the rack.

If questioned about the sermon that
morning, those sitting in that most ornate
and significant pew of the church wouldn't
have had an accurate answer. Jonny and
Angela were busy being children, watching a
ladybug crawl across the brim of Mrs.
Smith's hat, rolling their eyes at each other
as young lovers flirted across the room, and
stifling their giggles as the squire began to
snore. The earl and Sloane were simply and
exclusively thinking of each other.

10

Prescott Grayson, the Marquess of Sheffeld, watched in amusement as his tiny wife flitted back and forth between the library windows overlooking the lane.

"Where can those boys be? They should have been here hours ago," said the marchioness.

"Now, Olivia, don't be such a fussbudget. Your boys are grown men, quite capable of taking care of themselves."

"Oh, I know, Cottie. It's just that I'm so anxious to see them. It seems like it's been years instead of months." She perched for a fleeting moment on the arm of his chair, fussing with the lace ruff of her striped mauve silk dress, before jumping up to peer out the window again.

The marquess chuckled, moving to stand behind his wife. Right at six feet in height, he had to bend down to rest his chin on the mauve cornette hiding most of her gray-blond curls.

"I think I should have sent you out to play tag with the children."

"What? In these shoes?" She held out a delicate kid slipper. "I'd break my neck. Besides, that's expecting a bit too much even from a doting grandmother."

"You're a poor influence on Jonny, my dear. How is Mrs. Donovan to be expected to keep him contained when you are so agitated?" The marquess straightened, slipping his arms around his wife's shoulders to keep her in place.

"Pooh. She handles them quite well, in spite of my poor influence." She tipped her nose up in the air, a bit miffed.

"Now, don't get yourself in a huff. You know very well I didn't mean that you do badly by the boy in a general way."

She turned her head to look up at him. "No, I suppose not. At any rate, I dare say Mrs. Donovan could correct any grave misconduct I pass along to the youngsters. They seem to toe the line with her."

"I'm utterly amazed at the change in Angela. Even though both Cory and Tearle mentioned it, I was not prepared for the happy, talkative, little girl who bounced out to meet us yesterday."

Lady Sheffeld looked back out the window, snuggling against her husband. "Mrs. Donovan has worked wonders with the child. It's incredible what a little love will do. I wonder if she can do as much for Tearle."

"You mean in his relationship with Angela?"

"Well, partly."

"Olivia, why do I have this feeling of impending doom?" He looked down at the top of her head and said sternly, "You know I don't approve of you meddling in our children's lives."

"Humph! Meddling is a mother's natural right. Besides, I did quite well by Cory and Bailey. They are as happy as two peas in a pod." She looked up at him indignantly.

"True enough, but neither of them had been badly hurt before. Tread carefully, pet. See how the wind blows before you put your nose where it doesn't belong."

"Of course, dear." A smile flashed across her face. "You know I'm not a total peabrain. I simply think Mrs. Donovan is a lovely woman and since the children already adore her, it would be very nice if Tearle did, too."

"What of the lady in question? Doesn't she have a say in the matter?" He smiled as she heaved an exasperated sigh.

"Really, Cottie. Of course, she does, but how could she help but fall in love with my handsome son?"

"You forget that he is not the same jovial boy we used to know, pet. Handsome, yes, but far too cynical and brooding for many a woman's taste."

"From all the rumors I've heard, there are many women who don't find him too cynical or brooding; at least when weighed against his title and wealth." She stared wistfully at the racing curricle starting up the drive. "I wouldn't even demand marriage if she could make him truly happy, even if just for a little while."

"Come, pet. Let's go meet our sons, and please, try to resist your matchmaking. I would like to stay here for a while, not be asked to leave within the next week." He released his wife and stepped aside.

"Oh, botheration." Lady Sheffeld scurried to the door and down the hall; his lordship strolled along languidly a few steps behind.

The earl sprang lightly out of the curricle, tossing the reins to his groom. Jonathan joined him on the portico, and together they stepped into the great hall to meet their parents.

"What delayed you?" asked Lady Sheffeld, tipping her cheek up to her elder son for a kiss. "I thought surely you had been in an accident."

"We are fine, Mama. A stagecoach overturned on the road. The turnpike was blocked for hours."

"Oh, my. Was anyone seriously injured?"

"Yes, several of the passengers were hurt badly. The driver and two of the passengers riding on the top were killed. It was a ghastly sight."

Lady Sheffeld scanned Tearle's pale face, guessing the scene had brought back the memory of his wife's death. "Come, lads, let us go out in the garden where it's cooler. Grimley will bring us something to drink." She nodded at the butler, who bowed and left for the refreshments.

Jonathan and Tearle smiled at each other, then looked around behind them. "Ma'am, I do believe you're mistaken," said Jonathan. "I don't see any lads here."

"You'll always be boys to me, children." Lady Sheffeld smiled up at her two tall sons and stepped between them, hooking her arms through theirs. "Now, tell me all about town."

"It was hot, dull, and smelly," said Tearle.

"But there is always something to do in London, dears. Surely you found some amusement at White's or perhaps the opera."

"Or at least with the opera singers," said Lord Sheffeld, with a chuckle.

"Not even there, Papa. Tearle couldn't put up with the poor singing, so we left before the second act. You know how picky he is with music. I thought the lady's other assets were enough to balance out her lack of talent, but my dear brother didn't agree with me."

"She screeched like a dying cat, and though she was greatly endowed, her rather artificial beauty was not enough to merit suffering the headache," said the earl.

They passed through the conservatory and down the tier of steps into the garden. The children spotted them and raced across the grass to meet them. The earl picked up both of his children in turn, giving them each a hug and kiss.

"Ah, it's good to be home. Have you been behaving yourselves?"

"Of course, Papa. We hardly got into trouble at all while you were gone." At his father's frown, Jonny explained. "I found a snake and took it upstairs. Slo' didn't like it."

"I'm not surprised. Now, greet your uncle, imps." He sat Angela on the ground. Seeing the accident, and then Angela, had brought back the memory of his wife and her tragic death with painful force. He had thought he was over the guilt, that confused feeling of having somehow driven her into the arms of other men, and ultimately to her death. It had taken all his willpower to hug Angela, and he knew the child sensed his reluctance. Fresh feelings of guilt and uncertainty swept over him. For the first time in over two years, the earl felt he was floundering.

Lady Sheffeld watched her son closely. His pale face had grown even whiter when he saw Angela. Usually one to keep his feelings well-hidden, her heart had gone out to him as she watched the raw emotions play across his strained countenance. He stared down at the ground, fighting for control. She took a step toward him, but stopped when Sloane came into her line of vision.

"Welcome home, my lord," she said softly.

Tearle's head shot up. Slowly, he reached for the hand she held out to him, gripping it tightly, bringing it close to his heart. Lady Sheffeld watched in fascination as some color gradually returned to his face and the warmth of happiness filled his eyes. Biting her tongue to control her shout of joy, the older lady quietly turned away to talk to her other son.

"You look so tired, my lord. Was it a difficult journey?" Sloane's concern showed on her face and in her voice.

"There was a wreck on the road. It took some time for us to clear a way through."

"You weren't hurt, were you?" Sloane's gaze swept over him in alarm.

"No. It happened a few minutes before we arrived on the scene." He forced a smile. "You look tired yourself. Have the children been bad?"

"No, they've been good." She grinned at him. "Not angels, of course, but no more mischief than usual. I haven't slept well this week, probably due to the heat. Did Jonny tell you about the snake?"

"Yes, he said he brought it inside."

Sloane chuckled as he gave her hand a quick squeeze and released it. "He let it loose in the nursery."

"Did you catch it?" The earl smiled down at her, a small twinkle returing to his eyes.

"No, I can't stand snakes. Brian was my knight in shining armor and came to the rescue. If he had not, I fear it would still be there, and I would be sleeping at my parents' house."

The earl shuddered. "I'm glad I wasn't here. I don't like snakes either."

Grimley arrived with the tea tray, and they settled down in the garden for the refreshments and quiet conversation. An hour or so later, the marquess escorted his wife back into the house so she might rest before dinner. Jonny and Angela enticed their uncle down to the kennels to see Beau and a litter of kittens they had discovered in the hayloft at the stables. The earl stood also, and held out his arm to Sloane.

"Will you take a stroll with me, Sloane?"

"Of course, my lord."

His muscles flexed in response to her light grip, signaling his intense awareness of her presence. She stole a glance up at him, and instantly regretted it. His eyes burned with such fire that she found it difficult to breathe. They moved along the path, ignorant of their surroundings, until at last Sloane made an attempt at conversation.

"Did you have a pleasant time in London, my lord?"

"Not particularly."

"You did not find any of your friends in town?"

"I saw a few of my cronies at White's, but since I eventually handed over a great deal of money to them, I did not find their company enjoyable. I rarely lose, and it does not sit well with me."

"First in races and cards, is that not right, sir?" She smiled up at him, trying to lighten his mood.

"I usually achieve whatever I set out to do, madam." He smiled in self-mockery. "However, this trip proved I am not totally infallible." He glanced down at her, an un-readable expression settling over his face. "I even visited an establishment guaranteed to bring a smile to a gentleman's face. Surely, I do not shock you, my dear. Such behavior is not unusual among my peers."

He drew her off the path, guiding her into the darkening shadows of the old oak. "Unfortunately, I discovered that not one of the, er, ladies, appealed to me. As I scanned all those willing faces and luscious bodies, I saw only one exquisite face and one lovely body. The woman of my mind's eye had soft, light brown hair kissed by the sun, and the most beautiful gray eyes in God's creation." He slipped his finger beneath her chin and tipped her face up toward his. "I missed you, sweetheart."

"I missed you, too, my lord," she whispered, undone by the passion simmering in his eyes. There was something else hiding in the depths of those beautiful blue eyes, and she searched his gaze as he pulled her into his arms. Suddenly, she recognized the glint of fear and uncertainty.

"Say my name," he commanded, "let me hear my name on your sweet lips."

"Oh, Tearle, my dearest Tearle, I missed you so," she cried softly, leaning toward him, her arms going up around his neck. His mouth came down hard on hers, full of passion, full of need, and though he knew it not, full of love. He crushed her against him, molding his hard frame to her softness, kissing her with all the fierceness of a desire long held in check.

He tore his mouth away from hers,

spreading kisses across her cheek and down her throat. His lips worked their way back up to hers, taking them gently, tenderly delighting in the sweet nectar of her passionate response. His hand moved up her ribs to caress her breast, and Sloane shivered against him, clinging to him.

"Tell me I haunted your dreams; that your thoughts were ever on me," he whispered, kissing the sensitive spot just beneath her ear.

"Yes, my precious love, yes." Sloane was beyond rational thought. In this moment, she existed for him and for him alone. She did not realize until minutes later the words she had whispered, but the earl heard them and slowly raised his head, gazing at her intently in the lengthening shadows.

For the first time since the early weeks of his marriage, before he learned the harsh realities of that union, he acknowledged the existence of love. He could not deny the truth of that emotion for it glowed like a bright beacon on Sloane's face, calling him, luring him, daring him to share in that bittersweet pain.

He acknowledged, too, that the feelings he held for this woman went far beyond the realm of desire, but were they strong enough for a lifetime commitment? Was he even capable of caring deeply for anyone, or was trust so lacking that he would never be able to give all his heart? Would he only end up wounding her as badly as he had been hurt?

Caution replaced passion, and the earl

pulled her gently against him, cradling her head to his chest. He held her quietly for several minutes, until breathing resumed a somewhat normal pace and heartbeats ceased to be thunder. When he spoke, his voice was thick with emotion.

"You should go in now, sweetheart. The children will be dashing in soon, and it wouldn't do for you to look so enchantingly beautiful. I shall come up after dinner to bid the children good-night." He kissed her on the forehead and let her go.

"Yes, my lord." Sloane dared not look at him, now keenly aware of the endearment she had whispered only moments before. That his passions had cooled so quickly after she had spoken filled her with despair.

"My name is Tearle. It would please me greatly if you used it, at least when we are alone." His voice was warm and like a caress.

Her gaze flew to his face, searching, hoping. Slowly, a smile spread from her eyes down to her lips and across her face. She understood, as his lips came down to brush against hers, that all was not lost. She had not crushed the fragile blossom of his love; it only needed more time and the gentle nourishment from her own caring heart to open fully.

Two mornings later, Sloane was summoned to Lady Sheffeld's chamber shortly before ten. When Sloane entered the room, she found the marchioness dressed in a periwinkle muslin gown and ready to go down to breakfast.

"I would beg a few minutes of your time, Mrs. Donovan," said the noble lady, dismissing her maid with a wave of her hand. She waited until the woman shut the door before walking over to the window, looking out at the gardens.

"Come here, if you will, Mrs. Donovan. I would like you to see the splendid view." Sloane complied, and with a sharp churning in her stomach, stared across the grounds at the old oak. "Do you not agree that the scenery is quite nice, with an exceptional view of the oak?"

"Yes, my lady," said Sloane weakly.

"I chanced to look out the window a few evenings past and happened upon a most intimate little rendezvous, although I will admit I wasn't surprised at the players." Lady Sheffeld turned to Sloane, frowning slightly at the young widow's flushed face and downcast eyes. "Are you my son's paramour, Mrs. Donovan?"

"No, Lady Sheffeld, I am not." Sloane lifted her gaze to look directly at the marchioness and straightened unconsciously.

"Why not?"

"I beg your pardon, m'lady?"

"I have eyes in my head, child. You are obviously great attracted to my son, and he to you. From the way he reacts whenever you are near, you could bring him great happiness."

"Such happiness would be of the fleeting kind, m'lady. I love my family greatly, Lady

Sheffeld. I could not bring them dishonor. Perhaps in London such an alliance would soon be old news, but here in the country, the shame of such behavior would last for years."

"Yes, I suppose so." Lady Sheffeld subjected Sloane to several minutes of close scrutiny. "Do you love him?"

"Yes, m'lady, I do."

"You will only consider marriage?"

"There is no other choice open to me."

"I had hoped for an easier path of happiness for Tearle, but in truth, this can be the only successful one. Very well, my dear. You may be assured that I will do everything in my power to encourage a match between you and my son. I believe he has already realized how much he cares for you. It will take him a while longer, I have no doubts, to take what must be to him a fateful step. Men are so skittish when it comes to matriomony. Cottie was just the same. They can't stand the thought of being tied down to one woman, when in actuality that is exactly what they need—at least if the woman isn't a prig." She shook her head sadly, taking a chair near the window and motioning for Sloane to sit nearby.

"I'm not really sure why I'm telling you this, Sloane—but see, I already think of you as a daughter—for I've never told another living soul. It took many long years to learn how to be the woman my husband needed and to gain his love." She smiled at Sloane.

"If that little scene in the garden is any

indication, you already know how to be a woman. Now, quit staring, child. Close your mouth and gather your wits. I must go down to breakfast, or Cottie will be sending someone up to check on me. I'll have to send the men off hunting or something so we can make our plans." She rose quickly and Sloane followed suit.

"Our plans, m'lady?"

"What action to take, my dear. My goodness, didn't your mother help with your campaign to win your first husband?"

"Well, no ma'am. He worked for my father, and, well, everything just seemed to fall into place."

"Pooh, how boring. No, we must make careful plans, strategies to throw you and Tearle together as often as possible and in the most favorite situations for you. He knows of the passionate side of your nature, and your kindness to the children. What we must now show him is the side he will present to the *ton*. You must prove to him—whether he is aware of his need or not—that you are fit to be an earl's wife. He assumes that you are a lady, considering your manner and at least one side of your family, but you must prove to him that you can comport yourself with the proper dignity and style befitting his wife." Lady Sheffeld sat down by the window once again.

"Please don't miss my point. You must show him you are what he wants in a wife, not necessarily what someone else might be looking for. Mind you, you may be kind to other gentlemen, but under no circumstances should you flirt with one, not even a man as old as your grandfather. You must show him that you are completely above being unfaithful. You must give absolutely no hint if you find other men attractive." Lady Sheffeld gazed at Sloane, tears misting her eyes. "I daresay, if you cuckold him, it would be the end of him. He discovered within a year of his first marriage that his wife had the morals of a strumpet. She was not particular who she bedded; her tastes ran from the youngest footman to one of her great-uncle's oldest friends."

"Oh, my poor Tearle." Sloane sank down on the plush chair.

"He should not have tolerated it, but a divorce is a long and difficult process." Lady Sheffeld drew a deep breath and put on a smile. "Now, I have a thousand things to do. Since we shall all be attending the races in Cheltenham next week, I think we shall stay long enough to have a ball. Yes, that would be perfect; between the festivities of race day, the ball, and of course, a trip to the theatre, you will have an opportunity to show him not only how lovely and graceful you are, but how much fun you can be, too."

Sloane watched with a mixture of awe and trepidation as Lady Sheffeld leaped to her feet. It took her several seconds to remember that protocol declared she should stand also. "My lady, do you really think we should, um, try to ensnare him this way? It seems so devious."

"All policy's allowed in war and love, as the saying goes. We aren't being devious, my dear, simply feminine." With a laugh, Lady Sheffeld fluttered from the room, her mind whirling with plans for the ball, and the letter she had to write to Cheltenham's Master of Ceremonies.

Sloane stared after her for a few minutes in total silence. Slowly, laughter bubbled up within her, and she sank back down on the chair. "Oh, my dearest love, what are we in for?"

11

"Jon, pull in right here," called the earl, "there's plenty of room." He handed the reins to his groom and leaned back in the phaeton seat to watch his brother maneuver his team into the rather narrow space beside them. "I'll go bail it takes him three tries." He grinned lazily at Sloane, who sat next to him on the front seat of the four passenger phaeton.

"I think I'll save my money to bet on the races. I must mind my pence, you know," she said with a false primness, her twinkling eyes contradicting her statement.

"Are you hinting for a raise in wages, Mrs. Donovan? It could be arranged, with the assumption of a few more duties, of course," he said softly, his gaze moving slowly over her striped, powder pink, sarcenet gown. He wished she had not worn the muslin chemisette to fill in the low neckline of her gown.

Sloane returned his teasing smile from beneath the narrow brim of her small, straw poke bonnet. "I fear I could not handle any further duties, my lord. The children run me ragged as it is."

"You poor dear, perhaps I should hire another nurserymaid to help you, since Annie isn't enough. Do you think two would suffice, or shall I make it three?"

"Five would be perfect, sir, then we might be able to keep up with Jonny."

"I'm hungry," piped up a small voice from the back seat.

The earl shifted in the seat to look back at his son. "Jonny, you had breakfast less than an hour ago."

"I'm still hungry. Can we have our picnic, now?"

"Yeth, can we have a picnic, now, Papa?" asked Angela, standing on the floorboard and putting a tiny hand on his lordship's arm. "I'm tharved."

"You can't be thar . . . starved, imp, but we'll have a look to see what Mrs. Donovan brought for you. There's not much else to do for a while, since the races don't start for another hour." The earl climbed down from the phaeton and took a large basket from the partition in the back. He placed it on the seat next to Sloane, grinning as he climbed back up. Nodding his head toward Jonathan's phaeton, he said, "Three tries. Pity you didn't bet."

"Pity for you. Lucky for me." Sloane opened the basket and took out a couple of strawberry tarts, handing them to the children. "Please try not to make too big a mess."

"It looks like we have this section all filled up." The earl glanced down the row of carriages lining the top of Cleeve Hill. On his left, Jonathan and Roseanne shared a phaeton with her mother and her grandfather, Lord Atherton. To their left was a curricle occupied by Sloane's sister, Clarice, and her husband, Michael. Their four-year-old daughter, Beth, perched between them.

To the earl's right, the marquess and his lady shared a phaeton with Bailey and Corine, who had arrived in Cheltenham the day before. Tearle glanced at his sister's round belly and smiled tenderly. Her condition had become quite obvious although she kept a lacy shawl draped across her middle in an attempt to hide it. The racing festivities were the last she would be able to attend until after the baby was born. He shook his head slightly, amazed that in four months or so he would become an uncle.

His gaze fell upon Sloane, and he envisioned how lovely she would look cradling a babe in her arms. With a start, the earl realized the child of his imagination had curly flaxen hair and eyes the color of a dark crocus.

"It looks like all of Cheltenham and half the county have turned out for the races." Clearing his throat, he shifted uncomfortably in the seat. "I'm not surprised since it's such a beautiful, warm day for late August. Still, it's a very good turnout for the first one. With this great a success, it has a good chance of becoming a yearly event." He looked around at the colorful crowd, noting with pride that no other woman there came close to Sloane's beauty. She had no rival among the richly dressed gentry nearby or among the farmers' and tradesmen's wives and daughters clustered along the course.

Sloane glanced around the crowd, too, deciding no man there, be he gentleman, merchant, tradesman, or groom, was a match for her earl. He wore his favorite dark blue, superfine tailcoat and a crimson silk waistcoat. The wide turned-over edges of his top boots were a soft buff color, matching his leather breeches and leather riding gloves.

"Are you in the first race, Lord Beckford?" Sloane quickly wiped Angela's chin before a large drop of strawberry filling dripped down to her bright yellow dress.

"Yes, will you be betting on me, Sloane?" He looked at her, mischief twinkling in his eyes.

"Do you intend to win?" She glanced at him before turning back to keep watch on Angela and her tart.

"Of course. Trojan has never lost a race yet. I doubt that we will start now."

"Ah, but you have never raced against Tony, or one of my father's horses, have you?"

"No, I haven't. Do you think he'll give me a good run?"

"Why certainly; his animal is a beautiful bay stallion, much the same size as Trojan. Peaches has never lost a race either."

"Peaches?" The earl threw back his head and laughed.

"Tobie named him—after he ate all the ripe peaches on mother's prized tree."

The earl leaned back in the seat, gazing at Sloane warmly. As he watched her laugh, a glint of something more than humor lit his eyes. "Do you actually think I'd allow Trojan to be beaten by a horse named Peaches?"

Sloane occupied herself with washing the strawberries off Angela's hands and face with a damp cloth from the basket. Out of the corner of her eye, she watched the earl. He was relaxed, confidently arrogant, and giving her a very masculine appraisal. Her heartbeat quickened beneath his seductive gaze, and she admitted to herself that he would probably drive Trojan into the ground before allowing Tony to beat him. For once, she questioned her father's wisdom at allowing his children to name the horses. She was saved from answering by an interruption from Jonathan.

"Say, big brother, Michael and I have a little private wager going on. Care to join in? By the by, you'd better get a move on if you want to be at the start on time. Can't have you late for the race, my boy. I'll not lose a bundle because you were disqualified."

"I'm sure my throngs of followers would be terribly disappointed." The earl laughed and gracefully stepped down from the phaeton. Turning back to Sloane, he said, "Do you wish to place a wager with your brother-in-law, Mrs. Donovan, or do you still want to hang onto your hard-earned pence?"

"I think a small gamble could be allowed, my lord." She dug in her reticule for a moment and dropped the coins into his lordship's outstretched hand. His fingers closed over hers, trapping both the money and her hand.

"On which horse, my dear?" His thumb grazed the back of her hand; her silk glove only adding to the sensuality of his touch.

"On the winner, of course." Her eyes danced as she looked down at him, meeting his gaze with a coquettish smile.

"Done, madam." The earl grinned and swiftly brought her hand to his lips. In that instant, both of them wished the silk would vanish into thin air. Tearle released her fingers, and jangled the coins in his hand. "I'm off to make you a wee bit richer, madam."

"Ride carefully, Tearle," Sloane said softly. "I would much prefer to lose a few coins than to see you hurt."

He tipped his hat, stopping for a moment to talk to Michael Denton, before striding swiftly to the far end of the racecourse. Sloane spent the next half hour wandering around the carriages with the children, visiting with her relatives and the friends she spied along the way. By the start of the race,

the children were content to climb back into
the phaeton to watch.

It was apparent from the outset that the
contest was between Trojan and Peaches. A
third horse, Bengal, gave them a run for the
first mile, but then fell behind in the second.
The lead teetered back and forth between the
glistening black stallion and the powerful
bay. The crowd was on its feet as the horses
thundered by.

Jonny and Angela stood on the seat with
Sloane standing on the floorboard between
them. As the horses tore by, Peaches was
ahead by a nose.

"Go, my lord, go. You can beat him,"
cried Sloane. A lightning smile broke the firm
lines of concentration on the earl's face, and
he nudged his steed ahead just before the
finish line. Sloane and the children hugged
each other, laughing and jumping up and
down on the carriage until the groom was
hard-pressed to keep the team in check.
When the trio had calmed down and retaken
their seats, Sloane glanced over at Jonathan's
carriage. A laughing argument was taking
place between her mother and Jonathan,
since the first had bet on Tony and the latter
on the earl.

"Really, Sloane, wagering against your
own brother. I think we're in the enemy
camp, Roseanne." Libby Kincade shook her
head, but smiled at her eldest daughter's
blush.

"I'll root for him this afternoon. Lord

216216 Sharon Gillenwater

Beckford only entered the one race. Besides, Jonny would have pushed me out of the phaeton if I hadn't cheered for his father, wouldn't you, imp?"

"Don't be silly, Slo'. I'm a gentleman." A sly grin spread slowly across the youngster's happy, flushed face. "Of course, I might make friends with another snake."

"There, Mother," said Sloane, with a smile. "You see, I was only protecting myself."

A few minutes later, the victor joined them amidst cheers from his children and a bright smile from their governess. Jonathan slapped him on the back after the marquess had given his hand a thorough shake, and Lady Sheffeld dropped a kiss on her son's upturned cheek when he stopped to talk with them at their carriage.

The earl hopped back up into the phaeton, receiving enthusiastic hugs and kisses from his children.

"You won, Papa," cried Angela. "You won!"

"Correct, imp, and I owe it all to Mrs. Donovan."

"To Sloane?" Jonny frowned and looked at the object of discussion. "What did she do?"

"She bet on the winner, and I couldn't let such a lovely lady down, now could I?"

"She should have bet 'splicitly on you." Jonny continued to stare at Sloane in disapproval.

"Oh, I think she did, Jon," said the earl

softly. "I think she did. Did she not cheer me on to victory?"

"Well, yes, I guess she did." Jonny's frown faded and he was caught up in the excitement of the next race.

Sloane had been studying the strings on her reticule with great interest, but, now, she peeked up at the earl. His gaze held her hostage, and she thought frantically that everyone within fifty feet must be aware of the strong current flowing between them. The crowd's loud cheering set her mind to rest, and she relaxed slightly against the cushions.

"Surely, you could not hear me cheering, my lord."

"Oh, yes, my dear, I did. I would recognize your sweet voice anywhere. No one else calls me 'my lord' in quite the same way." He smiled tenderly at Sloane's blush. "It makes me wonder just exactly how you mean it."

"Oh, look, Squire Denton's horse is about to place second." Sloane turned quickly back to the event at hand, her fingers nervously plucking at her reticule. The earl took her evasion in good stride and turned his attention to the track also.

They watched the first three races before the midday break. During the two-hour inter-mission, they joined their families in a picnic beneath the shady elm trees nearby. The children pleaded with their father to take them to the other side of the course to what appeared to be a fair, but his lordship firmly refused.

He had no intention of exposing his young children to the avid gamblers and potential lowlife frequenting the hazard stalls and other games of chance. There might be a juggler or two among the crowd, true, but ruffians and thieves, strumpets and con artists strolled among the merrymakers plying their trades to a tidy profit.

They returned to the phaeton in time to watch the two final races. As expected, Tony won the first one easily. Sloane's other brother, Shawn, was a surprise victor in the last event. Both families returned to their various lodgings tired, but full of good cheer.

The next morning, Lady Sheffeld stopped by the nursery. After reading her grandchildren a story and observing some of the letters they were practicing, she drew Sloane aside.

"Are you planning to go to the theatre tonight with your family? Lord Atherton mentioned yesterday that most of the family intended to join him."

"I would like to go. It seems ages since I've been to a play, but there are so many Kincades in town that Grandfather's box will be overflowing as it is. I should decline, I think."

"Nonsense." Lady Sheffeld's eyes glowed like a child with a piece of candy. "You will go with us and sit in our box."

"Oh, my lady, I don't think that would be wise. It wouldn't seem right—there would be too much talk."

"Pooh. Let them talk. I consider you a friend, and why shouldn't I invite a dear friend to join us. But to make you feel better, I'll get Tearle's permission. After all, it is his box. He might be planning to take someone else."

"Do you think so?" Lines of worry creased Sloane's brow.

"Of course not, you silly goose. He would have mentioned it before now; besides, he only has eyes for you. Now, make certain you are especially ravishing tonight, my dear. If people are going to talk, give them something wonderful to talk about. And, for the love of heaven, remember, no flirting."

"Yes, my lady," Sloane said meekly.

That evening, she allowed Annie to help her dress and found she was happy for the company. If she had been alone, she knew she would have changed her mind and declined the invitation. The maid worked for an hour with her hair, turning it into a masterpiece of curls with one long sun-streaked ringlet winding down the side of her neck to frame her face.

After tucking tiny pearl combs into her hair and fastening a pearl pendant on a long golden chain around her neck, Annie very carefully lifted Sloane's gown over her head, guiding it until the material settled gracefully around her womanly curves. The rose-colored silk shimmered in the lamplight, picking up the soft flush of her cheeks, and putting silver stars in her large gray eyes. The wide, pale pink flounce ended at her ankles in deep scallops, or vandyking.

"Oh, Mrs. Donovan, ye look 'eavenly," exclaimed Annie. "Why, ye look just like a countess." The young maid turned crimson and stared at the floor. "I'm sorry, mum. I shouldn't 'ave said that." She raised her head and looked at Sloane militantly. "It's just that, well, all of us below stairs got eyes in our 'eads and we don't miss the looks 'is lordship gives ye. Lud, when 'e sees ye looking like a princess, 'e's liable to drop down on 'is knee and propose right there. At least 'e ought to."

"He might look a bit odd on his knee in the drawing room asking a governess to marry him, don't you think?"

"Oh, no, mum. I think it'd be the most romantic thing I ever 'eard of. Just like in them novels Mrs. 'oneycutt reads to us sometimes."

"Romantic, but highly unlikely. Now, let me see, do I have everything?" She checked her image in the mirror, pleased at the reflection. Annie was right; she did look fine enough to be a countess. The simple empire-styled gown was cut low over her bosom and shoulders, leaving a great deal of creamy white skin and decolletage exposed, although the gown was certainly not cut as low as some the ladies would be wearing. Picking up her reticule, Sloane gave Annie an uncertain smile and left the room.

The earl was alone in the drawing room when Sloane entered, since the marchioness had successfully drawn Jonathan, Cory, and

Bailey into her scheme. She had decided not to mention her strategies to the marquess, but merely detained him in his dressing chambers for a few minutes.

His lordship had been sitting near the window, his gaze fixed on the fading sunset, trying to picture how Sloane would dress for the evening. He was so deeply involved in his imaginings that he did not hear her come into the room.

She stopped by the door and watched him for a moment, wishing she were an artist. The dark corbeau of his tailcoat was a perfect contrast to the golden curls brushing against the collar of his white, florentine silk waistcoat. His sage green breeches ended in a tight band just below the knee, meeting the white, silk stockings that covered his shapely calves. Black kid shoes, polished to a mirror finish, adorned his feet.

"May I join you, Lord Beckford?"

Startled, the earl's head came up, then he rose in one smooth motion as if some invisible rope had pulled him to his feet. He stared at her, speechless. Slowly his gaze moved from the top of her shiny hair down to her face, searching her anxious eyes for a moment before dropping further down to that vast expanse of white skin. His gaze lingered there before going on down to her feet, slowly coming back up to her full bosom which rose and fell with each quick breath. A frown creased his forehead.

"Is something amiss, my lord?" asked Sloane, a note of uncertainty creeping into her voice.

"I can see I'll have to stand close guard over you tonight, madam. Your lack of modesty surprises me." His gaze dropped to the large pearl snuggled in the cleft of her bosom, and he asked irritably, "Don't you have a cloak or something?"

"No, I do not. The evening is quite warm and the theatre is hot even on a cold night." She watched his gaze flick back and forth from her face to her low neckline, and grew increasingly uncomfortable with each passing second. The warmth faded from his eyes, his jaw settling into a firm line. Suddenly, she knew if she did not retreat, she would humiliate herself further by bursting into tears.

"Forgive me, my lord. I . . . I really think it's best if I stay home. I can see I have displeased you greatly, and my presence will only spoil your evening. If you'll excuse me, I'll retire. Please tell Lady Sheffeld that I had the headache or something."

The earl watched with growing dismay as her eyes began to glisten with unshed tears and her rosy cheeks became scarlet. In that brief moment as she turned to go, he questioned his reaction to her gown. She had been radiant when she stepped into the room, and he wanted her—and so would every man who laid eyes on her tonight. Jealousy was not an emotion he had immediately recognized.

"Sloane, wait, please." He crossed the room and took her arm in a firm grip.

Turning her toward him, he took hold of her other arm also, caressing her smooth skin with his thumbs.

"I'm sorry I made you uncomfortable. You look ravishing tonight, and I find I do not want to share that beauty, or at least not quite so much of it, with the other gentlemen present."

"I am not yours to share, my lord." At least, not yet, she added silently. She raised her chin haughtily. "However, since I do wish to see the play, I will be happy to wear a stole; if it will put me back in your good graces."

"It would." He released her and stepped across the room to the bell pull. Just before his hand reached the tapestry, Grimley gave a discreet cough at the door.

"Excuse me, m'lord. It seems Mrs. Donovan forgot her shawl. Annie just brought it down." He crossed the room and handed the long scarf to the earl before shuffling out the door. The wrap was made of pale pink lace, highlighted with lace roses the exact color of Sloane's gown.

The earl calmly draped the material around Sloane's shoulders, adjusting the lace so that it covered a goodly portion of her exposed skin. The back of his fingers lightly grazed the upper curve of her breast as he straightened the edge of the scarf.

"You meant to wear it all along?" he asked softly.

"No," came her breathless reply. "I had decided against it. I think Grimley had a hand in this." His fingers smoothed the other side

of the delicate material, and Sloane forgot
how to breathe. His head slowly lowered
toward hers, his purple-blue eyes dancing
with fire. A muffled cough from the doorway
brought his head quickly back up again.

"Begging your pardon, m'lord. Lord and
Lady Sheffeld are on their way downstairs.
Shall I send for the coach?"

"Yes, please, Grimley." He stepped back
from Sloane and took her arm, escorting her
into the hallway.

"My dear, how lovely you look," boomed
the marquess, taking Sloane's hand and
bringing it to his lips. "We'll have to block
the doorway at intermission or our box will
be full of adoring young bucks."

"You're very kind, Lord Sheffeld, but I'm
sure the young gentlemen will be too
interested in the younger ladies present to
even give me a second look."

"I wouldn't go bail on that, my dear," the
earl said so softly that only she could hear.

"Humph," said the marquess. "The
younger ones are easy to handle. 'Tis the ones
old enough to know better that create the
problems."

"You should know, dear," teased his
wife, pulling him toward the front door.

Many of the theatregoers were still
lingering in the lobby when the earl and his
party arrived. In the country way, members
of the *ton* mingled with the local gentry,
exchanging the latest *on dits* right along with
tips on hunting or agriculture. As the party
moved among the earl's various friends,

Sloane was introduced as Lord Atherton's granddaughter. Taking her cue from his lordship, Sloane simply introduced him as the Earl of Beckford to the few of her friends they encountered that he did not know. They were only a few yards away from the entrance to the earl's box when they came face to face with Lord Carlisle.

"Why, good evening, Beckford, Mrs. Donovan. Did the earl give you a night off from the children, madam?" Conversations around them ground to a halt as Carlisle's voice carried across the lobby. "You are in rather exalted company for a governess, are you not?" For a split second, the room buzzed with whispers. Carlisle smiled, enjoying being the center of attention. "Or did Beckford finally decide to publicly raise your status and show off his prize? I might add that you look exquisite tonight, my dove." Several women gasped, then the room was as quiet as a still night.

"You go too far, Carlisle. Keep quiet." The earl's voice was low and menacing.

"Why should I? You're the one dangling your little trinket before the world. Such beauty is bound to stir up comment, as well as a man's blood."

"You jackanapes!" The earl's hand doubled into a fist, and he brought it back to take a swing at Carlisle.

"Tearle, please don't," cried Sloane, hanging onto his arm.

"There you are, children." The marquess and his lady stepped out of a doorway several

boxes away and hurried to their side. "Sorry
to detain you, Tearle," said the marchioness.
"We were just visiting with your grandfather, Sloane. Come, my dear friend, let us
go in and sit down. The play is about to
begin." Lady Sheffeld put her arm around
Sloane's waist and drew her inside the box as
Lord Sheffeld stepped in between the earl
and Carlisle. Bailey and Corine, along with
Tearle and his father, joined the ladies in the
box moments later.

"What a dreadful man," exclaimed Lady
Sheffeld. "Now, hush, all of you. Let's not
have any further scenes. Sit back and try to
enjoy the play."

The earl settled in the seat beside Sloane
and took her trembling hand in his as the
curtain rose. He held her fingers in a strong,
reassuring grip, resting his hand on his thigh
well out of sight of any interested onlookers
from the boxes around them. He kept it there
until the curtain fell for the intermission.

"Do you want to step into the lobby,
Sloane?" the earl asked, as the rest of their
party migrated toward the doorway.

"No, I think it best if I stay here. Please
go ahead if you like."

"No, I'll stay here. Why don't we just
stand up here behind the seats?" He gently
took her hand and assisted her to her feet. At
the same time, he signaled an attendant to
bring them some refreshments. Moments
later, several men, most of them in their early
twenties, crowded into the box.

"Beckford, you scoundrel, how unkind of

you to keep the lovely lady in hiding. You could have at least brought her out into the lobby so we might worship at her feet; dreadfully hard to kneel down in such a small room, you know."

Sloane smiled coolly at the Honorable Edward Spears, the young dandy flirting so proficiently. "Surely there are several young ladies who have reserved just such a space for you, sir. I am confident any of them would be delighted to have you paying them such outrageous compliments."

"Ah, but none of them deserve the praise half as much as you, m'lady." The owner of the warm bass voice shouldered his way past the younger men. "Beckford, you are remiss in not allowing the rest of us to become acquainted with such an exquisite creature."

"Mrs. Donovan, this is Viscount Remington. Mrs. Donovan is Lord Atherton's granddaughter." The earl's coolness was unmistakable. Remington had a way with the ladies. Tearle had heard rumors that Linette had been one of his conquests, but had never known if they were true or not.

"Yes, I can see the family resemblance. You must be Mrs. Kincade's daughter. Are you in Cheltenham for long, Mrs. Donovan?"

Something in Viscount Remington's manner and the earl's coolness signaled a warning in Sloane's mind. Unconsciously, she shifted her weight closer to Tearle, a movement which did not go unnoticed by either of the men.

"We are to be here for a forthnight or

more, my lord.''

"Might I have the honor of strolling with you on the Well Walk, say, day after tomorrow?"

"I must regretfully decline, my lord." Though they were not touching, she had sensed Tearle's tension. "I do not often go to the Pump Room for it takes me away from Lord Beckford's children. I have taken them with me on occasion, but I do not think you would enjoy strolling with a three year old."

"Then you are truly Lord Beckford's governess?" asked young Spears, a look of surprised disappointment slowly spreading over his face.

"I am, sir."

"We have long known Mrs. Donovan's family," the earl lied, "and are extremely grateful that she consented to help with the children. Until she began to care for them, my daughter was a painfully shy child who rarely talked. While I was away, Corine discovered that our previous governess had been cruel to Angela, only worsening her condition. She sought Mrs. Donovan's assistance, and the lady graciously consented to help." The earl slid his arm about her waist, looking down at her with possessive tenderness. "She has worked miracles with Angela, and I am forever in her debt."

Young Spears and the older, more worldly viscount, as well as the other young men who hovered at the back of the box, recognized the earl's declaration of ownership. They chatted a few more minutes about trivial matters before taking their leave. Spears and the viscount had just passed through the doorway when their voices trailed back to where Sloane and the earl remained standing.

"Say, Ashley," asked the young dandy, "do you think she's really his paramour like Carlisle hinted? Certainly doesn't seem like just a governess."

"Ah, lad, you've a lot to learn about our world. No man, not even Beckford, would have his cyprian and his mother in the same theatre box. You can bring your light skirt to the theatre, my boy, but definitely not with your mother along."

The rest of the earl's party returned to their seats just then, cutting off anything further the viscount might have said.

As Sloane sat down, she happened to glance across the theatre to a box a little to their left. For a moment, her gaze locked with that of Lord Carlisle, then moved to meet Lady Wentwood's glare. She was shaken by the undisguised hatred both expressions held. She would have paid more attention to the cold feeling that swept over her, except just at that moment, the earl took hold of her hand and began a delicate attack on her senses.

Later, after their return to the townhouse, Sloane peeped in on the sleeping children. She drew the cover up over Angela's bare feet and turned to go.

"They both look like angels, don't they?" the earl whispered from the doorway. Sloane nodded and joined him in the hall as he pulled the door closed behind her.

"However, madam, you don't have to be asleep to look like an angel," he said softly, slipping his arms around her to hold her loosely. "You were the most beautiful woman in the theatre tonight. I was proud to have you by my side."

"Thank you," she whispered, lifting her hands to rest on his chest. She gazed up at him in the flickering light of the hall tapers, her bursting love-filled heart shining in her gray eyes. "I would never want to be an embarrassment to you."

"You could not be." His arms tightened, pulling her against him as his mouth claimed hers, and her hands slid to the nape of his neck. His urgent, demanding kiss was different from all the other times he had touched her. There was no reserve, no holding back as his soul shouted his love.

Her lips parted for him eagerly, welcoming him as her tongue danced with his. He growled low in his throat, shuddering at her invitation, and tore his mouth from hers. Driven by the need to feel her skin beneath his lips, he pressed firm, fervent kisses along her jaw and down the side of her neck.

Sloane's head dropped back, giving him access to the expanse of soft, smooth skin above the low-cut gown. His touch was like morning dew upon a rose as he brushed kisses across the hollow of her throat and collarbone and down to the sensitive curve just above the edge of her gown. She wove her fingers in his hair and clung to him, her breathing rapid and shallow.

Her head spun crazily and she gasped for air. "Tearle, oh, love, you make me weak," she whispered.

Trembling, Tearle raised his head. With each taste, each touch, his ardor had increased until his control was a thread away from the breaking point.

He forced his hands down to his sides. "Flee, my precious love," he whispered hoarsely, "or you will become that which you detest."

Drugged with passion, Sloane stared up at him through a warm haze. He gently pulled her hands from behind his head, kissing the back of each before letting them slip from his fingers.

"Sloane, go now, I beg you. I do not want guilt and shame between us on the morrow." He gently pushed her in the direction of her room.

Sloane hesitated going through the portal but then shut the door. Leaning against it, she closed her eyes, reliving the delicious pleasure of those last several moments. Her eyes flew open, and a happy, silly grin spread across her face. She was his *precious love!* Slowly, tears trickled down her cheeks. Carlisle's opinion nothwithstanding, the Earl of Beckford made her feel like a rare treasure, and he certainly knew how to treat one.

12

Sloane nervously smoothed the skirt of her silver satin ball gown and checked the mirror one last time to make sure the material fell straight. When she looked up at her face in the glass, she realized she was smiling, an expression she had worn almost continuously since last night.

She studied her reflection critically. The silver satin glistened in the light, matched only by the diamond sparkle of her eyes. Lavender ribbon trimmed the edges of the tiny puffed sleeves and neckline, accenting the smooth white skin of her throat and shoulders. The lavender showed up again in a soft flounce at the bottom of the gown, shot through with delicately embroidered threads of silver. Silver satin slippers and gloves almost completed the ensemble, with the final touch being a rather old fashioned amethyst necklace which had belonged to her grandmother. Sloane looked at the bauble and frowned. It really was a trifle large and gaudy, but the color was right, so she gave a resigned sigh and left the room.

As she slowly descended the townhouse staircase, she was met with unusual silence. Only a lone underfootman stood uneasily by the front door, all the other servants having gone ahead to the Assembly Room. Even Annie and the children had left a few minutes earlier to take their place in a small out-of-the-way alcove, allowing the youngsters a glimpse of the glamorous guests as they arrived.

Race week had been hectic for the Grayson family, with balls or assemblies every night. Sloane had not participated in most of the festivities since few had known of her arrival in Cheltenham until the previous evening at the theatre.

The earl stepped from the drawing room, wearing a dark blue coat, white satin waist-coat, and white kerseymere breeches. He stood at the bottom of the stairs, watching her graceful descent. He had been absent most of the day, attending to last-minute details for his mother, so Sloane had not seen him since the previous night. She had prayed fervently all day that she had not read more into his words last evening than he meant. Now, his look of adoration sent her heart into flutters.

Without a word, he offered her his arm and escorted her out into the garden. Night had fallen, but the bright moonlight turned the garden, with its fragrant flowers and bubbling fountain, into a fairyland. The earl stopped, remaining in the fringe of the light shining from the doorway.

"You are breathtaking, my love. Lovely enough to be a princess."

"Thank you, my lord." She wanted to return the compliment, for he truly looked more handsome than she had ever seen him, but something in his look literally took *her* breath away.

"Yes, lovely enough to be a princess," he said quietly, his voice low and husky. "But would you settle for a mere countess? My countess?"

"Oh, Tearle, I . . . I—" She thought frantically that she was a fool, but she needed to hear the words, those three oh-so-important words.

The earl frowned down at her confusion. Then, slowly, so very slowly, his countenance relaxed, and he allowed her to see into his heart. "I love you, Sloane. I cannot go on living without you by my side and in my arms. I would be the most honored among men if you would become my wife."

"Oh, Tearle, yes. Yes!" She threw her arms around his neck and stood on tiptoe to kiss him soundly. When they came up for air, she laughed and gave him a quick kiss on the chin. "I love you, Tearle Louis Grayson, and I always shall."

"I will hold you to that promise, madam. Now, reach into my coat pocket. I have a little trinket for you. If you are a good girl," he said, grinning wickedly, "I shall shower you with many such toys over the next forty years or so."

Sloane smiled up at him and eagerly delved into his pocket, pulling out a long, slender, flat black box. Opening it carefully, she gasped at the beautiful diamond and amethyst necklace and earrings nestled on black velvet. The jewels were mounted in delicate silver leaves running the length of the chain.

"Oh, Tearle, I've never seen anything so beautiful," she breathed. "Help me get these monstrous rocks off my neck."

The earl chuckled at her eagerness and gallantly complied, removing grandmother's necklace and dropping it into his pocket. "May I?" he asked, lifting the intricate silver chain from the box, purposefully holding it so the diamonds sparkled in the light.

"Oh, please. My hands are shaking so badly, I'll drop it."

He fastened the clasp with care, then stepped back to admire his gift and his glowing bride-to-be. "You'll have to do the earrings; my fingers are too big." He took the box from her hand, holding it open. She removed the jeweled leaves and slipped them on her ear lobes.

"Thank you, my dearest. They are lovely." Standing again on tiptoe, she kissed him gently. "Now, let's go inside where I can find a mirror."

The earl laughed and slipped his arms around her once again. "Not so fast, minx. You have to continue with your treasure hunt."

"There's more?" Her eyes widened in disbelief.

He nodded, a smug grin on his face. "Try the other pocket."

Sloane reached in the other pocket and pulled out a ring box, but she was too overcome with emotion to open it.

"Go ahead, my love. If you wait much longer, our guests will arrive at the ball before I can slip my betrothal ring on your finger." He, too, felt the emotion of the moment, and his low, hoarse voice reflected his feelings.

With trembling fingers, Sloane opened the box. Her eyes brimmed with tears as she stared down at a perfect silhouette of the old oak. The outline of the tree was done in silver, its center filled with one large amethyst surrounded by diamonds.

"I can no longer look at the old tree without thinking of you. I realize now that I fell in love with you the very first night beneath those wise, ancient branches." He traced the outline of the tree with the tip of his forefinger before taking the ring from the box and slipping it on her finger. "I claim you as my own," he whispered.

"And you are mine," she whispered fervently. He cupped her face in his hands and leaned down to her, the tender sweetness of his kiss bringing fresh tears to her eyes. Several beautiful moments later, he reluctantly lifted his head, brushing the tears from her cheeks with his thumbs, and gently put her away from him.

"If we do not go now, there will be no time to share the news with the family. I asked them to go on ahead, so I might talk to you unhampered." They left the garden, stopping only in the entryway where Sloane admired her new jewelry in a gilt wall mirror while the earl picked up her light cloak from the underfootman. As an afterthought, Tearle handed the servant the necklace Sloane had been wearing earlier with the instructions to give it to Annie to put away. When they rushed down the steps, the earl's landau was waiting.

The trip to the Assembly Room took less than ten minutes; still, they hurried inside the magnificent Corinthian pilastered ballroom. The earl cornered his mother before she flew off to check on the oysters for the third time. The marquess looked over his wife's head as his son unsuccessfully attempted to give Lady Sheffeld a stern look. Lord Sheffeld took stock of the situation immediately and beamed a smile at his son and Sloane.

"Mother, there is a grave matter I wish to discuss with you."

"Oh, dear, do you think the oysters are a little overripe, too? Jonathan says we should throw them out, but whatever will I use to replace them?"

"Obviously, you have enough food to feed all of Cheltenham and half of Evesham to boot, so throw out the oysters. We don't want all of our guests sick for the rest of the week. However, madam, that is not my bone of contention."

"Oh, did I put too many palms by the doors? Surely not; even Prinny could get through, if he were here, which, of course, he isn't, and I can't say that I'm sorry." She glanced up at her husband, a spark of devilment in her eyes, and the gentleman choked back a snicker. Glancing quickly at Sloane, she confirmed her suspicion that her elder son had proposed.

"No, Mother," said her son, slightly exasperated. "You have been matchmaking, and it is to cease this instant. Do you understand?"

"Me? Matchmaking? Why, I would never do such a thing." She grinned at Tearle, and he began to laugh.

"Baggage! You guessed."

"Of course. You both are beaming like lanterns in a lighthouse. In fact, I think we could snuff about half the candles in the room and still have plenty of light. It would save on the horrid expense of this party, too." Laughing, she threw one arm around her son and the other around her future daughter.

Moments later, Jonathan, Cory, and Bailey rushed up to see what all the commotion was about. More hugs, handshakes, and a slap or two on the back followed. Sloane and Tearle decided to tell the children their happy news privately on the morrow since the first carriage rolled up in front of the Assembly Rooms before they could extricate themselves from their enthusiastic loved ones. They had just enough time to smooth the wrinkles from their slightly rumpled clothes before Grimley regally announced the arrival of the first guests.

The room was fairly teeming with people when Sloane's parents and Roseanne arrived. Sloane was thrilled to see her former employer, Countess Landan, walk into the room with her mother. She worked her way through the crowd to greet them.

"Lady Landan, how wonderful to see you again," cried Sloane, throwing her arms around her friend. "You look as lovely as ever."

"Thank you, my dear. Before I forget, the children send their love. They do miss you, Sloane. But, here, let me look at you." The countess studied her for a moment, then smiled at Libby. "It has done your daughter good to come home. I have never seen her more radiant."

"Nor have I, Priscilla. Sloane, do you have a surprise for us?"

"Yes, Mama, I do, but I can't tell you here. Come with me for just a moment." She took her mother's hand and led them into a small antechamber. Roseanne had been captured by Jonathan the moment she came through the ballroom door, but Sloane knew he would be sharing the good news with her. She closed the door and held out her hand, proudly displaying her ring.

"The earl has proposed," she said softly.

"Oh, darling, how wonderful!" Her

mother swept her into an embrace, followed by Galen, and lastly, by Lady Landan.

"It's about time he threw in the handkerchief," said Galen. "After last night's fiasco at the theatre, I was ready to take matters in hand."

"Were you there, Papa?"

"No, but I certainly heard about it. Your mother came home in a tizzy and your grandfather was pounding on my door at midnight, trying to decide who was the worse rascal, Lord Beckford or Lord Carlisle. I tell you, daughter, if he hadn't come up to scratch soon, I was ready to take his lordship to task."

"It wasn't his fault, Papa. Carlisle was the one causing all the problems. Unfortunately, we may be in for more of it tonight. Lady Sheffeld insisted on inviting him and Lady Wentwood since she has known the elder Lord Carlisle for years. She could not deliberately snub such an old neighbor, although Tearle protested greatly. Of course, the invitations went out over a week ago, and she had no way of foreseeing last night's events."

"Perhaps they will not have the audacity to show," said Lady Landan. She smiled at Sloane. "I, too, heard the pounding in the middle of the night and was given a full account of the tale this morning."

"Poor Pris," soothed Libby, "she had only arrived a few hours before, and then to be awakened after such a short rest. We have not treated you well, I'm afraid." She released a heartfelt sigh. "However, I am acquainted with both Lady Wentwood and Lord Carlisle, and I'm certain they would not pass up this ball unless they were on their deathbeds. It is the highlight of race week." She grinned at her husband's indignant look. "As far as the parties go at least."

"We must go back to the ballroom. I hear the orchestra tuning up, and I'm to lead out with Tearle." She smiled mischievously. "Now, I understand why he insisted the first dance be a waltz."

"When did he propose?" whispered Libby as they walked through the doorway.

"Only about an hour ago." As they entered the ballroom, she looked up to find Tearle watching her. He worked his way through the crowd to her side, stopping every few steps to greet another guest or two.

"It appears Sloane has shared our little secret. I hope it meets with your approval, sir." Although he smiled at Galen, his eyes were cautious.

"Yes, it does, my lord. My only peeve is that it took you so long to come to your senses."

The earl smiled and nodded briefly. "A point well taken, Mr. Kincade. I am only thankful your daughter is blessed with a great deal of patience. Now, if you will excuse me, I believe I have promised this dance to the most beautiful woman in all of England." He took Sloane's hand and led her onto the dance floor, smiling at his parents as they joined them. He gave Roseanne an encouraging wink as Jonathan guided her through the steps of the waltz. Other dancers quickly followed until the room was a blaze of swirling, undulating color.

Long before the song ended, the room buzzed with speculation. Even if Sloane's ring had not sparkled like exploding sky-rockets in the candlelight, their glowing faces gave them away to the more practiced observers. When the waltz ended, several young bucks dashed up to Sloane, begging for a dance, but the earl sent them all scurrying back to the outer regions of the room by announcing that Mrs. Donovan's dance card was full. With the innocently slow grasp of those new to society's ways, some of the young men did not realize until several dances later that his lordship's name filled almost all of the lines on the pretty widow's card.

About this same time, the earl and Sloane were moving through the steps of a country dance when he spied Jonny waving frantically at him from the alcove. He had instructed Annie to let the children watch for the first several dances, but gathered quickly that Jonny's panic-stricken face and Annie's grim expression had nothing to do with the proposed bedtime. At the end of the set, he excused himself and crossed the room to talk with the youngster. Moments later, he returned to Sloane's side, his expression a mixture of worry and amusement.

"I'm afraid to ask, but it was too noisy to hear Jonny clearly. Who is Georgie?"

"His pet frog."

"Frog?" The earl's voice cracked, making him sound a little like a frog himself. "When did he acquire this newest addition?"

"This afternoon. He and Brian found it in the park. Why?"

"Because Georgie has decided to drop in—or should I say, hop in—on the ball."

"Oh, no."

"Oh, yes. You skirt around that side of the room and I'll look on this side."

"Tearle, I can't. I classify frogs in the same category as snakes."

"You're no help. Oh, well, come along with me. Let's try the side nearest the alcove." They moved around the room, visiting with the guests and surreptitiously scouting for Prinny's namesake. The room was crowded and the going slow.

Suddenly, a shriek resounded across the room. By the time they ascertained its direction of origin, the musicians had stopped and all conversation ceased—just in time for a second scream to rattle the windows.

The crowd parted as the earl and Sloane hurried to the far side of the dance floor to a group of chairs clustered in the corner. There, they beheld Georgie, calmly making himself at home on the lap of a very large matron who was dressed in a voluminous green gown, decorated with nothing less than a dozen huge silk flowers. Georgie stared up at the woman with his big, bulging eyes, and she stared back at him in horror, her eyes equally wide. Sloane put her hand over her mouth to stifle a giggle.

"My most humble apologies, Lady Ingles." The earl grabbed for the frog, but the nimble pet leaped. The earl's fingers brushed across the lady's fat thigh and came up with a handful of green silk. At her startled gasp, he dropped the fabric as color flooded his face. "I do beg your pardon, m'lady." With a rather ungraceful leap of his own, the earl captured the villian and held him up for all to see.

"Nothing to worry yourselves about, ladies. It is only a frog. May I introduce Geo . . . er, Charley, my son's erstwhile friend. Undoubtedly, he only thought all the ladies were lovely summer flowers for his enjoyment. I shall exile him to the garden where he belongs. Again, my deepest apologies, Lady Ingles."

The lady in question nodded, raked the earl's agile frame with her gaze, completely ignoring the frog, and resumed fanning herself furiously.

Embarrassed, the earl turned toward Sloane, still clutching the wayward pet. "Can't blame him; poor creature probably thought she was a giant lily pad," he muttered.

Sloane burst into giggles, and the earl began to chuckle. Soon, practically the whole assembly was laughing over the incident. Even Lady Ingles managed a dreamy smile.

Two members of the party did not join in the hilarity. Lady Wentwood and her brother

mingled with the other guests, always
keeping themselves at the opposite end of the
room from the earl and Sloane. Lady Wentwood struck up a conversation with one of
the elderly ladies and gave a slight nod to
Lord Carlisle. At her signal, he moved over to
the punch bowl and began talking to a
middle-aged dandy hovering nearby, who just
happened to be the worst gossip in the whole
county.

"I say," said the Honorable Mr. Brownstone, straightening his already perfect
waistcoat, "that Mrs. Donovan is a ravishing
beauty. Beckford's a lucky fellow if the
rumors are true."

"What rumors?" asked Carlisle casually,
although he knew full well Brownstone
referred to the stories flying around about a
probable wedding announcement.

"Don't say you haven't heard? Why, the
lady is sporting a huge new ring and Beckford can't take his eyes off her. He's only
allowed her to dance with her father, and
more important, his father. And, then only
one dance apiece, mind you. No, if I were a
betting man, which I'm not, mind you, I'd
wager a case of brandy that he's asked the
little beauty to marry him. If that's not a
betrothal ring on that finger then I don't
know how to dress."

Carlisle glanced at his lime green jacket
and red waistcoat and grimaced. The man
might recognize a juicy bit of gossip, but
never could it be said he knew how to dress
with anything even remotely akin to style.

However, he would serve his purpose well.

"Yes, I would suppose we'll be hearing an announcement of that sort soon enough. It's a pity, though. You'd think after his first wife's, um, indiscretions, Beckford would be more careful."

"Whatever do you mean?" The dandy shifted closer to Carlisle, and the baron could almost swear he saw his ears prick up.

"Oh, it doesn't signify."

"Tell me, do you know the lady? You have some reason to believe she might be anything like his first wife?"

"No, no, she's nothing like Linette. It's just that, well, she has been working as the earl's governess for several months now—"

"His governess. How very convenient."

"Well, yes, convenient for her. I visited Beckford not too long ago, and thought to, um, entertain the lady, but she declined my invitation, piously declaring that she had only given herself to her husband. She said if she ever shared a man's bed again, it would be a marriage bed. Of course, I didn't believe her, figured she was just protecting her, uh, relationship with Beckford."

"Yes, yes, go on." Brownstone plucked at his jacket once again, smoothing an imaginary wrinkle.

"Well, he came to her defense, and I'll admit, his manner left me puzzled. Didn't act like a man defending his mistress, if you know what I mean."

"Oh, yes, I believe I understand."

"Then, last night, I ran into an old

acquaintance at the theatre. Somehow or other, the conversation got around to Beckford. I mentioned Mrs. Donovan's name and Ridgeway about went through the ceiling.''

"Sir Spencer Ridgeway?"

"The very same." Carlisle dropped his voice, forcing Brownstone to lean closer to hear the confidence. "It seems Ridgeway has an estate up near York and has just returned from there. Until Mrs. Donovan went to work for Beckford, she lived in York with the Countess Landan.''

"Ah, yes, a lovely lady."

"At any rate, Mrs. Donovan and Ridgeway carried on quite a passionate affair right under the Countess' nose. It was all very discreet, of course, although I don't know how they kept some of their more illustrious adventures from the lady.''

"Adventures?" The dandy's eyes glittered as he soaked up the tale.

"Well, yes, it seems Mrs. Donovan has a passion for riding that beautiful bay mare of hers bareback—in nothing but her shift.''

"You don't say!" Brownstone's eyes grew wide as he turned to watch Sloane across the room, his vivid imagination portraying the scene with great relish. Then he frowned.

"But it's cold in Yorkshire."

"In the winter, yes, but only chilly in the summer. He said she would ride across the moor in the moonlight on . . . let me see, what did he call that horse . . . oh, yes, Windsong. Anyway, she would go for a ride and then come back to their secret little hideaway so he could, uh, warm her up."

"Oh, my, that does sound exciting. What broke up the little love nest?"

"She began pushing him to marry her."

"Ah, I see, and, of course, Ridgeway wasn't about to marry his light skirt." Brownstone held out his cup for more punch, making sure the servant only filled it half-way.

"Precisely, and that's why I think she changed her tactics with Beckford. She found being a plaything didn't work, so she kept the poor devil drooling so long that the only thing left for him was to propose. 'Tis a pity. No doubt she'll grow tired of him before long and seek her amusement elsewhere. That would be a terrible blow. One harlot for a wife was bad enough, but two—well, it could cost him his life."

Carlisle's last few words were spoken with such apparent sincerity and concern that Brownstone was quite moved by what might possibly be the outcome of such a disastrous marriage. He quickly excused himself, and with all the righteous indignation he could muster, began to spread the tale to the far corners of the room.

Much later in the evening, the earl returned to the ballroom from a brief conciliatory visit with some friends in the card-room. Just as he stepped into the room, the story reached a small group of people clustered nearby. Hidden by the large palms framing the doorway, those embroiled in the

conversation did not know that Tearle stood
rigidly beside them, hearing every word. He
would have sent the plants crashing to the
floor and personally escorted the gossips
from the ballroom had he not spotted Sloane
talking to Viscount Remington across the
floor.

In her happiness, even the viscount did
not seem disturbing, and she forgot to be
cautious. He made some amusing quip, and
she laughed up at him, her eyes sparkling
more from the joy of her love than from the
humor of his joke. By now, practically everyone in the room, except for those most
closely connected to the tale, had heard
Carlisle's careful fabrication, with the usual
embellishments that come when a story is
told many times.

As Tearle stared at Sloane's happy face,
another image projected itself over that
beloved countenance. For the space of a
heartbeat, it was Linette's face looking up at
the viscount, flirting, teasing, inviting with
her beckoning eyes. Sloane sensed his gaze
and looked toward him. Once again, it was
her face, but all he could see were her eyes; a
different color, but those same beckoning
eyes.

13

Sloane's smile faded as she watched the earl speak to a passing footman and then stride rapidly across the room to her side. She did not wonder at the way the crowd parted to let him through for her gaze was fixed upon his unsmiling face. As he stepped up beside her, she searched his eyes for the warmth shining there only moments before, but it had evaporated. His countenance was cold, an immobile mask, and when she met his gaze, she felt as if she were crashing through the dark blue, icy waters of a frozen pond.

"You will excuse us, Remington, I need to talk to Mrs. Donovan." Tearle took her arm and propelled her toward the doorway.

"Tearle, what's wrong?" She searched his face in alarm, ignoring the staring guests.

"I prefer to talk to you in private, madam."

His hard, distant voice sent a shiver down her spine. She could only stare at him in confusion, her feet moving automatically down the corridor and out the front door amid the knowing looks and whispers of the guests. She stumbled a little on the last step, and his fingers tightened on her arm, snapping her back to a stable position. He lifted her into the waiting landau, practically throwing her into the driver's seat.

"Tearle, in the name of heaven, what is wrong?"

The earl ignored her anguished expression and moved swiftly around to the other side of the vehicle, jumped up into the seat, and snatched the reins from his attending groom. "Ride with my parents," he snapped to the bewildered groom. He waited until they were some distance down High Street before he spoke again.

"A friend of yours is in town. You should have told me of his arrival, and I would have invited him tonight. It would have made the ball even more interesting, if that is possible." He kept his face on the street, carefully averted from her anxious gaze, but she did not miss the unusually tight grip he held on the ribbons.

"Tearle, I don't understand. Who are you talking about?"

"Sir Spencer Ridgeway." His voice was hollow and cold, sending a dart of fear into her heart.

"Why would I want him here? I don't even know the man." She frowned as he slowly turned to face her, his stony countenance clearly visible in the light from the new gas lamps lining the street.

"Oh, I would say you know him, and know him very well. Let's see, how does the story go—oh, yes, you were his paramour while in York, all very discreet, of course, engaging in secret little rides and rendezvous. Being close to home does have its disadvantages. You would be a fetching sight riding bareback in just your shift." He ignored her gasp and continued. "But, from what I heard tonight, you grew a little too anxious. You should have known a man seldom marries his mistress, even if she is a fringe member of the *ton*."

"What in the world are you talking about? I never had a love affair with Sir Ridgeway. I've never even met him. He lived on the other side of York and did not move in the same circles as Countess Landan and certainly not in the same society as me."

"The gentleman says different. You should have been more careful, Sloane. If you had parted with more grace, perhaps then you would not have made an enemy of an old lover."

"He was not my lover!"

He stared at her as if he didn't even hear her words. "It would seem you learned one lesson well. Having discovered the inability to move from mistress to wife, you decided to portray the pious little widow, never yielding to temptation, yet ever luring me on."

"No, Tearle, no. Please don't say such things. Everything I said was true. There has been no one since Casey."

"Don't keep lying to me!" The horses

shied as his hands jerked, his grip tightening
even more, and it took several minutes to
bring them under control. "I knew better
than to trust you. I swore once to never trust
a woman again. You're all the same—cheats
and liars." He partially turned away, closing
his eyes briefly against the pain, his lips
drawn in a thin, harsh line.

Though his words were like arrows
piercing her heart, Sloane found she could
not reply in anger. In that brief moment, she
had glimpsed his tortured soul. Her love was
too great to inflict more wounds, and she
prayed with all her heart for a way to convince him of her love and regain his trust.

She turned toward him and gently placed
her hand on his outstretched arm. His
muscles jumped at her touch, and he winced
as if in pain. With growing despair, she
removed her hand and let it drop in her lap.
Silence reigned for several minutes while she
tried to gather her scattered wits.

"Tearle," she said softly, "I have not lied
to you, not this evening, nor any other time. I
don't know why Sir Ridgeway would malign
me so wickedly. I do not know him, nor do I
know how I could have made him my enemy.

"I love you with all my heart and wish I
had never kept you at bay," she said with
quiet fierceness. She shook her head, fighting
back the tears. "No, that is not true. If I had
submitted, then I would not be the person
that I am, and you would not love me, nor
could you ever have trusted me." With
trembling fingers, she unfastened the

necklace and the earrings, letting them slide from her lifeless fingers into her lap. As the earl stopped the landau in front of the Royal Crescent, she slipped the ring from her finger and placed all the jewelry on the seat between them.

"With your permission, my lord, I shall not leave until the morrow. I . . . I cannot bear to leave without saying farewell to the children." The earl nodded briefly, and Sloane scrambled down from the landau, ignoring the startled underfootman who rushed out to assist her. She stopped a few feet away from the carriage and turned back to look up at the earl. "I never deceived you, Tearle. Someday, perhaps you will learn to put your trust in those who love you instead of in vicious rumors." Choking back a sob, she turned and fled up the steps into the townhouse.

The earl swung down from the carriage and tossed the reins to the young man. He stomped up the stairs into the entry hall and threw the jewelry on a small Queen Anne console table not far from the door.

"I will be in the library," he barked over his shoulder to another still younger underfootman who dashed into the hall and skidded to a halt, buttoning his livery. "I do not wish to be disturbed—by anyone." He slammed the library door so hard that the lad barely had time to catch an expensive porcelain vase as it toppled from its perch nearby.

Once alone, Tearle poured a generous

splash of brandy and threw it down his throat. He poured himself another, but hesitated, his fingers hot against the cool glass. Deciding the drink would only further muddle his mind, he left it on the table. Crossing the room, he dropped into a large, comfortable chair, suddenly feeling very, very tired. He closed his eyes, giving in to the pain. Not even the small, cheerful fire nor the pleasant smell of the fine leather book-bindings could ease his hurt. The rich, powerful Earl of Beckford was not at all surprised at the trickle of moisture on his cheeks.

Sloane moved as quietly as possible to the back staircase, her hands clenched in an effort to hold back the tears. Just as she reached the first landing, the library door slammed and she jumped. She hurried up the stairs, reaching the sanctuary of her room before a sob escaped. Not heeding the wrinkling of her gown, she threw herself on her bed and buried her head in the pillows, trying to muffle her heart-wrenching sobs.

Quite some time later, after her heart-break had settled into occasional shudders, she heard the sounds of carriages on the street below. After a few minutes, the subdued voices of the returning family drifted up to the second floor. By the time a knock sounded softly on her door, Sloane had dragged herself from the bed and splashed cold water on her swollen, red eyes.

The door opened and Sloane's mother and Lady Sheffeld stepped cautiously into the room. Sloane sank down on the edge of the bed.

"Sloane, dear, are you all right?" Libby sat down on the bed next to Sloane and put her arms around her.

"I feel so helpless, Mama. If Tearle were simply angry at me, I could scream and yell and perhaps pound some sense through his thick skull, but he isn't just angry, he is terribly hurt. Sir Ridgeway is saying I was his paramour. Why would he do such a thing? I don't understand. I don't even know what has been said about me; how can I fight it?"

"Well, we heard what was being said, didn't we, Lady Sheffeld?"

"Indeed, we did. Jonathan got wind of it, although our delightful guests were extremely careful to spread the tale to everyone else but us." Lady Sheffeld shook her head bitterly. "Sometimes I think you are right, Libby. I'm not sure society is worth my time."

"Mama, what was said?" Sloane watched her mother warily.

Libby quickly related the tale exactly as she heard it, her arm tightening around her daughter's shoulders as Sloane's face grew hot and her eyes widened in alarm.

"Lady Sheffeld, you do not believe such lies, do you?" Sloane earnestly searched the lady's face, hopeful, yet afraid of what she might find.

"Of course not. I'm an excellent judge of character, and am of the opinion that you

would make the finest possible wife for my
son. But you must understand, dear, Tearle
was cruelly hurt by Linette. She was no
better than a street strumpet, open and
flagrant in her misdeeds, exposing him to the
worst form of ridicule. The *ton* had a
heyday." She blinked back tears. "He is very
tender in this area. Even a strong, proud man
is little more than a small boy where love is
concerned."

"I can't understand why Sir Ridgeway
would say such things," said Sloane, shaking
her head in confusion.

"I wonder if he did."

"What do you mean, Lady Sheffeld?"
asked Libby, her eyes narrowing.

"I am somewhat acquainted with Ridgeway, and I do not find it in character for him
to spread such lies. In fact, it is not like him
to have paramours and such in the first
place. It seems he was converted to the
Evangelical persuasion a few years back. Of
course, the gossips love to have an *on dit*
about anyone who seems too pious, so no
doubt they relished the tale even more. However, what signifies is that unless he has
become totally disillusioned with his faith,
he would not cast such stones."

Lady Sheffeld jumped to her feet and
began to flit about the room. "The more I
consider it, the more I am convinced poor
Ridgeway knows nothing of tonight's events.
True, he does own an estate in York, and he is
in town. I saw him at the Pump Room two
days past." She spun around toward the two

women sitting on the bed, stamping her foot for emphasis. "No, he did not spread the lies, but I think I know who did. Oh, I must have had a maggot in my head for inviting them."

"Carlisle." The color slowly faded from Sloane's face.

"Of course. Who else could it be? We gave him a fair set down at the theatre last night, and we mustn't forget the confrontation earlier in the summer. Oh, why didn't I listen to Tearle when he tried to stop me from inviting him and his sister."

"My lady, it is not your fault. I never dreamed he would try to malign me in such a way."

"You can be sure Lady Wentwood had a hand in this," said Libby. "She has made it no secret that she would like the Earl of Beckford as her next husband. If you were shamed, she could just step in to console his lordship."

"But how can we prove it?" asked Sloane.

Lady Sheffeld smiled. "I don't think we will have to. I believe Jonathan is already working the problem. He walked through the doorway tonight, took one look at your ring lying on the table, and left immediately, muttering something about getting to the bottom of this. If I know Jonathan, he will not rest, nor will he let anyone else sleep, until this whole matter is cleared up."

Sloane's heartbeat picked up speed and for the first time since entering her chamber, she felt a glimmer of hope. She sat up straighter and took a deep breath. Libby's arm slid from her shoulders.

"I was kept so busy when I worked for the countess that there was no time for secret rendezvous or rides. In fact, I didn't even have a horse. I'm certain Lady Landan would vouch for me. Is she with you, Mama?"

"No, dear. She had a terrible migraine, so Roseanne accompanied her back to the townhouse. However, I will speak with her as soon as she arises in the morning. Now, I really must go. The marquess and your father are downstairs in the drawing room. Since I have not heard the sounds of a brawl, it would seem his lordship has effectively restrained Galen, but I do not dare test his patience too long. He is extremely angry with the earl."

"We are all vexed with my son," said Lady Sheffeld, "but do not give up hope, Sloane. He'll come up to scratch." Her eyes twinkled. "After all this has blown over, I intend to take him down a peg or two for meddling in my matchmaking. Now, young lady, we all have need of rest. Do not be surprised if Tearle is in no condition to talk in the morning. He is not a drunkard, mind you, but after tonight's events, I suspect he is taking his comfort with a bottle of brandy. 'Tis considered good *ton*, you see."

Lady Sheffeld rang for Annie, and moments later the young maid appeared. "See that Mrs. Donovan gets into bed immediately, Annie." With an abrupt nod of her head, she scurried from the room.

Libby kissed her daughter's cheek, whispering, "Do not despair, but have hope and pray for your earl." With the regal carriage befitting a queen, she swept from the room.

The maid stared at Sloane's mother as she departed, then turned quickly and began to help her undress. Once in her nightclothes, however, Sloane refused to rest. Instead, she dismissed Annie and paced from one end of the room to the other, leaving a path of delicate footprints on the thick Turkish rug.

Downstairs, Tearle listened curiously as Galen and Libby Kincade departed. He had recognized Galen's voice when they arrived at the house and fully expected him to burst into the library, demanding a public aplology. He grew somewhat bemused when the man did not even request an audience with him, and surmised that Sloane's poor father was convinced of his daughter's guilt. After the Kincades left, Tearle waited for his father to come into the library, but the older Grayson simply paused outside the doorway and bade his son good night.

The quiet of the house settled over Tearle like a cloak of gloom. He stared at the delicate pattern of the fanlight above the hall door, going over the confrontation with Sloane again and again. His heart protested her innocence, but his mind played devil's advocate, riddling each protest with doubt.

For, in the beginning, hadn't Linette portrayed the innocent, too? Hadn't she been able to smile and dismiss the rumors as just vicious gossip? Rumors which began within a month of their marriage. Tearle shook his head bitterly. What a fool he had been. How easily she had been able to sway him, to convince him that she was his alone, that only his touch made her cry out in the night. He was brought back to the present by a discreet tap on the door. When the earl grudgingly acknowledged the interruption, Grimley stepped into the room, closing the door behind him.

"Do you need anything, my lord?"

"No."

"Smythe was inquiring if you would be retiring soon."

"Tell him to go to bed. I can undress myself."

"Yes, my lord. Is there anything else, sir?"

"I do not wish to be disturbed again, by anyone. Not my father, not my mother, and especially not Jonathan."

"Mr. Jonathan has gone out."

Tearle frowned and glared at Grimley. "Where did he go?"

"He did not confide in me, sir."

"Very well. Leave me."

"As you wish, my lord."

Seconds before the old butler reached the door, he stopped, turned slightly, and watched his lord for a long minute. He cleared his throat, gaining the earl's attention. "You did not ask, but I know you are wondering. Mrs. Donovan went directly to her room. She is still there—wearing a hole in the carpet."

"That will be all, Grimley."

"Ring if you need me, sir."

"Thank you, Grimley, I appreciate having your permission," the earl said, with a glare.

"You are quite welcome, Lord Beckford." With an aloof snort, the elderly butler shuffled from the room, letting the door close with a loud click.

The earl spent several disgruntled minutes considering replacing his butler before once again turning his thoughts to the woman upstairs. He shifted his gaze to the marble chimney piece and decided to view the situation as rationally and logically as he could, but found it nearly impossible. He mulled the story over and over in his mind. The clock struck one, then two. Weariness gradually took hold and memories began to weave themselves into his thoughts.

Each memory of Sloane brought a fresh, poignant pain. Sloane mopping up the spilled water and prattling on about Napoleon. Sloane clinging to the tree. Sloane racing across the grass with the children. Sloane sliding from Windsong's back into the circle of his arms.

Suddenly, he sat upright. What had she said about Windsong that day? He searched his memory frantically. As so often happens when a simple truth makes itself known, her words crashed over him—"My father gave him to me when I moved back here. He had named him long before I ever acquired him."

Tearle groaned and dropped his head, letting it rest in his hands, his elbows propped upon each knee. Surely, she would not have been lying then. She could not have fabricated her history so thoroughly as to think of the best time in the story to acquire her horse. Or could she? If Windsong played a role in her affair with Ridgeway, wouldn't she want to disavow having owned him at the time?

Tearle moaned in despair. Was there no end to this? Could he never find a way to clear her from his mind's accusations? Another polite tap sounded at the door, and Tearle glanced at the clock. It was half past three.

"Yes?"

Grimley opened the door and slowly crossed the room. "I am sorry to disturb your solitude, my lord, but this missive just arrived." He held out a silver tray which held a note on delicate, pink stationery.

The earl picked up the letter, dismissing the butler with a nod of his head. He broke the seal and flipped the page open, glancing first at Countess Landan's signature.

"I regret that I left the ball early due to a migraine; therefore, I have only just learned of this evenings ridiculous events. I find it difficult to believe that you would give any credence to such malicious dribble. My children took up much of Sloane's time; the rest was spent as a companion to me since

my husband travelled a great deal. She had
two days a month free and generally spent
those days with the vicar and his wife—I
repeat, the vicar and his wife. To my
knowledge, she never made the acquaintance
of Sir Ridgeway. During much of the time we
spent in York, the gentleman was in India.
Shortly after he returned to his estate, he was
thrown from a horse and broke his leg and
consequently spent several months abed. I
can assure you Sloane did not join him
there!"

In spite of his own inner agony, the earl
gave the letter a wry smile. There was a sharp
knock at the door before it burst open,
revealing Jonathan and, to the earl's
astonishment, Sir Spencer Ridgeway.

Jonathan stepped aside, allowing Ridgeway to limp into the room. He eyed Tearle
warily as he stopped in front of him, leaning
heavily on his cane.

"Sit down, Ridgeway," the earl said,
motioning toward a chair. "I just heard about
your accident. How's the leg?"

"Mending slowly." Sir Ridgeway took
the chair with a grimace. "I would like to get
to the point if you don't mind. Lord Grayson
dragged me out of a very warm, comfortable
bed, a bed which I share nightly with my
beloved bride and have for the last year and a
half, except for the months I spent recuperating from this blasted leg. I have never had a
tete-a-tete with your fiancee, never kissed
her, never made love to her, never even met
the lady. Now, may I please be excused to go

back to my home?'' the poor man said, in exasperation.

"Yes, Ridgeway, by all means, go on home. I apologize for the trouble you have been put to." The earl shot an irritated glance at his brother. "However, my brother's intentions were good, I assure you. You will have to bring your bride out to visit Beckford Hall sometime. We would be honored to have you as our guests."

"Doubt that, m'lord. She's an Indian."

The earl looked a bit surprised, but stood and extended his hand. "That doesn't signify with me. You'll still be welcome."

"Thank you, m'lord." For the first time since Jonathan had insistently pounded on his door at a quarter to three, Ridgeway smiled. "We might just take you up on the offer."

As Grimley showed the man out, Jonathan sprawled in a chair across from the earl. "So, you've already heard the truth. How did you find out?"

"Lady Landan sent a terse message." He picked up the note and waved it to the room in general. "It's a pity I'll not be able to get better acquainted with the countess. She has spirit."

"Why won't you be able to get to know her? She's a good friend of Sloane's. Surely she'll want to have her visit Beckford Hall."

Tearle sank in his chair, his shoulders sagging. "Jon, do you really think she'd forgive me for tonight? It is asking too much. I fear I have wounded her as badly as before, if not more so. Not only did I believe the accusations without giving her a chance to defend herself, I dragged her from the ball. I forced her to leave with me in front of everyone, further raking her good name through the mire. No, she will never marry me now."

"Have you asked her?"

"No, nor do I intend to." He quickly changed the subject before Jonathan could protest. "Did you find out who started this catastrophe tonight?"

"Yes. I went to see Brownstone, since he loves to wag his tongue. He said Carlisle told him about it."

The earl swore softly. "I should have guessed. No doubt Ebony put him up to it. He's not bright enough to think of it on his own."

"But certainly talented enough for Brownstone to fall for every word. What are you going to do about it?"

"I don't know; call him out, I suppose."

"If you kill him, you'll have to leave England. That's not what you want, Tearle."

"Does it matter, Jon? I've already lost the one I love. It wouldn't matter whether I'm alone here or in some foreign land." He leaned his head back against the chair and closed his eyes, his features ragged. "Without her, my life is meaningless."

"What about your children? Don't they mean anything to you?" Jonathan asked softly. "Aren't they worthy enough to have their father alive and to have the Grayson name remain honorable?"

"Yes, of course they are." His eyes remained closed. "I'm very tired, Jon. I'll have to think these things through when I've rested."

Jonathan rose and reached in his pocket, pulling out the jewelry Tearle had given Sloane earlier in the evening. He carefully laid the jewels on the table near Tearle's chair. Fingering the ring, he looked his brother straight in the eye. "Don't miss your chance for happiness, Lou. Don't give up now." He crossed to the door. "I'll see you in the morning."

When he was certain Jonathan had gone upstairs, Tearle rang for Grimley. The butler appeared a short while later.

"Fetch me my dueling pistols, Grimley."

The elderly man nodded and returned in a few minutes with the firearms. "You have discovered who is responsible, my lord?"

"Yes, it seems Baron Carlisle carries a grudge against Mrs. Donovan and myself."

"Do you intend to fight him?"

"I don't know, Grimley." He fingered the weapons on his lap. "Perhaps it would be simpler if I put the gun to my own head."

"Either method would be beneath your dignity and intelligence, my lord. I would suggest that you announce your marriage to Mrs. Donovan as quickly as possible and with as much pomp and splendor as you can manage. That would effectively show Carlisle and the *ton* that the rumor was false and that you never believed a word of it."

"A clever idea, my old friend, but I fear Mrs. Donovan will never consent to such a proposal. I have wounded her too deeply this time. She will never forgive me."

"Has she said so?"

"No, but 'tis true." He placed the guns on the table, and smiled at Grimley. "However, you are right, as usual. Dueling or suicide would not solve matters. I must think of a better method of retaliation. Go to bed, Grimley, you look done in."

"Will you be going up shortly, my lord?"

"Soon. I think I shall have another glass of brandy, then I'll retire."

Grimley left his lordship to his drink and went straight away to Sloane's room. Candlelight shone underneath the door and the old man knocked softly. Sloane opened it immediately.

"What is it, Grimley? Is something wrong with Tearle?"

"Aye, Mrs. Donovan. He's in a very bad way. He has discovered the truth about the matter this evening, and now, he is convinced you will never forgive him."

"Of course, I would. All he has to do is ask."

"He won't do it, mum. I just left him in the study. He requested his dueling pistols."

"He's not going to fight, is he?" Sloane cried in alarm, her fingers clutching the pink lace lapel of her wrapper.

"No, I don't believe so. However, he did mention something; well, he mentioned something about taking his own life."

"Oh, no! He mustn't!" Sloane flew from the room and down the stairs, not noticing Grimley's tired but satisfied smile.

14

Tearle rose from his chair and stretched his
arms above his head, turning it from side to
side to ease his weary muscles. He stared at
the pistols sitting on the table beside him,
letting his imagination run with the fantasy
of putting a bullet through Carlisle's rotten
heart. He lowered his arms and ran a finger
over the fine cherrywood handle. The
weapons had been a present from his father
upon his graduation from Oxford, more a
symbol of manhood than anything else. The
gift had been accompanied by a stern lecture
about the imprudence of using the pistols in
an actual duel.

"Ah, Father, how much simpler life
would be if dueling were still legal." He
picked up one of the fine instruments,
fingering the trigger. The library door burst
open, and he swerved toward it, pistol still in
hand.

"Tearle, I beg of you, put the gun down,"
Sloane cried, flinging herself across the room

and grabbing his arm. "I don't care what happened tonight. Nothing matters except that I love you and want to spend my life with you. Please, put down the gun. I could not bear it if you were dead."

The earl stared at her for a few stunned seconds before letting the pistol slide from his fingers onto the table. Sloane threw her arms around his midsection and buried her face against his chest. His arms went around her, clinging to her as if to life itself. He buried his face in her fragrant hair, breathing deeply of its lavender scent, and strongly reminded himself that men don't cry.

"Does this mean you forgive me?" he whispered incredulously.

"Yes," she breathed against his satin waistcoat. "A thousand times, yes." She lifted her head, gazing up at him openly and lovingly.

"How can you? I have wronged you terribly. I mistrusted you, believed those preposterous lies, and never even gave you a chance to defend yourself or explain. I do not deserve your forgiveness."

"But you have it." Sloane moved her hand up to caress his face and smiled. "I have no choice; you are lord of my heart." Her expression shifted to one of mock seriousness. "Yet, you will be forever in my debt. You are doomed to a lifetime of repaying me. You may begin now." She slid one hand behind his head, curling her fingers in his hair, and pulled him down toward her. "Kiss me," she commanded softly.

Tearle complied willingly, touching her lips with a gentleness approaching reverence. Soon, however, gentleness was not enough as their overwrought emotions turned to passion. Sloane sought his mouth hungrily and his fiery response threatened to consume them both.

"Enough," the earl said roughly several minutes later, putting her away from him. He smiled down at her and ran a shaking hand through his flaxen hair. "I will not give truth to the gossip and speculation. You will be Lady Beckford when we consummate our love, with a properly executed marriage license on the bedside table."

"Yes, my lord." Her eyes twinkled up at him. "However, I do not believe in long engagements."

"In this instance, neither do I. We shall post the banns tomorrow and shout it to the world. I will give you two weeks to plan our wedding. Not one second more." He picked up the betrothal ring. "I gave you this ring once in love. It is given now with even deeper affection." He slid the ring on her finger and lifted her hand to his lips to kiss the palm. Clearing his throat, he added, "There was a time I thought it impossible to care deeply for another. You have taught me differently."

"Tearle, tell me about Linette. If I am to banish her ghost forever, I must know how she hurt you." She curled her fingers through his and led him to a small pale blue brocade sofa tucked contentedly by the fireplace.

"I suspect you have heard much of it."

"I know she was unfaithful, and that she flaunted her promiscuity in your face."

"I can see mother has been talking to you." Sloane nodded. "Even mother does not know the half of it." He tensed, leaning his head on the back of the sofa.

"She was so beautiful the season of her comeout. She was the Incomparable. Everyone flocked around her, paying her court. I was as bad as the rest, but it wasn't long before I knew she was interested in me and, I thought, me alone. I fell in love and thought I was in heaven—until my wedding night. Though she played the part well, I knew she had already been with a man. I did not mention it, at least not then. She was so passionate; I convinced myself that it didn't matter, that she had probably had a sweet summer love affair with some young fellow with dots on his face.

"We had been married just over a month when the first *on dits* began to circulate. She could act so innocent, shrugging off the whispers as other's envy. I wanted to believe her, so I did. Jonny was born ten months after our marriage. Six weeks after his birth, she announced that since she had given me a son, her duties to me were fulfilled. I was no longer interesting. I had already fallen prey to her charms." Tearle sighed and felt himself begin to relax. With the sharing of his deepest hurts, he unknowingly began the healing of those very wounds.

"She taunted me with her conquests. I returned from a ride one day to find her naked with the stableboy in Trojan's stall. She knew when I would be returning and deliberately seduced a poor lad who hadn't even had his first woman. A week later, my father discovered her in the arms of one of his oldest friends in his garden while I played a game of billiards in his game room."

"Oh, Tearle, how could she be so unkind?"

"She was a spoiled, only child. She had been given anything and everything her heart had ever desired. She hadn't reached womanhood in some sweet summer fling. She had intentionally seduced a young farmer whose prowess as a lover was giggled about among the maids."

"What of Angela?" Sloane watched him carefully, painfully guessing what his answer would be.

"After Jonny was born, I never touched her. Angela is not my daughter."

"Oh, Tearle," Sloane whispered sadly, resting her head on his shoulder and putting her arm around him.

"She wouldn't, or couldn't, tell me who the father was. God was merciful to the child when she arrived looking the picture of her mother. I found myself studying every man I met, young or old, wondering if he had sired the child I was compelled to claim as my own."

"Oh, love, no wonder you couldn't bear to be around Angela."

He lifted his head from the back cushion and smiled down at her. "I'm glad you helped me change my feelings for Angela. I had never considered how she felt until after you came while I was away. Cory wrote long, excited letters about the wonders you were working, and it caused me to think. For the first time, I considered what it must be like for a little girl to grow up without a mother and with a father who couldn't stand to touch her. I had determined to change the situation, but I didn't have a feather to fly with. You showed me the way from that very first day."

Sloane started to ask about Linette's death, but held back, sensing Tearle needed to talk about it at his own pace. She waited patiently, snuggling against him as the fire burned low in the grate. She thought perhaps he had fallen asleep, but he began to speak again, his voice low and restrained.

"Finally, Linette decided to deal me one last crushing blow. I never really figured out why she hated me so much. Oh, I could see it at the end—all we ever did when we were alone was to scream at each other, but I never really understood what started it all. Her final gesture of spite was to run away with her latest lover, an Italian artist. She left a note saying she was going to Florence, renouncing me and her children. She was a wealthy woman in her own right, with an inheritance from her grandmother that was protected in such a way as not to become mine upon our marriage. She didn't need me, nor her children. She didn't even reach Dover. The coach overturned, and both she and her lover were killed instantly. I was plagued for months by a double guilt—I found I was relieved she was gone, but at the same time haunted by the feeling that somehow I drove her into other men's arms and ultimately to her death."

"Oh, love, none of it was your fault. Surely, you can see that. Her pattern was stamped long before you met her. You must forget the past. Bury it along with Linette. The future belongs to us and our children. I love Jonny and Angela as if they were my own. I'll not love our children any more."

Tearle's arm tightened around her shoulders, and he kissed the top of her head as it rested against his chest. "My love, I like the thought of having children with you. But not too many; I don't want you fat for years and years."

"Won't you love me even when I grow fat and waddle down the hall?"

"Will you look like a duck?"

"Only the walk."

Tearle laughed for the first time in hours. "No wonder women hide themselves until after the baby is born. I have to admit I wasn't around too much toward the end of Linette's confinements. The sight of me only antagonized her, so the doctor recommended I keep busy with other things. She would go into such a temper that he feared for the child."

"I will want you close by, have no fear.
Now, my love, we are both exhausted. Please
let us hasten to our beds before the dawn
breaks. If you are going to flaunt your
betrothed to the world, I don't want to look
like a hag."

"You could never look like a hag, but you
do need rest." He stood, taking hold of her
hand, and drew her to her feet. "Sleep until
you awaken naturally. If we rouse at a decent
enough time, we will begin giving our
neighbors something new to talk about."

Although some considered it fashionable
to arrive at the Pump Room shortly after six
in the morning, most waited until shortly
before midday or early afternoon to stroll the
tree-lined walks around the spas, the original
drawing card in Cheltenham.

On the day following the ball, the Earl of
Beckford joined the members of the *ton* out
for an afternoon stroll near the Montpellier
Spa. To the amazement of those he encountered, the notorious Mrs. Donovan
walked at his side, her arm possessively
linked with his. Some ladies even gaped in
astonishment at the way the earl's other hand
often strayed to absently caress those
graceful fingers resting upon his right arm.

The earl was not neglectful of his
neighbors and bestowed his most charming
smile upon all he met. As the Honorable Mr.
Brownstone remarked to his companion, it
seemed as if the Earl of Beckford and Mrs.

Donovan were the two happiest people in all
of Cheltenham, and that apparently no harm
had been done by the vicious rumor spread
the evening before by some unscrupulous
person.

Since they did not suffer from any
stomach ailments, gout, asthma, or a variety
of other complaints, neither the earl nor
Sloane cared to drink the waters, but they
decided to go to the Pump Room itself just to
see who might be about. They paused for a
moment outside the entrance to listen to the
small orchestra playing for the enjoyment of
those passing by, and then entered the room.

They spoke with a few of their friends
before the earl spotted the gentleman for
whom he had been secretly searching. He
expertly guided Sloane through the crowd,
chatting about unimportant things until they
stood face to face with Sir Spencer
Ridgeway.

"Sloane, my dear, this is a gentleman I
think you should meet." The earl paused,
giving Sloane time to look expectantly at the
man standing in front of her. As he had
planned, her open expression plainly stated
that she had never met Ridgeway, a fact commented upon by more than one observer.
"Mrs. Donovan, may I introduce Sir Spencer
Ridgeway. Sir Ridgeway, I present Mrs.
Sloane Donovan."

"I am delighted to meet you, Mrs.
Donovan. Although I am not one to entangle
myself with women, at least the gossips did
me the honor of picking a beautiful lady for

my partner in our supposed indiscretion."

"You are very kind, Sir Ridgeway. I do so regret the horrible mischief done last evening. I hope that your wife realizes there is no truth to the rumor." Sloane gave him a pleasant smile, though her face was becomingly flushed.

"There is no need to worry on that quarter, madam. I have rarely been out of my beloved's sight since we were wed, so she gave no credence to the intended scandal. She is quite aware that you and I had never even met until just now." Sir Ridgeway did not seem to speak loudly, yet his voice conveniently projected to the ears of those hovering nearby. The earl silently applauded the man's expertise in oration.

"May I wish you happy?" asked Sir Ridgeway, dropping his voice so the eavesdroppers could not hear.

"Yes, Ridgeway, you may. Sloane is to be my bride within the next two weeks." The earl smiled warmly down at his love. "You are not bound to keep it a secret. I would be delighted for the world to know."

"Rightly so, my lord; however, I will leave that to others more experienced in such matters. Now, if you will please excuse me, I grow weary and must rest this blasted leg. I have had enough fresh air and conversation for one day."

"Good day, Sir Ridgeway. Thank you," Sloane said softly.

"You are welcome, my lady. Another time, Lord Beckford."

The earl nodded his appreciation to Ridgeway, his eyes thanking him for going to the trouble to meet them as he had requested. He watched the man limp away, leaning on his cane, and wondered if there wasn't something more that could be done for him. As he determined to write to a doctor of his acquaintance in Scotland, Viscount Remington stepped into his line of vision.

The earl tensed immediately, and Sloane glanced up at him, a question in her eyes. She followed his gaze to see the viscount walking toward them.

"Good afternoon Mrs. Donovan, Beckford. I will not murmur behind my hand and cast my speculations to the wind as most of our companions seem to be doing. You will forgive my surprise at seeing you here today." The viscount studied Tearle's cool expression for a long moment, then turned his gaze on Sloane's cautious one.

"You have no reason to be surprised, Remington. I believe I have made it plain the last several days that I prefer Mrs. Donovan's company above all others."

The viscount smiled, first at Sloane and then the earl. The earl was startled to discern genuine warmth and friendliness in the other man's twinkling eyes.

"So you have. I am pleased to see last night's whisperings did no damage. I have always thought you were a man of good sound common sense, Beckford." He turned his gaze and smile back to Sloane. "Now, I must admit I do not always adhere to good sense, but even I, rakehell that I am, can tell a lady of integrity.'' His smile faded. ''I owe you both an apology. When I heard the gossip last evening, I did little to stop it because the whole idea seemed so utterly incongruous. I did not think anyone could believe such dribble, but then I must have had more punch than I thought, for I forgot how many of our peers will believe anything simply because they want to.''

''There is no need to apologize, my lord,'' Sloane said quietly. ''As you said, no damage was done.'' She pressed her fingers against Tearle's arm when she felt his muscles tighten beneath her hand.

''Good. Would you both care to join me out on the Walk? It grows crowded in here.'' He waited until they reached the shady walk with no one else close by before he spoke again. ''Now, Beckford, I will ask the question everyone is dying to know, but politely refuses to bring up. Have you proposed to this beautiful breath of fresh air? If not, tell me quickly, so I might beat you to the punch.''

Tearle nodded his head and found himself smiling at Viscount Remington, something he had never thought he would do. ''Properly proposed and properly accepted.''

Remington's face broke into a smile. ''Then, I wish you both happy. I trust the ceremony will not be long in coming?''

''In a few weeks. I sent the announcement to London this morning, so we will give it time to appear in the papers. It will be a small family affair at our local church."

"Rightly so. You will be returning to Beckford Hall soon then?"

"Within the next few days. We have a few loose ends to tie up here." The earl looked at him thoughtfully, wondering what he was driving at.

"I will be visiting in your area for the next several weeks. Would it be convenient for me to stop by some afternoon before the wedding? I have a lovely little mare who might be a good mate with your stallion. But, of course, you will probably be much too busy."

"No, Sloane will be doing most of the planning. Feel free to drop by." The earl extended the invitation but with reservation. He could not rid himself of the nagging thought that the handsome viscount might have been one of Linette's admirers.

"Very well, I shall. Please feel free to send me packing if it is not a convenient time. Mrs. Donovan," he said, giving Sloane a radiant smile, "you may assure your future husband that I will not try to steal you out from under his nose. I deeply regret that he saw you first, but the die is cast. Though I freely admit to enjoying a beautiful woman's company, I draw the line at other men's wives or those so promised." He gave Tearle a look full of meaning.

The earl appraised him carefully, finally tipping his head ever so slightly in acknowledgement of the message. So, perhaps all the rumors about Remington and Linette weren't true, he thought. He was well aware of the effort the viscount was making toward furthering their acquaintance and made a quick decision to see how much they had in common.

"We are giving a dinner party this evening to officially announce our engagement, Remington. I would be pleased if you could attend, if you do not have plans."

"I will change them, sir, and accept the invitation with honor. Now, if you will excuse me, I have an appointment at Wilson's. I can't keep such as esteemed personage waiting, you know." He chuckled, his chocolate brown eyes sparkling.

"Of course not," said the earl with a smile. "If you irritate him badly enough, he'll make you a social hermit for the next month or two."

The viscount tipped his hat to Sloane and walked quickly down the sidewalk several blocks to a shop next to the Ball Rooms. Wilson was a successful haircutter and dresser transplanted from London, who humbly proclaimed the establishment to be a paragon of fashion and repository of taste.

The earl and his love strolled back toward the Royal Crescent, deciding at the last minute to continue north a few blocks to High Street. There, they paid a visit to Williams Library nearby the Assembly Rooms, not for the purpose of borrowing a book, but to weigh themselves on his famous weighing chair. Feeling giddy with happiness, they took turns sitting in the chair to be weighed and have their weights recorded in the logbook.

Laughing at their silliness, and solemnly promising to return in ten years to be weighed again, they left the library to visit Tinkler's Basket Shop. From there they proceeded to Mr. Cook's china warehouse which sold goods from the Worcester factory. When they left Cook's, the earl carried a pretty porcelain figurine which had caught Sloane's eye.

They made a stop at Mr. Riviere's jewelry store where Tearle had purchased Sloane's betrothal ring and matching jewelry. They did not leave the store empty-handed for the earl spotted a tiny cloisonné butterfly pin which matched Sloane's gown perfectly. He insisted on purchasing it for her and took the liberty, putting Sloane to the blush, of pinning it on her bodice.

Finally, growing tired, they walked back to the townhouse, past other terrace homes under construction. These brick homes, faced with stucco and painted in imitation of limestone, would be adorned like the Royal Crescent in Cheltenham's specialty, beautiful wrought-iron balconies, porches, and railings often painted green.

That evening, the wedding announcement came as no surprise to any of the guests assembled around the earl's twenty foot dining room table. The few who had not heard the latest *on dit* of the afternoon quickly ascertained the circumstances by the intimate and possessive way the earl kept his arm around his beloved's waist during the small talk before the meal.

Moments before dinner was announced, Tearle drew Sloane to the center of the drawing room and cleared his throat, catching everyone's attention.

"Most of you know our cause for celebrating this evening, but I would like to make the announcement official. Mrs. Donovan has graciously consented to become the Countess of Beckford." He smiled down with unspoken devotion at his love as his guests applauded and gave a small cheer. "We will be married within the fortnight, and since some of our peers might miss the announcement in the paper, you have our permission to share our joy with all you meet. In fact, do not be shocked if you find me standing on top of the Montpellier shouting our intentions to the world." He then proceeded to amuse his guests and embarrass his betrothed by kissing her soundly in front of them all before leading the way into the dining room.

Poor Mr. Brownstone fidgeted through all the courses. He simply did not think he could contain himself until the morrow. He knew he would not sleep a wink in anticipation of the delightful pleasure of passing this bit of news on to that dastardly Baron Carlisle and his sister.

15

"What an odious little man. I detest him."
Lady Wentwood drummed her fingertips
angrily against the windowsill as she
watched the Honorable Mr. Brownstone
swagger down the street.

"I told you it wouldn't work," whined
Carlisle, pouring himself a large glass of
Madeira.

"You did no such thing," yelled his
sister, whirling from the window. "It would
have worked just fine if you had picked someone besides Ridgeway to be her lover. *I* told
you he wouldn't do. He's as pure as fresh
fallen snow. If you recall, idiot brother, I
pointed out he was too pious and that Tearle
wouldn't believe such things of him. But, no,
you insisted he be the one. How could you be
so stupid?"

"Don't call me stupid," shouted her
brother. "You were the one who said we
needed someone who lived in York and was
currently in Cheltenham. Ridgeway was the

only one who fulfilled those requirements."

"You should have been more careful in telling the story. You weren't convincing enough."

"Rot! Brownstone bought it and so did everyone else at the party. Beckford just wasn't as gullible or as suspicious as you thought he would be." Carlisle threw himself into a chair, ignoring the wine he sloshed on the carpet. Slumping against the cushion he stared at his drink and pouted. "Now, I'll never know what she is like. I'll never touch her lovely hair, or see all of that white skin, or—"

"Stop it! I don't want to hear a recital of that chit's attractions. I can't see what is so special about that country bumpkin." Ebony dropped down on the couch, kicked off her slippers, and curled her feet up under her, her expression matching her brother's sullen glare. "I wanted the exhilaration, the power that would have been mine if I had the mighty Earl of Beckford wrapped around my little finger. Curse it all. I hate to lose."

"Yes, it does rub, doesn't it. I can't remember ever being denied what I really wanted. What I resent most is that we let a little-miss-nobody, a simple governess best us. She's a witch."

Ebony jolted upright, her feet hitting the floor. "Yes, that's what she is, and she must be punished."

"It'd never work, Eb, people don't believe in witches anymore. We'd never get the courts to go along with it."

"Of course not, dolt, so we'll have to hand out the justice ourselves."

"I'm not going to burn anybody at the stake, especially a body as desirable as that one."

"We don't have to kill her, but I think I know how to get revenge, both on Sloane Donovan and Tearle Grayson. We'll pay them back for the suffering they've caused us, and then, who knows, eventually Tearle might turn his attentions back to me."

Carlisle shifted in his chair and tossed his glass on a table nearby, his eyes narrowing. "What will I gain from your scheme?"

"Sloane Donovan, to do with as you wish until you grow tired of her, and a tidy little sum of pocket money."

The lure of having Sloane in his control was more than enough to make Carlisle sit up and pay attention, but the mention of adding to his dwindling coffers sweetened the pot even more. He and his sister discussed her plan for over an hour before he left the townhouse, driving his curricle toward the seedier part of town.

Two days after the earl and Sloane announced their engagement, they returned to Beckford Hall with the rest of the family. Within three days of their return, Sloane had completed all the details of the wedding—invitations had been sent, a gown purchased, a dinner menu agreed upon, arrangements made for flowers, and the basic plan for a wedding trip to Italy had been made.

The fourth morning found the occupants of Beckford Hall relaxed and discussing their plans for the day.

"Viscount Remington should be here by eleven," said the earl, finishing his cup of coffee. "He's bringing over his mare. I think I'll give him a tour of the estate, and perhaps do a little hunting. How will you pass the hours, my love?" He watched Sloane put down her teacup and daintily dab her mouth with her napkin. He checked the temptation to lean over and kiss her, deciding to give her a chance to speak first.

"I've promised the children a picnic down by the pond. We should be well out of your way there during the hunt."

"True, just promise me you won't let Jonny bring home another frog."

"He'll be so terribly disappointed. He was hoping to convince you to persuade me to let him capture a new friend. He doesn't want to believe it is truly in the frog's best interest to remain at the pond."

"It is in all our best interests if the frogs remain at the pond. I doubt if I'll ever be able to look at Lady Ingles with a straight face."

"Poor lady, I think you sent her into worse palpitations than the frog." Sloane laughed, then tipped her head haughtily in the air. "I do hope you refrain from molesting the older ladies after we are married, dear. It is so irritating to have them go off in an attack of vapors simply at the sight of you."

The earl threw back his head and

laughed. "I did get to the old girl, didn't I? Well, you'd better keep me pleasantly occupied after we're married, or I'll see what she has to offer."

"Oh, no you won't. I'd hate for you to cause the woman's demise." She smiled at him seductively. "She's not up to your sultry kisses."

"But you are." He leaned across the corner of the table, his burning gaze sending showers of sparks over Sloane. His lips came down over hers, and though no other part of their bodies touched, both hearts were pounding when he lifted his head several moments later. "I picked up a Special License yesterday. Are you sure we must wait another week?" he asked softly.

"No, I'm not," came her equally soft reply.

He was about to suggest an impromptu visit to the vicar, when Grimley discreetly coughed from the doorway.

"Your pardon, my lord, but Viscount Remington has arrived."

The earl flashed Sloane a wistful smile. "Perhaps we can sneak away this evening. Do you think your brother-in-law would object to a quick evening wedding?"

"Not if he thought he was keeping us from sin," whispered Sloane, smiling impishly.

"Minx!" The earl kissed her quickly and wandered out of the breakfast room and across the great hall to where his guest stood patiently studying the tapestries.

"Good morning, Remington."

"Good morning, Beckford. These are splendid tapestries. Sixteenth century Belgian?"

"Yes, you have a good eye."

Lord Remington smiled. "I have a mother who loves art of all kinds, but has a special fondness for tapestries. She grew up in a very old, drafty castle in the Scottish Highlands and spent many of her early years mending the thick wall coverings. After my father's death some years ago, she redecorated her apartments in the manor house to resemble a medieval castle, complete with tapestries on the walls and claymores and targes over the fireplaces. She says it brings back fond memories of her childhood." He laughed at Tearle's surprised look.

"I'll admit she's a bit eccentric where her private rooms are concerned, but she never asked to change the rest of the house. Thankfully, she chose only the finest tapestries to line the walls, otherwise it might prove terribly depressing to anyone else who might venture in."

"Somehow, I cannot picture your mother enjoying a country house. I would have thought she preferred the London social whirl." The men walked out the front portico to find Remington's groom walking both the animal the viscount had been riding and a lovely midnight black mare.

"Oh, she never misses a season, but I suspect her devotion to the gala life will diminish once I have given up bachelorhood.

In truth, I think she prefers a quieter life among her books and flowers."

"It must be inborn in women to help their children find mates. It seems to be second nature to them." The earl smiled as he carefully inspected the mare. "She's a beauty." He continued to stroke the smooth firm muscles and glistening coat until Remington had completed the recital of her lineage. "Yes, I think breeding Trojan and this little lady would be an excellent idea." He instructed the groom to take her down to the stables and place her in a paddock by herself. After she had been given a chance to grow familiar with her surroundings, Trojan would be turned into the same area.

A few moments later, Sloane watched the earl and the viscount canter across the meadow. For the briefest of moments, she relived the touch of his lips on hers, then shook her head briskly and went up to see if Annie had the children ready to go on the picnic.

As she entered the nursery, Jonny commanded Angela to keep the lid on the basket. "You already know what's in there. It's no fair if you go poking your fingers into every pie to see what kind it is. Mrs. Honeycutt said there was beef and ham, so you don't need to look."

"I wath looking for dethert."

"Then you sure don't need to punch holes in the pie crust. She said there was chocolate cake." Jonny stepped between his sister and the basket, hands on hips, his chin defiantly in the air.

"I don't think this is any way to begin a picnic, children," Sloane said quietly. "We want to have a good time and enjoy each other's company, not bicker all the while. Jonny, do you have your butterfly net?"

"Yes, ma'am."

"Do you have your parasol, Angel?"

"Yeth, ma'am." She grinned up at Sloane. "Annie thaid I would turn brown if I didn't take it."

"Well, you certainly might get burned since you're so fair. Now, what are you going to play with?"

"My dolly and Beau. He can come, too, can't he?" Her forehead wrinkled up in concern.

"Of course, he can, dear." Sloane ruffled her curls. "He will be our champion."

"Our champion?" asked Jonny. "Against what?"

"Oh, grasshoppers, snakes, and things. He'll probably love to help you chase butterflies."

"Let's go."

An hour later, the little entourage was happily sprawled on blankets on the grass beside the pond. They were completely out of sight of the house, and the only sounds to be heard were their happy chatterings, the hum of bees, the songs of the birds, and the gentle rustle of the wind as it blew through the willow trees.

Most of the contents of the picnic basket had been quickly devoured after their long walk. Sloane dozed in the sunshine while Annie kept a sleepy eye on the children playing a few yards away. Eventually, the children and puppy grew tired of the inactivity, and Jonny pulled out his butterfly net.

"Don't go too far, Mr. Jonathan," called Annie.

Sloane slowly roused from a lovely dream and pushed up on her elbows to watch the children. "Jonny, stay here in the meadow where we can see you."

"Yes, ma'am," called the little boy, spotting a large yellow and black butterfly. He tore after it, net at the ready, with Angela on his heels.

"Well, that should occupy them for a while," Sloane commented to her maid. Both women kept a watchful eye out for the children, satisfied as long as they could see their heads bob up and down fairly often in the tall grass. Sloane eventually stood up as the children ran closer to the woods.

"Sloane, come here," called Jonny, waving his hands in the air.

Annie and Sloane left the remains of the picnic scattered on the ground and hurried across the meadow to the children.

"What is it, Jon? Did you catch the butterfly?" asked Sloane as they approached the children.

"No, I let him go. Listen."

Everyone was quiet for a few minutes before they heard a tiny mewing sound coming from the woods.

"Why, it sounds like a kitten," exclaimed Annie. "Whatever would a tiny kitten be doing way out 'ere?"

"Perhaps the mother hid here for them to be born," said Sloane.

"Can we go investigate? What if he's hurt or something?" queried Jonny.

"Yes, we should check on it. Your father isn't hunting in this part of the estate, so I think we're safe enough." Carefully the small band threaded their way through the underbrush, seeking the crying animal. Finally, they broke into a small clearing.

"Well, I never saw the like," cried Annie. For a brief moment, they all stared at a tiny kitten tied to a tree. The rope was small and the animal was in no immediate danger of choking itself, but it certainly was an easy prey for a larger animal. Annie moved to the little fur ball and quickly untied the rope.

Jonny and Angela joined Annie, arguing about who was to hold the kitten first. Jonny won the argument and took the kitten from the maid. He glanced over his shoulder at Sloane and asked, "Slo', who would tie up a poor little kitten?"

Suddenly, his eyes grew large, and he opened his mouth to call out, but in that instant a huge, dirty hand clamped over his mouth, stifling his cry. Jonny dropped the kitten, which scampered off in the woods, Beau hot on its heels. Jonny wiggled and kicked, but the man would not ease his hold.

"Let him go," cried Sloane, taking a step toward the boy before someone grabbed her arm, twisting it behind her back viciously. The tiny clearing grew crowded as another man joined the two holding Sloane and Jonny.

"We ain't 'bout to let 'im go, dearie," growled the large, wicked man holding Jonny. "You three is our ticket t' the good life. Now, keep quiet and do as yer told and nobody 'as to suffer. If you don't go real quiet like, I might just 'ave to break an arm or somethin'."

"What do you want? Where are you taking us?" Sloane tried to keep her voice calm for the children's sake, knowing, too, that if the men knew how terrified she was, they would use it against her.

"You'll find out soon enough." He glared at Annie and then barked an order to the third man. "She'll just get in the way. Thump 'er."

"No!" Sloane cried as the man grabbed Annie. Although the young maid put up a frantic struggle, he quickly overpowered her, bringing the handle of his pistol down on her head with a sickening crack. He let her drop to the ground, picked up Angela, and turned his attention back to the leader.

"Take 'em to the coach."

Jonny started to kick and pound on his assailant, but Sloane called out for him to stop. "It will do no good, Jon. Don't provoke him into hurting you."

Jonny obeyed, but glared up at his captor. They wormed their way through the woods to the waiting carriage where they were roughly pushed inside.

One of the men climbed in the coach, sitting across from Sloane and the children, blocking the door. The other door had been barricaded with a piece of wood nailed across it. The curtains had been pulled almost closed, shutting out most of the light.

They traveled for several hours; the children finally fell asleep huddled against Sloane. She pretended to sleep, but kept a watchful eye on the guards.

She had almost given up hope of determining their direction when the coach stopped at a posting inn to change the horses. The man stayed in the coach so Sloane could not venture a peep out the window. Moments before they pulled away from the inn, church bells rang out across the town. As the top guard climbed aboard, she heard a passerby comment on visiting the home of the bells they had just heard—Worcester Cathedral. Sloane chanced a secret glance at her watch and was surprised to discover it was almost six.

The kidnappers themselves gave her another clue a short while later. The man riding guard beside the driver opened a small window to check on the passengers. As he turned to shut the door, a shaft of sunlight shot through the trees behind him, and Sloane caught a glimpse of the sun low in the western sky. Shortly afterwards, the tilt of the coach proclaimed they were going up an incline, and for the next hour, the vehicle wound around in a gradual climb. An hour and a half out of Worcester, they stopped.

"Wake up the brats. You can get out now."

Sloane gently prodded the children and held them as they struggled to awaken. The kidnappers barely gave them time to open their eyes before they were hauled from the coach. Angela started to cry, and one of the men gave her a quick shake.

"Don't you be drippin'. You ain't got nuthin' t' cry about."

"Let her be. She's afraid and half asleep," scolded Sloane. She was surprised when the man released Angela and let her run to Sloane, who picked her up. She took a quick look around as she scooped up the child, noting the lane that wound around the stone house, and the ivy completely covering one wall. At one end of the house, a chimney had crumbled to the ground, and Sloane was relieved to find that particular portion of the house had been closed off from the rest of it.

"Yer to go upstairs." One man led them up the wooden steps until they reached the third floor attic. It wasn't particularly spacious, but at least it was reasonably clean. Three mattresses had been thrown on the floor, covered with fresh linen.

"I'm hungry," complained Jonny.

"Me, too," piped up Angela.

The kidnapper glared at Sloane. "And, I suppose ye're 'ungry, too? Well, we all are. Can you cook?"

"Yes."

"Then get downstairs and cook up some

eggs. All we got fer now is eggs and a side of 'am. We'll get more food tomorrow when we send the ransom note.''

"Why not send it tonight?" asked Sloane quickly.

"We're goin' to let the earl stew about things fer a while. It's all part o' the plan." He grabbed Sloane's arm and jerked her to the top of the stairs. "Now, get down there and cook."

"Let the children come, too," pleaded Sloane. "They won't be so frightened if they are with me."

"Yer probably right there." He glanced at Jonny as he shifted uncomfortably from one foot to the other. Angela was doing the same. "I'd better take 'em outside first. This fancy inn even 'as its own little convenience out back." He glared at Sloane. "You need to go, too?"

Sloane's face flamed but she nodded her head. A short while later, the group returned to the kitchen, having taken care of at least one immediate problem.

The children discovered an old tomcat curled up beside the fireplace, and to Sloane's relief, the animal was content to lazily play with a piece of string Jonny found. While Sloane scrambled the eggs and fried the ham, the cat kept the children occupied and helped them to relax.

There were only two chairs at the table, but the kidnappers let the children have them to eat. The men either stood or slumped down on the floor to greedily devour the eggs, ham, and a few slices of stale bread. After Sloane had eaten and washed the dishes, she and the children were ordered back upstairs.

Once inside the room, the door locked from the outside, Sloane breathed a sigh of relief. Even though the situation was deadly serious, she felt much safer away from the men. Jonny raced to the window, trying to peer out in the feeble moonlight.

"Hey, Sloane," he said softly, "there's a tree right outside the window. Maybe we could climb down and escape."

Sloane went pale. "Perhaps, Jonny. We'll have to wait until sunlight to check it out. We're very high up, and it might not be a good climbing tree."

"What are we going to do? I don't have anything to play with."

"I want my dolly." Angela looked up forlornly at Sloane, her lower lip drooping. Large, glistening tears welled up in her eyes as that tiny rosebud lip began to quiver. "I want my Papa."

Sloane swept her into her arms. "I want to go home, too, honey, but we'll have to make do for a little while. We'll be home in a few days, I'm certain. Now, don't cry, please."

The little girl bravely wiped away her tears, but her lips remained in a pout.

"Why don't we make up stories? I'll start a story and you can each add to it." Just like gossip, thought Sloane whimsically. Oh, dear, she thought, I must be extremely tired to find anything humorous in this situation.

The game kept them busy for half an hour, but by then both children were restless. They sang a few songs, but slowly quieted. Although they had slept in the coach, it had not been a restful sleep, and the ordeal was beginning to take its toll. The house creaked and groaned in the dark; the lone candle they had been allowed did little to dispel the ghosts from the shadows.

"I'm afraid," sniffled Angela. "I want to go home," she sobbed. In seconds, her sobs became wails. Jonny watched his sister for a moment, trying to be brave, but soon giant tears rolled down his cheeks, and his sobs and sniffles joined hers.

Sloane gathered them in her arms, and they curled up together on one of the mattresses. "Hush, children, hush. It won't do any good to cry." She rocked them gently back and forth, smoothing their hair with her fingers, murmuring words of comfort. Angela's sobs reached the point of hysteria, and the little girl's brokenhearted screams echoed throughout the house, reaching the darkness outside.

The door burst open and the leader of the kidnappers stomped into the room, glaring at the trio huddled on the mattress on the floor. "Make those brats be quiet, or I will," he shouted. He turned abruptly and slammed the door, leaving a startled, cringing Angela staring silently at the closed door.

Sloane acted quickly. "There, now, children, you must be quiet so we don't anger

him further. If you promise not to cry anymore, I'll tell you a story." She looked down
at Angela as the tired little girl sadly nodded
her head. Sloane gave them each a squeeze
and began the story of David and Goliath. For
the next hour, she told them as many Bible
stories as she could remember, until they
finally dropped off to sleep.

Once they were tucked safely beneath
their blankets, Sloane snuffed out their
candle and moved to kneel in front of the
window. Gazing out at the clouds skittering
across the face of the moon, tears stung the
back of her eyes.

"Please, dear God," she prayed softly,
"keep us from harm. Let Tearle find Annie in
time, and please don't let her die. Help me to
think of some way to let him know where we
are. Please, Lord, help me to think."

She made her way back across the
darkened room to her makeshift bed, too
exhausted to even cry. In a matter of
minutes, she was fast asleep.

16

Sloane woke at the crack of dawn. Carefully drawing back the blanket, she crawled from her bed and tiptoed to the window, opening it quietly. The tree was large, and a sturdy branch grew near enough to the building to reach by stretching; however, the branches were too far apart for Jonny and Angela to climb down safely. Sloane looked down at the ground and grabbed the windowsill when the world swirled in front of her. From this height, it would take a guiding angel to get her to the ground safely, especially with a child clinging to her back. Even if their lives depended upon it, she doubted if she could climb back up to bring down another.

Sloane shut the window softly and crossed the room to listen at the door. She could hear the men stirring below, their voices only an indistinct rumble. She left the portal and searched the attic, hoping she had overlooked something in the dim light the previous evening that could be used as a weapon. The only thing she discovered was an old dust-covered trunk shoved in a dingy corner.

Sloane tugged at the latch for several minutes before it sprang open, then she carefully lifted the lid, grimacing as the hinges gave a small squeak. A mouse scurried out a thin crack near the bottom, and Sloane bit back a cry. Gingerly, she poked around the pile of shredded paper. There were no weapons to be found, not even a cane or umbrella. However, she did discover a tattered Bible and a packet of whist cards, worn but with the deck intact.

She took out the treasures, blowing the dust from them, and breathed a thank you for small blessings. The children were beginning to stir when a key rattled in the lock and the door swung open. Sloane expected to be ordered downstairs to cook breakfast, but instead, a young girl of about fourteen entered the room.

The girl glanced curiously at the trio but placed a chamber pot in a corner without a word, then hurried from the room. One of the men stood in the doorway, yawning and scratching his overhanging belly. Moments later, the girl returned, carrying a pot of gruel, bowls, and spoons. She sat them on the floor near Sloane, giving her a timid smile.

"From now on, you won't leave this room," ordered the man at the door. He jerked his head for the girl to leave, turning to follow her, and closed the door.

Sloane convinced the children to choke

down the thick mush by promising to teach them some card games if they ate all their breakfast. When the bowls were empty, she hugged each child, agreeing that the food was horrible, but reminding them that if they stayed healthy, they would have a better chance of escaping. She had just taken out the promised pack of cards when the door opened again.

Another man lumbered through the doorway carrying a small table. The man who had come up earlier, evidently the gang's leader, walked in behind him with a rickety chair, paper, and a pen and ink.

"I'll tell you what to say, and you'll write the ransom note. Don't try no tricks 'cause I can read, and I know 'ow many words they's supposed to be."

Sloane's mind raced frantically, going over the plan she had conceived in the early dawn hours. She wasn't certain it would work, but she had to try something. She nodded her head and looked at the kidnapper gravely.

"Don't worry. I'll cooperate."

"There's a good wench. You just do wot ol' Jack says and nobody will get 'urt."

"May I tell his lordship that we are unharmed?"

"No, let 'im worry. 'e's more likely to come through with the money if 'e thinks you might be 'urt."

Sloane shuddered at the way he looked at her and sat down at the table, trying to hide her revulsion and fear. She wrote as he dictated, praying silently he would not decipher her carefully coded message. In the hours to come, she would pray just as fervently that the earl *would* understand the directions she was giving him.

Sloane blew on the ink, then handed the missive to the kidnapper. He painstakingly read the request for two hundred thousand pounds in return for the children and Sloane, and the directions for leaving the money at Worcester Cathedral during the Sunday morning worship service. When the man did not notice the various misspelled words, Sloane almost breathed a sigh of relief. She decided to proceed with the second step of her plan.

"Did you say someone was going into town today for food?"

"Aye, why?" The man's eyes narrowed as he looked up from the note.

"Would it be possible for someone to go to the circulating library and pick up a few books for us?"

"I ain't paying no money so's you can enjoy yer stay."

"I didn't expect you to." Sloane removed a small pearl pin from her dress and held it out to the man. "This is not worth a great deal, but it could be exchanged for enough to pay for the loan of the books. There is so little up here to entertain the children, and I'm sure you don't want them crying for hours at a time. They are frightened and need something to occupy their minds. They love to have stories read to them." Sloane looked up at him hopefully. "It would help to keep them quiet."

The man scratched his head, frowning. At last, he reached out and took the pin. "Well, I don't want no noise. All that screechin' last night 'bout drove me out o' me noodle. I guess it'd be all right. I could get 'arley to run over there while Sally's at the market."

"Oh, thank you so much. I'll make out a list if it is all right. So many times the books are already checked out, so I'll put down several. We only need three or four."

Sloane took another piece of paper, hoping she could insert enough letters to send a message without Jack catching on to what she was doing. She wrote sloppily so her misspellings would appear to be a product of carelessness.

Again, the man struggled over the words, thinking that for a governess, she didn't write very well. "I ain't never 'eard o' some o' these."

"Those are probably the religious ones. I use them for textbooks for the children. It won't hurt to keep up with their studies."

The man shot her a scornful look before he went to the door and yelled down at Harley. A few minutes later a young man stuck his head through the door opening. He was not one of the original kidnappers.

"What'd you want, Jack?"

Jack gave him the instructions for what he was to do in town, tossing him the pearl pin.

"I ain't never been to no library before. I won't know wot to do." The young man looked uneasily at Sloane.

"All you have to do is read the list to the librarian. He will get the books you need."

Harley looked down at the floor and shifted uncomfortably. "Can't read."

"You can just give the note to the librarian. He would probably prefer having the list in front of him anyway so he won't have to try to remember the titles. It's done all the time, Harley." Sloane smiled at the young man, somehow feeling that he was not cut from the same cloth as the others. "If you act confident, the librarian will never guess that you can't read."

The young man flashed her a grin and nodded.

"Don't dawdle," snarled Jack. "Be back by midday. I'm goin' to deliver the ransom note. Ed and Joe'll stay 'ere." He turned back to Sloane and the children as Harley disappeared down the steps. "You keep those brats quiet, and don't try to get away. It wouldn't bother those two downstairs to handle you rough." His leering gaze traveled over her slowly. "Now, me, I like to treat my women real gentle, but I can get rough if I 'ave to."

Sloane forced her gaze away from his and picked up the cards, frustrated that he could see her hand shaking. "I found these cards in the old trunk in the corner. We'll keep busy. Is it all right if I open the window?"

"Aye." He watched closely as she crossed the room and pushed the window up. Before she could turn around, he moved swiftly across the room to stand behind her, wedging her between him and the windowsill. Sloane leaned forward over the window ledge, trying to keep her body from touching him. The ground seemed to sink even further away, and suddenly, the trees and bushes began to spin. Nauseous, Sloane jerked back from the window, her body pressing against his.

Closing her eyes, Sloane tried to ignore the stink of his sweat, concentrating instead on halting the swirling image in her head. He put his arm around her, his fingers splaying across her midriff. He shifted slightly, drawing her back from the window. To her dismay, Sloane's prevalent emotion was one of relief as she fought the fear that blocked everything else from her mind. She could not think about what he might do in the next moment, or even feel shame at the intimate way his body was pressed against hers.

"I was told you 'ad spirit," he softly, tilting his head to look at her white face. "I wondered if you would try to escape out the window, but I don't think I 'ave to worry about it, do I?"

"No," whispered Sloane and as her fear subsided, she grew angry and embarrassed at the way he held her. "Let me go," she commanded through clenched teeth.

His fingers slowly moved across her flat stomach until he dropped his hand at his side. "I 'ope the cove gets tired o' you real quick," he whispered, as he stepped back.

Sloane whirled around to face him, edging away from him and the window. "What do you mean?" she demanded, her eyes glistening with anger.

"The ransom ain't for you, missy. The tykes'll be sent 'ome, but the cove's got other plans for you. When 'e's done, we'll turn you over to a London Abbess, after we're through with you. Aye, 'tis a sweet pot ol' Jack fell into this time. The governor pays us to nab you and we get 'alf the ransom. 'e keeps you for awhile, then me and the boys 'ave a little fun before we takes you to Town and gets the bunt from the Abbess. Aye, she'll pay dear for the likes o' yer pretty face."

Sloane stared at him, stunned by the revelation that someone else was behind the kidnapping. As her mind began to function again, she realized who had to be the one who had hired these thugs. "I'll kill myself before I let Carlisle or you touch me," she said quietly, grimly satisfied by Jack's startled look at the mention of Carlisle's name.

"You won't 'ave the chance." He spun abruptly and left the room, pulling the door closed and locking it.

The children had sat mutely wide-eyed at this exchange. As soon as the door closed, Jonny jumped to his feet and raced to her side.

"What did he mean about the ransom not being for you? Aren't they going to let you go, too?" He stared up at her, his little face wrinkled up with concern.

"Of course, they will, darling. He was just trying to scare us, that's all. I have a lot of faith in your father, Jonny. He'll rescue us, and those stinking thugs won't get one ha'penny."

"Do you really think he'll rescue us, Slo'? Will he come charging in on Trojan? Do you think he'll have a whole band of men with him?"

"Well, I don't exactly know how he'll go about it, but I do think he'll get us away from these men. Now, let's sit down and try to pass the time with a game." Sloane curled up on the mattress with the children and dealt the cards, sending another fervent prayer heavenward.

Later that morning, Harley self-consciously stepped into the lending library in Worcester. He hesitated for a brief moment, then lifted his chin and approached the librarian with a confident swagger. The coins from pawning the pin jangled in his pocket, and he hoped it wouldn't cost the whole amount to borrow the books. Stopping in front of the desk, he handed the note to the man standing behind it.

"Me mistress wants to check out some books. The little lord is feelin' poorly, and she wanted somethin' to keep 'im busy. She said you didn't 'ave to send 'em all; three or four would do."

The librarian took the missive and perused it quickly, frowning slightly when he noted the strange spellings and the two very unusual titles and authors.

"Somethin' wrong?" Harley's eyes narrowed, and he studied the man intently.

"Oh, no, nothing at all." The clerk looked up at Harley and smiled. "I was just trying to remember if all of the titles are in. If you would like to be seated, I'll get these books for you in just a few minutes. I do have to take a report in to the head librarian first, so I'll be delayed a bit." He grinned and winked at the younger man. "He's a bit absent-minded, so I'll have to explain why it's important we get the report in the post right away. I'll try not to keep you long."

He picked up a stack of papers and headed for the office near the back of the building. Just before reaching it, he glanced back to see Harley sitting where he had indicated, staring about the room at the books and well-dressed patrons with undisguised awe.

Since the head librarian was out for the day, Anders, who was the assistant librarian, did not bother to knock on the office door. He simply opened it and stepped into the room pretending to talk to someone. When the door closed, he trotted across the room to the desk and scanned the note again; his brow furrowing as he pondered the poor spellings and the unusual titles.

William Anders had graduated from Oxford just the year before. Bright, quick of mind and wit, he did not intend to remain a librarian for all his days. He planned to become a gentleman's secretary, to work for a man who had either made his fortune himself or who had no qualms about investing his money in trade or some other lucrative endeavor. William knew such a position would give him the knowledge to place some of his own hard-earned money into profitable investments.

However, making money was not his greatest dream. Nothing delighted him more than solving a mystery, and he spent many hours reading about time-proven methods of investigative work as well as the newest theories of the day. He longed for the opportunity to put what he had learned, as well as some ideas of his own, into practice. He had even toyed with the thought of joining the Bow Street Runners, but being a man of slight build, he knew he did not have the physical power necessary to overcome a strong opponent. No, his power lay in his mind, in attention to detail, and in the logical, careful thinking required to resolve a mystery.

His frown disappeared and a slow smile spread across his face. Either the writer of the note was playing a prank, or he had just been drawn into a real-life adventure. He sat down at the desk and read the note carefully.

"*Mothher Goose's Melodey* by Jolhn Newpberry; *Follow the Messenger* by W.E. Rabducted; *Swiss Famikly Robiinson* transdlated by Williamn Godwain; *Gullipers Travelds* by Jonacthan Swieft; *The Buatterrfly's Ball and the Grasslhooper's Feast* by Willbiam Roesckoe; *The Peafcock at Home* by Mrs. Catherrine Dordset; a volumee of fairvy tales; *Robinsson Crusoe* by Dahniel Demfoe; and *Angel's Deliverance* by Beck Fords Earl."

"You're one clever lady," he murmured, smiling to himself. He went through the list slowly, circling each inappropriate letter. He then wrote down the letters and the phony titles and authors. It took him a few minutes before he divided the letters properly so they made sense, then he gazed down at the message triumphantly.

"Help Follow the Messenger We R Abducted Kidnaped C Earl o Bekfrd Evshm Angel's Deliverance by Beckfords Earl."

He stared down at the missive, the seriousness of the situation settling over him. He pictured Harley in his dirty worn clothing. That boy was no more a servant than he was. Instinct told him the message was real, and the fate of another person lay in his hands.

With a grimace of determination, he jumped up from the desk and walked swiftly to the door. He roamed up and down the shelves, gathering the required books, and tossing a wave to Harley when he looked his way. When the boy looked away again, Anders caught the attention of his helper and motioned for him to meet him in the back of the room. Once they were hidden from Harley's view, he showed the youngster the note.

"Edgar, I think we've received a call for help." Edgar read the note, his eyes widening in amazement.

"Do you think it's for real?" he whispered.

"I can't be certain, but I believe so. At any rate, we must treat it as authentic until we discover otherwise. It would be terrible to shrug it aside, only to find out later we could have kept someone from harm. I want you to follow the boy who delivered the message. I've collected some of the books requested, but left a few out so it won't be too obvious that the only ones missing are the fake ones. Do you think you can follow him, even if he goes out of town?"

"That's no problem. I've been all over the countryside many a time. Me uncle don't pay no mind to when I comes or goes."

"Good. I don't dare follow him because he might see me. You follow him to his destination and then come back here. I'll wait here until I hear from you, then you can show me where she is being held." He reached into his pocket and took out some coins. "Can you ride?" At the boy's nod, he said, "Here's some money in case you have to rent a pony to follow him. If he's going to the country, he'll probably have a cart and horse. You'd never keep up on foot."

"Aye, Mr. Anders, I'll not let 'im get away from me."

Anders went back to the front desk with the books while Edgar moved near the front door and began rearranging a display. Harley stepped up to the desk when Anders smiled at him.

"Here are the ones I could find. Un-

fortunately, some of the titles are loaned out.
To whom do I check them out?"

Harley looked startled. "Uh, Lady Mary
Smith."

The librarian dutifully wrote the name
on the cards. Picking up a piece of paper, he
wrote a quick note to Lady Smith. "Lady
Smith, some of the volumes you requested
are not currently in our library. I shall
inquire at the appropriate establishments
around the area to see if I can locate the
particular items and authors mentioned.
Your patronage is greatly appreciated. I hope
our service will be satisfactory."

"Wot's that?" asked Harley, looking at
the note suspiciously.

"Just a brief message advising Lady
Smith that some of the books are not
available today, and thanking her for her
patronage. Always wise to show one's
appreciation, you know. Good for business."

"I suppose so. How much?" Anders
named an amount. Harley carefully counted
out the coins, putting the fee on the desk and
the remaining money back in his pocket. He
picked up the books and left the library,
totally unaware of the boy following him.

Anders quickly penned a message to the
Earl of Beckford, giving him what details he
knew of the situation, as well as a copy of the
note from Sloane and the decoded message. A
friend of his, James Rogers, was currently
sitting in the library's lounge reading the
London Times. Taking him into his confidence, Anders explained what had

happened and asked if he was willing to ride to Evesham and try to find the Earl of Beckford.

"I'd go myself, but with old Higgins out for the day, there's no one to mind the store."

"I'll go," said Rogers. "It's a good day for rescuing damsels in distress. Do you want me to bring the earl back here if I find him?"

"Yes, I'll stay here. If Edgar gets back soon, I'll have him show me where the kidnappers are. If it takes him a long time, we'll both wait here until the earl arrives. If you can't find him, we'll go the local magistrate, but I hate to do that since we both know how inefficient he is."

"Right. Well, I'm off. Let's hope the trip is worth it."

"Yes, and let's hope the earl is as quick of action as the lady is of mind." After his friend departed, William Anders tried to attend to the business at hand, checking out books, accepting overdue fines, and answering queries from customers. Years later, he would tell his grandchildren that it turned out to be the longest day of his life.

17

The earl and Viscount Remington had ridden
slowly up to the stables, laughing at an
amusing antedote about a mutual friend, not
a great hunter, and a confrontation he had
with Colonel Berkeley, a powerful member of
Cheltenham society and an avid fan of the
hunt. Their laughter stopped abruptly when
they beheld the near panic around the stable
yard.

"Oh, thank goodness you're home, my
lord," exclaimed Grimley, conspicuously out
of place in the stables and obviously in a state
of near hysteria, a condition so unusual that
the earl could only stare at him in amazement. "Tom has gone to try to find you."

"Whatever is the matter, Grimley?"
asked the earl, coming out of his shock.

"It's Mrs. Donovan and the children,
m'lord. They went for a picnic early this
afternoon and haven't come back. I sent
Brian to look for them and he just returned.
He found the remains of their luncheon but

321

cannot find a trace of them anywhere." The old man wrung his hands helplessly. "Lord Grayson, Brian, and the stableboys were going to search the meadow. Something bad has happened, m'lord. I can just feel it."

"Calm down, Grimley. Where is Brian?" The earl remained in the saddle, tossing his brother a wave as he came down the lane from the house. Jonathan nodded and quickly hopped onto the back of the horse one of the grooms had saddled for him.

"I'm here, m'lord," cried Brian, running from inside the stable. "I looked all around the meadow, Lord Beckford, and called and called, but there wasn't a sign of the little ones or Mrs. Donovan or Annie."

"Then let us begin the search immediately. You lead the way to where they had luncheon, Brian."

Jonathan turned to Grimley. "Miss Kincade is in the drawing room. Understandably, she is upset. I entrust her into your care, Grimley, until my parents return from their afternoon visit. I know you will remain calm and not upset her further." He nodded as his old friend took a deep breath and straigthened, with great effort once again assuming the unruffled demeanor of his station.

The small band galloped across the meadow to where the blanket was still spread on the grass, the picnic basket open and attracting flies and bees. The only sounds to fill the late afternoon air were the singing of the birds and the hum of insects busily storing away the last bit of food for the day.

"Brian, you and the rest of the men spread out at five foot intervals and sweep across the meadow. The pond is not deep enough to pose a threat. We will search the parameter of the woods. Give a shout if you find anything."

Brian, ever so proud at being called a man, waited until the rest of the group spread out, then gave the order to commence with the search across the meadow. The earl, his brother, and Remington walked their horses slowly to the edge of the woods and began their search there. A fruitless half hour later, they stopped their horses, trying to figure out where to go next.

"Lou, listen. Do you hear a dog whimpering?" The three listened intently until the sad, faint sound came again. "It's coming from in the woods, down to our left, I think."

The earl jumped from his horse, followed by Jonathan and the viscount, and pushed their way through the underbrush, moving slowly so as not to frighten the animal. Every several steps they stopped and listened, continuing on when the sound came again. In a few minutes, they broke into a small clearing.

Beau lay beside the still form of Annie, whimpering and licking her ashen face. At the sight of the men, he jumped up and ran to meet them, giving an excited bark.

The earl knelt at the maid's side, noting

her bloody mobcap and fearfully searched for a pulse. "She's still alive." He gently turned her and removed the cap, examining the large purple knot and cut on the back of her head. "The wound has clotted, but she's had a nasty blow." He looked up at the other two, who had been searching the surrounding area. Pain and worry filled his eyes. "Is there any sign of the others?"

"No, Lou," said Jonathan quietly, "but there's been a struggle. It looks like someone has gone through the brush back this way. You take Annie on back to the house, and we'll see what we can find."

The earl nodded, unable to speak for the heartache in his throat. He knew Jonathan would not find his loved ones, for if the children or Sloane were about, Beau would have been with them instead of Annie. Carefully picking up the maid, he carried her through the woods to where Trojan stood nibbling the grass. He laid her on the ground, and cupping his hands around his mouth, called to Brian. A few minutes later, his loyal servants arrived at the scene.

"Is she dead, my lord?" asked Brian softly, his eyes filled with pain. The earl shook his head. "Did you find the others, sir?"

"No, Brian. Jonathan and Remington are following a trail through the woods, but it appears they have been taken. You men help me get this poor woman up on the horse." Tearle climbed up on Trojan, then cradled the maid gently when the men lifted her into his lap. "Brian, ride to Evesham and fetch the physician."

The young man jumped on his horse and rode across the meadow as fast as he could. Tearle instructed the men to wait until Jonathan came out of the woods before they returned to the hall. With great care, he made his way across the meadow, shielding the maid from as much jarring as he could.

His father met him at the stables and took the young woman from him as Tearle briefly explained the situation as he dismounted. The marquess started toward the house with her, but Tearle caught up with him.

"Let me carry her, Father. She's my responsibility." Lord Sheffeld relinquished his burden, grieving at his son's gray, haggard countenance.

"I agree that it appears to be a kidnapping. It is common knowledge that we are wealthy and that you have children. Of course, now most people know about the wedding. Unfortunately, this type of thing is not uncommon. I suspect you will be receiving a demand for ransom soon." He rested his hand upon his son's shoulder. "When you were children, I lived in fear of this happening; it was even more prevalent then. From most instances I have heard about, the victims are usually returned unharmed once the money is paid."

The earl stopped and looked at his father. "As you said, Father, usually." A look of agony swept over his face. "Do you honestly think a man who stoops to kid-napping could keep his hands off someone like Sloane?"

His father grimaced and gripped his son's shoulder tightly. "It will not do to think the worst, Tearle. We must pray that they are not harmed, and trust that it will be so. You must clear your mind of such a fear. You can't think rationally if you do not."

"I know." He moved through the back door as his father opened it, meeting his mother, Roseanne, Mrs. Honeycutt, and Grimley as he stepped into the room.

"Oh, dear God," cried Lady Sheffeld, scurrying before them, pushing open the hallway door as they proceeded to the back stairs. She clung to the door, stepping aside as Tearle carried Annie through. "You didn't find the children or Sloane?"

"No, Mother," Tearle said gently, stopping by his mother's side. "It appears they have been abducted."

"No, oh no, not my babies," Lady Sheffeld moaned and collapsed into her husband's arms, sobbing.

Poor Roseanne stared at Tearle's back as he disappeared up the stairs. Her gaze shifted to his parents as the marquess helped his weeping lady up the stairs to her room. Frightened and bewildered, she turned pleading eyes to Grimley.

"Please," she begged, "tell me what has happened. Where is my sister?"

Tears welled up in the old servant's eyes, and he took the young woman's hand in his.

Carefully and slowly, he explained what they knew, then put his arm around the young miss and comforted her as she began to cry softly.

Mrs. Honeycutt, wiping her eyes on her apron, called for Bess to attend Lady Sheffeld as she hurried up the stairs to tend to Annie herself. Tearle gratefully turned his charge over to the capable woman, advising that the doctor should be arriving shortly. Assured that she would take care of her and call him immediately if she should come around, he took his leave and went back downstairs.

He stepped into the drawing room to find that Jonathan and Viscount Remington had returned. Jonathan cradled Roseanne in his arms, offering the best solace he knew—his love.

Remington held out a glass of brandy. The earl numbly accepted the drink, sank down in a chair, and stared at the floor after he downed the liquor.

"We found coach tracks not too far from where we discovered the maid," said the viscount. "The ground was damp so there were footprints, too. Three men, a woman, and one child. They must have carried your daughter because her prints were back with the others in the clearing. We followed the coach tracks out of the woods. They took the road to Evesham."

Tearle's head jerked up. "Someone might have seen it."

"I'll ride to Evesham and ask around. We

might at least discover which way they went from there," suggested the viscount.

"Yes, that's a good idea. I don't dare leave in case they try to contact me. If Tom has returned, take him with you. He knows everyone in the village."

"Of course. We'll leave immediately."

Tearle looked up at his new friend as he stood, ready to depart. "Thank you."

"I only wish I could help more."

"I'll send someone to fetch your valet. I'd like to have you stay here. I may need all the help I can get."

The next few hours seemed like a dream to the earl. Jonathan took Roseanne home and informed Sloane's parents of what had happened. The doctor came and left, indicating that Annie was fortunate to still be alive and that if she regained consciousness soon, she might have a good chance of survival. He promised to return early the next morning to check on her.

Jonathan returned, bringing a message from Galen that he and ten men could be ready to ride at a moment's notice, and that the family planned to come to Beckford Hall early the next morning. Soon afterward, the viscount and Tom returned to the Hall with the news that a well-guarded coach had thundered through the village at mid-afternoon, its curtains drawn, and a fierce-looking coachman handling the reins. They also discovered the coach had been seen on the road not far from Worcester.

The earl ordered a late supper for everyone, though most of the plates returned to the kitchen with half the portions left on them. Finally, around eleven o'clock he suggested everyone go to bed. He followed the others from the drawing room, stopping when he saw Brian snuffing the candles in the great hall.

"Brian, I completely forgot about Beau. Was he brought back to the kennels?"

"Well, yes and no, m'lord." The young man's face turned red. "I carried him back from the woods, but seein' as how he's like a little hero, I didn't have the heart to take him to the kennel. I mean, if it hadn't been for him, we wouldn't have found Annie and she might have died. He was muddy and tired so I gave him a bath and fed him, and well, er, he's asleep over in front of the fireplace in the servants quarters."

"I see. Does he like being indoors and treated with special favor?"

"Well, yes, m'lord, he seemed to like it." Brian shifted uncomfortably. "I know he's not supposed to be in the house, m'lord, but it's like he knows somethin' bad has happened to the children. He kept lookin' at me with those big, brown, sad eyes, and I didn't have the heart to take him back to the kennel."

"I understand, Brian. Take him for a walk and then bring him up to my chambers for a little while. Perhaps we can console each other."

Smythe was somewhat surprised when Brian knocked on his lordship's door some

twenty minutes later with the happy bundle
in his arms, but he left the room with a sad
smile as the earl gathered the pup in his arms
and began scratching it behind the ears. As
he turned to shut the door, he caught a
glimpse in the mirror of the earl holding the
animal close, one cheek resting against that
black, wavy fur, the other glistening in the
candlelight from his lordship's silent tears.

Dawn was just breaking when Smythe
knocked gently on his master's door. Opening
it slowly, he found the earl and the puppy
curled up together on the bed asleep. Smythe
gently shook the earl's shoulder.

"My lord, Mrs. Honeycutt has sent for
you." Tearle awoke with a start. "Annie has
regained consciousness, and she wants to
speak to you."

The earl eased his arm from beneath the
pup's head and jumped from the bed,
hurrying to the guest room where Mrs.
Honeycutt nursed the young woman. He
pulled the chair up beside the bed and took
her hand gently in his. Annie opened her eyes,
struggling a minute until they focused on his
concerned, anxious face.

"My lord," she whispered, "I don't know
who took them. I 'ad never seen them before.
Three men, ragged, dirty, large, mean thugs.
One said your family was their ticket to the
good life."

"Did they give you any indication of
where they were taking Sloane and the
children?"

"No. 'e told them to cooperate and no one

would be 'urt. Then, 'e said I wasn't no use to them so one of 'em 'it me.''

"You just rest, Annie. I'm sure we'll find them. You just concentrate on getting well. There was nothing you could do against three men.''

The earl left the maid, changed his clothes, and went downstairs. Soon, the other members of the household joined him and shortly after an early breakfast, Galen and Libby Kincade arrived, accompanied by Tony, Shawn, and Michael Denton. The group spent a long, tedious morning waiting for some word from the kidnappers.

The missive finally arrived in mid-afternoon. A small boy walked cautiously up the steps to the portico and knocked timidly on the front door. Grimley opened it immediately and ushered the child into the library where the earl jumped to his feet and rushed across the room to meet him.

"Do you have something for me, young man?''

"Aye, m'lord. I wuz told t' give you this.'' He held out the note with trembling fingers. Tearle took it, his own hand trembling somewhat, and looked down at the youngster.

"Were you instructed to wait for an answer?''

"No, m'lord. 'e wuz to watch until the door opened and then 'e would leave. I don't know where 'e wuz watchin' from. I didn't see 'im anymore after 'e give me the paper.''

Jonathan dashed from the room, Galen and his sons following him. "We'll see if we find any sign of him," Jonathan called back over his shoulder.

The earl thanked the lad and gave him a few coins, then instructed Grimley to take him to the kitchen for a cake. Walking slowly to the window, he unfolded the message, unconsciously holding his breath. He read it, releasing his breath, his brow furrowed in a puzzled frown.

"Tearle, what does it say," his mother asked impatiently.

"They are demanding two hundred thousand pounds. We are to wrap the money in a cloth and put it in a basket, the kind bakers use to deliver their goods. The basket is to be left on the back right pew in Worcester Cathedral during Sunday morning worship. Once they have the money, they will free Sloane and the children."

"Why, that's two days from now. Why couldn't the delivery be made tomorrow?" exclaimed Libby.

"They probably thought I would need time to raise the money, which is true. No one keeps that amount lying about." He studied the note and turned toward his study. "I'll be back in a few minutes." He glanced up at Libby with a faint smile. "Either I've employed a governess who can't spell, or your brilliant daughter has sent me a message. Keep Mother in here so I can have enough quiet to think."

He stepped into his study, sitting down at his desk, and read the note once again. "Deliver twwo huwndred thouosand pounds to Worrcester Cathsdral during Suntay mornning worshhip. The money shousld be wraepped in a clocth and put in a bakerr's delivury basmket with harb rolls covcring the clothh. Put the basmket on the back rignht peiw in the cathadral. Two hours aftter the money is diliverced lecve Worcesler by Evisham roab. You will find yourr famaly wirting on the roid. Don't try two foollow the one carrrying thhis messege or try to caltch the person picking upp the mowney. Doen't crross us or youw'll never see your famelly again."

He stared at the words and began to circle the misspellings and list the letters on a sheet of paper. It took him several minutes to get even a semblance of what she was trying to tell him. Knowing they took the road to Worcester, he first circled the letters "wor" which appeared twice in the note. Gradually, he worked with the letters, putting them together in sequences that finally made some sense. At last, he leaned back in his chair and read the message he had written: w wor stn hse crumb chmni atic c librari wor help we r wel. He shook his head and leaned back against the chair, closing his eyes, saying the sounds over and over. He stopped and a slow grin spread across his face.

He again picked up his pen, this time writing out the words he thought she wanted to say: W—that would be west, Worcester, stone house, crumbled chimney, attic, see library Worcester help, we are well.

"My darling, you are a genius!" The earl threw back his head and heaved a sigh of relief. He then laughed until tears rolled down his cheeks, tears of mirth, tears of joy, tears of relief. Eventually, he wiped his eyes, still chuckling, picked up the paper and strolled into the library. His mother and Libby looked at him cautiously as if he had lost his mind.

"Mrs. Kincade, you have my compliments."

"Why?"

"For not only having the most beautiful daughter in the world, but also the brightest. She did indeed send me a message. It would seem they are somewhere west of Worcester in the attic of a stone house with a crumbled chimney. They are well, and if I understand her correctly, she has somehow enlisted the aid of the Worcester library or more probably the librarian."

"Tearle, you aren't serious, are you?" asked Lady Sheffeld, as both women jumped to their feet.

"Quite," replied the earl, his eyes twinkling. "As of this morning, at least I assume she wrote this letter this very day, not only was my love well, but she had her wits about her." He grew serious. "As soon as the others return, we shall set out for Worcester. I intend to find this librarian and see if Sloane has somehow contacted him, and if he has any better idea of where they are being held. Then, I think we shall attempt a rescue if all things seem favorable. Otherwise, the money will be delivered as required."

"May I see the note, my lord?" asked Libby. "I'd like to see how my daughter told you all of this."

Tearle handed her the note and his translation, grinning as her gaze flew from one to the other, her eyes growing ever wider. She sank back down on the couch, passing the papers on to Lady Sheffeld when she reached for them.

"I never would have been so clever," muttered Sloane's mother. "She must have inherited it from her father."

Lady Sheffeld read the note and slowly eased back down on the sofa. "I hope the librarian can tell you more. It will take hours to search around Worcester for the house she described."

"Yes, I hope so, too. If he does know something, it may just mean the difference in whether we are able to rescue them before the ransom drop or not."

At that point, Jonathan, Galen, and the others returned. There were several minutes of commotion as they learned the contents of the message and exclaimed over it. They were about to go to the stables and mount up for the ride to Worcester, when Grimley announced that a Mr. James Rogers from Worcester had arrived and asked to speak to the earl immediately.

"Send him in," commanded the earl, anxious to see if Sloane had indeed enlisted other help.

"Good afternoon, my lord. My friend, Willian Anders, is the assistant librarian in Worcester. This morning, a lad came in requesting some books. When he gave Anders the list, he noted the poorly spelled words and the peculiar titles. Being something of an amateur investigator, he decided to see if the lady was sending some kind of message." He handed the earl the copy of the list. "It did not take long to figure out that they had been abducted and that we were to notify the Earl of Beckford." He smiled. "He also deduced that she wanted the lad followed. I don't know where he went because I left shortly after he did, but Anders had the stock boy follow him. If you care to return to Worcester with me, my lord, Anders will probably have a good idea of where the lady is being held." His voice softened. "And, I would assume from the list that there are children involved?"

"Yes, my children and my betrothed. Grimley, tell Mrs. Honeycutt we are leaving within the quarter hour. I believe she was packing a lunch for us." He turned back to the messenger. "You will be generously compensated for your ride today. I can never thank you enough."

"I don't expect any payment, m'lord. I'm along for the adventure. Count me in on any rescue, that is if you intend to try one."

"If the circumstances appear favorable, we will indeed." He frowned thoughtfully. "It will not do if we all ride out together. A large group will only attract attention, and we cannot take a chance that some of the gang are still in the area. Father, Jon, Remington, and I will accompany Mr. Rogers. Tom, you and a groom come along with us in the coach. We will need a means of transporting Sloane and the children back home."

"The boys and I will return home, now," said Galen. "I'll give you time to get on the road and then we'll follow in about half an hour from the time you go through Evesham. I'll instruct the rest of my men to split into two smaller groups and follow at quarter hour intervals."

"Yes, that's good," replied the earl. "Tom, have the other two grooms and the two older stableboys leave in about an hour. Tell Brian he can come along, too, if he wishes. He has proven his worth the last few days. We don't know how many men are involved in this scheme, but I want a small army with me."

Before leaving, the earl went upstairs to get his pistols and to check on Annie. He knocked softly on the door and stepped inside, walking over to the foot of the bed when Bess informed him the young maid was awake.

"How are you feeling?"

"Me 'ead aches somethin' awful," she said weakly, "but it'll take more than a bump on me noodle to do me in. Are you goin' after Mrs. Donovan, now?"

"Yes, we are. We've received a ransom note, which I will pay if we don't rescue them first."

"Rescue them, and give them brutes a sharp knock or two for me, m'lord."

"That I will, Annie." The kindness in his expression vanished, to be replaced by grim determination. "When I'm through with them, they'll wish they had never heard of the Earl of Beckford."

18

The library was closed when the earl and his companions arrived, but the door opened quickly after a sharp knock by Rogers. He made the introductions, then the men rapidly got down to the business at hand.

"Edgar followed the lad to a house west of Worcester. He stayed for a while to make sure it was the place we wanted. During that time, he saw two men go in and out of the house as well as the boy and the young girl he had followed from town. He didn't see anyone else, but he did hear a woman and some children singing. He said it sounded like they were somewhere upstairs."

The earl turned to Edgar, who had listened intently while Anders gave his report. "Is the house made of stone and does it have a crumbled chimney?"

"Aye, m'lord, it does. Looks like the whole thing just up and toppled over. 'ow did you know?"

The earl smiled. "Mrs. Donovan is adept

339

at coded messages. Do we have time to go there before dark?"

"Aye, if we 'urry. It took me about an hour to get back, but then I was on an old nag. Mr. Anders got me a right smart little filly for this trip." The boy grinned at the librarian, who obviously had become something of a hero in the space of the afternoon.

"I wanted to wait for Mr. Kincade, but we can't wait any longer."

"I'll stay here if you want, m'lord," said Rogers reluctantly, tired from his afternoon's work, but not really wanting to miss out on anything. "I can tell them what we're up to."

"Thank you, Rogers. I don't want to attempt anything until I've had time to check the place out and consider all the options. If it looks peaceful, I'm inclined to wait until morning, although I hate to leave them in jeopardy any longer."

The men left the library and to Rogers' immense relief, spied Galen and his sons riding up the street. They were quickly briefed and in a matter of minutes, the road going west out of Worcester shook with the pounding of hoofbeats.

Some forty minutes later, Edgar signaled for the earl to slow down. "The house is just up the road. There is a lane off to the right. It winds around for a little way, then breaks through the trees into a nice big clearing. The house is right in the middle of it."

"Are there trees all around?"

"Aye, m'lord."

The earl held a brief discussion with his father and Galen. It was decided that Anders, Jonathan, and Remington would work their way through the woods on foot to the other side of the house. The earl, his father, and Galen would walk down the lane with Edgar and survey the house from the nearby brush. The others would stay and keep the horses quiet.

Ten minutes later, the earl hid in the lengthening shadows, and pushing aside a small branch, had a clear view of the building. It appeared that someone had just arrived. As the man dismounted, two other men came out of the house to greet him. A young man, whom the earl suspected had been the one to fetch the books, came out of the house and took the horse off to a make-shift pen.

His gaze left the men and searched the attic portion of the house. There were two small windows in the front, but there was no way to get up to them. They watched until the men went inside and it began to grow dark. Just as the earl was turning to leave, he caught the dim flicker of candlelight glowing from the attic window.

They returned to where the others were waiting and moments later, Jonathan, Anders, and Remington joined them. Jonathan was grinning from ear to ear.

"I saw Sloane in the attic window," he said quietly, but barely able to control his excitement. "The candle must have been nearby because I saw her clearly. The window was open and the wind was blowing our way." He grinned at his brother and put a hand on his shoulder. "I heard Jonny fussing at Angela. He said she as taking up too much of the bed."

"Thank God." The earl's eyes filled with tears of relief. He looked away from the others for a moment until he regained control of his emotions. He turned back in time to see Galen dab his eyes with his handkerchief.

"Something else," said Jonathan, "the lane winds around behind the house. There's a big tree in back, and it's sitting right next to an attic window. A man could climb up that tree easily and slip in the window; there's plenty of room." He looked Tearle straight in the eye. "A man could climb out again with a child on his back and get back down the tree easily. The branches are close enough together to make it simple."

"I don't know if Sloane could manage it, m'lord. Not with her fear of heights," said Galen.

"She'll make it, Mr. Kincade, if I have to carry her down on my back, too." The earl glanced up at the sky as a gentle rain began to fall. "Now, gentlemen, let's go back to Worcester. The others have probably arrived by now. I'm sure Mr. Anders and Mr. Rogers can show us an inn where we might lodge for the night. We have some plans to make." He smiled at Galen. "Let's see if we can come up with a good rescue strategy; something as ingenious as Sloane's messages."

* * *

The next morning, Sally lingered upstairs when she came to pick up the breakfast dishes. Harley stood in the hallway talking with Jack, while Sally carefully stacked the bowls. Casting a quick glance at the door, she sidestepped over next to Sloane.

"Me and 'arley picked these up for the little ones," she whispered, reaching in her apron pocket and producing four pieces of taffy. "It ain't much, but we feels just awful 'bout the way they're keepin' you locked up 'ere."

"Thank you, Sally. I knew you and Harley weren't like the others. Why are you here?"

"Jack's me uncle. Me pop ran off years ago, and me mum died last month. I don't 'ave no other place to go."

"And Harley?"

The young woman's face flushed, giving life to her dull complexion. " 'arley's me sweetie. We're goin' to get married if 'e can find a decent job somewheres. Times are 'ard, mum, and there ain't no work. 'e stays around to 'elp me fetch and carry for Jack." She glanced nervously at the door. "Got to go, mum. Jack can be real mean when 'e gets riled."

About nine o'clock, after a game of fish, an attempt at whist, and a vigorous time of Ring Around the Rosie, Sloane surprised the children with the treasured taffy. She quietly explained it was a gift from Harley and Sally, and instructed them not to say anything

about it in front of the men so their bene-
factors would not be punished.

While the children enjoyed their taffy,
she touched her pocket which held the note
from the librarian. Jack had seen nothing
amiss in the message when he read it, but she
hoped the words carried a deeper meaning
than what appeared on the surface. She had
just picked up the book of fairy tales,
planning to read the children another story,
when they heard singing in the distance.

They raced to the front window, opened
it, and peered out. It was a clear, crisp, early
September day, and, as so often happens
when the hint of fall is in the air, sound
seemed to travel farther and with greater
clarity than at other times.

An old, heavily laden tinker's cart was
coming down the lane, pulled by an equally
old horse wearing a straw bonnet with holes
appropriately cut out for her ears to poke
through. As the cart grew nearer, the singing
grew more distinct, and Sloane recognized
the slightly bawdy tune the earl had sung
that night long ago after returning home
from Lady Ebony's ball.

She gasped as that beautiful and beloved
voice drifted to her on the wind, and clamped
her hands over Jonny and Angela's mouths
just in time to prevent their excited
announcement of their father's arrival.
Kneeling down between them, she warned
them to be quiet.

"We must not give them away," she
whispered, "or something bad might happen

to your father. You stay here and wave. Don't worry if he doesn't look up. He knows we're in this house, or he wouldn't be here. I expect someone will come up shortly and make us stay away from the window, so I've got to signal him somehow."

"If we had a flag, we could wave it," whispered Jonny. "Flags are easier to see than hands."

"That's a good idea, Jon." Sloane quickly tore a long piece from her petticoat and raced on tiptoe across the room to the back window. Leaning out, she tied the lacy cloth to a branch just below window level. Only when she started back across the room did she realize she had not grown dizzy from the height.

She peered out the window with the children, studying the two men in the old cart. Anyone looking at the tinker's apprentice would never imagine the man was a titled earl. The man slouched lazily in the seat, his sometimes slurred and mispronounced words giving evidence to his lower-class upbringing. His clothes were worn, the pants torn at the knee and several inches too short. His cap sat on top of straight, dirty brown hair that hung almost to his shoulders.

The man driving, evidently the tinker, sat hunched over in the seat, his elbows resting on his knees, and reins held lightly in his hands. His clothes were ragged and somewhat dirty, and his hat looked like the horse had stepped on it a few times. His hair was gray and straggled, badly in need of cutting. As the cart neared the house, the apprentice stopped singing, and the tinker began calling his wares.

"Pots 'n pans, buttons 'n lace. Put a smile on yer lassie's face. Pots 'n pans, buttons 'n lace."

Sloane smiled and blinked back a tear. The brogue's a bit thick, Papa, she thought, but it's every bit as beautiful as Tearle's singing.

She heard boots stomping up the stairs and took one last look at those below. The apprentice scratched behind one ear, then tipped his head back and scratched beneath his chin like one in need of a shave. In the split second before the door burst open, his purple-blue eyes met hers, sending a multitude of messages.

"Get away from that window," the kidnapper growled in a low voice. He stepped across the room to stand between them and the window when Sloane and the youngsters moved out of the way.

"There's no need to stop, tinker," barked Jack from the front stoop. "Ain't nobody here in need of frilly women's things."

"Mayhap ye gentlemen would be in need 'o some tools, or a new knife? I got some bonnie little blades in back. There's candles 'n flints, leather fer reins, a bucket fer water." He shifted and leaned toward Jack, as if telling a secret. "I've even go' a wee bit o' good ol' English gin."

"Gin, you say?" Jack licked his lips,

thinking about how good he'd feel after a few swigs of the drink. "I could use something to drink." He pulled out a coin and flipped it to Galen.

The earl lazily climbed down from the cart and opened up the side, fetching the gin. "Want anythin' else while she's open?" he asked.

"Naw, this'll do. Now, get on out o' 'ere. We don't like 'aving anybody else around."

The earl closed up the cart and climbed back on the seat, looking as if even that slight movement was a hardship. He slumped down in the seat and eased his head forward, dropping his chin and tipping the bill of his cap over his eyes.

Galen clucked to the old horse and gave her a slap on her flank with the reins. She gave her head a shake and began to plod down the lane as it wound around behind the house.

The earl stayed on the cart until they reached his father and the others in the woods. Jumping down from the seat, he pulled off his cap and wig and threw the wig on the ground.

"Blasted scratchy thing," he muttered. Motioning for the others to gather around, he quickly advised them that Sloane was still there. "She recognized us." He smiled, glancing down at his clothes. "One of the men went upstairs when we got too close. I saw him through the window. I'll give him a few minutes to get back downstairs. With a little luck, they'll decide to have a few drinks now.

There's not enough laudanum in it to put them to sleep, but they'll be groggy.

"It looks like there are only three men, the boy, and a girl. Still, once I get Sloane and the children to the edge of the woods, I want you to surround the house like we planned. Be ready to take cover in case they haven't had any of the gin. They may shoot. Don't take any unnecessary chances. Once Sloane and the children are safe, we'll burn them out if we have to."

When the earl returned to the edge of the woods, Sloane was standing in front of the window, Jonny and Angela by her side. She had removed the cloth from the tree and scanned the woods anxiously. The earl hunched over and crept across the clearing; the wet leaf-covered ground muffling his steps. He hid briefly behind the outhouse and a nearby tree.

Determining the coast to be clear, he swiftly scaled the tree. Sloane and the youngsters stepped back to let him inside, then smothered him with silent hugs and kisses. He broke free, and touched his finger to his lips for continued silence. Picking up *Robinson Crusoe*, he indicated that Sloane should read out loud.

She took the book from his hand and began to read. The earl hoisted Jonny to his back, climbed out the window, and after making sure no one was in sight, quickly descended the tree.

"You stay here and wait for Angela," he whispered to Jonny. "Stay behind that bush out of sight." The earl repeated his climb, transferring Angela to the ground quickly. "Grandfather and Uncle Jonathan are over there in the trees." He pointed to a cluster of three maple trees jutting out slightly from the others. "I want you to run to them, but you must be very quiet, and try not to be seen. Can you do it?"

Two little heads nodded up and down, eyes wide and expressions serious. Jonny took his sister's hand and carefully led her across the yard, keeping a watchful eye on the house. Once they were closer to the woods than the yard, he broke into a run, pulling her along with him. When the earl saw they had reached the safety of the trees, he climbed back up after Sloane.

"That's enough for now, children," she said. "Why don't you lie down and take a little rest. Thank you, dears, that's very nice." She took a deep breath and started out the window, but stopped and drew back. "Someone's coming," she cried softly to the earl who was waiting in the tree.

He scrambled in the window and dove to a corner a few yards from the doorway just as the door opened. Jack staggered through the portal and leered at Sloane.

"I don't care what Carlisle says, I aim to 'ave a taste of you now. 'e might decide to keep you locked up forever." An angry shout exploded from the corner, and Jack turned toward the sound just in time to receive a powerful right fist to the jaw. Seconds later, he was sprawled on the floor from the earl's attack. He looked up at the man sitting on top of him and squinted his eyes. "Who're you?"

"The Earl of Beckford," Tearle snapped.

"Oh, lud," Jack moaned, seconds before the earl's left fist met his jaw. Tearle hit him again with the right. The man's eyes drifted closed, his head lolled to one side, and he lay perfectly still.

The earl listened anxiously for the sound of someone coming up the stairs, but all was quiet below. He winked at Sloane and pushed against Jack's rib cage, lifting himself off the man. Once on his feet, he stepped quickly to the window and gave a sharp whistle.

"Stay here," he commanded, pulling a pistol from his pants. "I'm going to check out below. Since it's so quiet, I assume they all had a drink of Jack's gin." He crept down the stairs and looked around the corner into the kitchen. Straightening, he motioned for Sloane to join him. As she came down the steps, she saw the earl's army encircling the house. She hurried to the door and waved to her father, who quickly dismounted and ran to encompass her in a bear-hug.

"Who was behind the kidnapping?" The earl stood in the middle of the kitchen, hands on hips, glaring at the two drunken souls trying to remain upright by leaning against the wall.

"Some cove named Carlisle."

"Jack said somethin' 'bout the cove's sister, too. A real gentry mort, but nasty to deal with."

The earl nodded grimly, his suspicions

confirmed. "Which of you blackguards hit the maid in the head?"

" 'e did." A grimy finger pointed to the culprit. "I was 'olding the brat."

The earl strode across the room and punched the man in the stomach. "That's from Annie." The man doubled over, then slowly raised his head, and the earl hit him again, this time in the chin. "So's that." He released a sigh of satisfaction and turned to Sloane, holding out his arm. "Let's go home."

"Yes, please," she agreed, snuggling against his side. "Wait, where's Harley and Sally?"

"We're 'ere, mum." The young couple pushed aside a loose board and emerged from the part of the house that had been closed off when the chimney collapsed. Harley's face grew red. "We sneaked in there when we saw 'ow drunk they were gettin'. They didn't even know we was gone. Thought we'd 'ave a little time to ourselves, and all of a sudden, this 'ere gent's standin' in the kitchen, and the 'ouse is surrounded. We didn't know wot to do but stay 'id."

"Tearle, can't we find someplace for these two to work? They didn't really have a part in the kidnapping, and they've been nothing but kind to us. They even bought Jonny and Angela some taffy and gave it to me on the sly."

The earl smiled down at his love and squeezed her side. "Oh, there must be something around the estate they can do. Anyone who buys taffy for children can't be all bad."

He looked back at the wide-eyed pair. "Gather your things and put them on top of the carriage coming down the lane. I'll give you five minutes to grab what you want to take and to climb up top with Tom." He turned to Remington, "Will you take some of my men and deposit these hooligans and the one upstairs with the magistrate in Worcester?"

"Of course. Anything else?"

"Yes, please convey a message to Baron Carlisle and his vile sister. Inform them I know they were behind this whole affair and that if they do not want to be brought before the courts, they should leave the country. I recommend they pay an extended visit to India, say for the next twenty years or so."

"A splendid suggestion. I'll have my man make sure they are on the next ship sailing for India."

The earl thanked him and helped Sloane and the children into the carriage. Once they were settled, he turned his attention back to the commotion in the yard. His men threw the kidnappers across their horses, feet dangling on one side, head on the other, but the criminals were too drunk to care.

Stepping up to Remington, Tearle stopped him before he mounted. "You may miss the wedding," he said quietly. "Unless she is adamantly against it, I intend to marry her this evening. I'll not rest easy until I know Carlisle is out of the country, and I want Sloane with me."

"I'll ride hard," said Remington, with a grin, "but don't wait for me."

"Agreed. Come back to Beckford Hall as soon as you can. I would like you to be our guest, for tonight at least." Remington nodded and mounted as the earl returned to the carriage. He climbed in, sat down beside Sloane, and dropped his arm across the seat behind her.

"Are we going home now, Papa?" asked Jonny, sitting opposite his father. "Has anybody been taking care of Beau?"

"Yes, we're going home now, son, and yes, all of your pets have been well cared for. Beau has been treated like royalty, and he should be since he's quite the hero."

"A hero, Papa?" Both Jonny and Angela's eyes grew wide.

"Yes, if it hadn't been for him, it would have taken much longer to find Annie. He stayed right by her side until we came along. His whimpering is what led us to them."

"Tearle, how is she?" Sloane looked up at him, trying to foresee his answer. When he smiled, she relaxed.

"She'll be fine. It will take a while for her to get back on her feet, but the doctor says she has passed the crisis point."

"Thank God," Sloane whispered fervently.

The earl nodded, then smiled at his children. "When we get home, we'll have a celebration. Knowing Mrs. Honeycutt, she has been cooking your favorite things all day."

"Chocolate cake?" Jonny licked his lips and closed his eyes.

"Yeth, chocolate cake?" cried Angela. "And loth of clotted cream on top."

"You may have as big a piece of cake and as much cream as you want, pet."

"But only after a good meal," interjected Sloane. "Our food has been adequate, but just so."

The earl smiled down at Sloane, his expression soft and full of love. "I'd like another reason to celebrate tonight. Are you up to a wedding?"

Sloane looked down at her gown and made a face. Leaning over, she glanced at his short, torn trousers and grinned. "I'd rather not marry a tinker's apprentice. The earl has much more style."

When she straightened back up, he hugged her close. "You'll have your earl; if I get my countess. I'll give you two hours from the time we arrive home to transform into an exquisite butterfly. I'm certain all the family will be there anyway, waiting for news."

"Are you saying I look like a caterpillar?" Sloane met his eyes with a forced frown.

"Of course not, love." Tearle grinned and kissed the tip of her nose. "You just look like you've been in a cocoon for a few days."

Sloane laughed. "I feel like it, too." She snuggled against him, her head nestled on his shoulder, and her hands sliding around his waist. "I was so glad to see you riding down the lane. If you hadn't come when you did—"

"Don't even think about it, sweetheart. It's over now, and no one can threaten you again. By the by, you're a clever little minx. How did you come up with your secret messages?"

"It was a game we used to play on rainy winter days, when we were supposed to be studying."

"Quiet, madam," he said softly, "you'll give the children ideas." He looked across at the youngsters. Their eyelids were growing heavy from the rocking motion of the coach, and soon they were curled up on each end of the seat asleep.

Tearle and Sloane spent the trip wrapped in each others' arms, sometimes sitting quietly, sometimes talking low, and sharing quite a few gentle kisses.

As expected, when they arrived at Beckford Hall, they were met by a large crowd of family members, including Sloane's grandfather. After the commotion settled down and everyone moved inside to the library, Tearle conferred with the vicar, who happily agreed to perform the ceremony.

Before Tearle had an opportunity to make the announcement, Grimley proclaimed that a buffet dinner had been set out in the dining room. The earl listened to his growling stomach and held his tongue. After they had all eaten, and Jonny and Angela finished off their second piece of chocolate cake covered with clotted cream, the families moved en masse back to the library.

"May I have your attention, please?" Tearle spoke up in a commanding tone and waited a moment until an expectant hush fell over the group. He looked around at the happy faces and smiled. "Since all of you are already here, Sloane and I decided to have our wedding tonight." He motioned at his clothes and winked at his sweetheart. "For some unexplained reason, my bride-to-be doesn't think my attire is suitable for a wedding." He waited until the laughter subsided. "If you will excuse us for an hour, we will go and make ourselves more presentable."

Sloane stopped off to see Annie on her way to her room. She was surprised to find Brian sitting beside the bed, the maid's hand clasped carefully in his. When she entered the room, Brian dropped Annie's hand and jumped from the chair.

"I was just checkin' on Annie, my lady. I'll be on my way, now."

Sloane could see the regret his words brought to the maid's eyes, and she hastily stopped him from leaving. "There's no need for you to go, Brian. I can only stay a minute, since we're going to have the wedding in a little while. I just wanted to make sure you were all right, Annie. How do you feel?"

"I'm growin' stronger every day, mum. I'll be right as rain in no time, but I still get mighty weak when I get up."

"I'm so thankful you didn't fare worse. I insist you take as much time as you need to recover." Sloane smiled at the maid and

Brian. "Stay as long as you like, young man, but don't tire her out too much."

The footman blushed and looked at the floor before slanting his gaze over towards Annie. "Thank you, mum. I'll be careful of her, mum."

"I know you will. Good-night."

Sloane went to her room and found Libby and Roseanne waiting to help her bathe and dress. Exactly fifty-five minutes later, Galen tapped on her door, stepping through when Libby opened it.

"Ah, lass, you do make a lovely bride. Are you ready to go down, daughter? The earl has been pacing around his study for over ten minutes now, and the wee ones are gettin' a mite sleepy."

"I'm ready, Papa." Sloane took one last look in the mirror. Her pastel pink, satin gown draped over her curves gracefully, the row of pearls at the bottom of the flounce whispering around her ankles as she moved. Though the neckline was plain, a row of tiny pearls trimmed the band of each short, puffy sleeve.

The earl's necklace and earrings adorned her throat and ears, speaking of a treasure more precious than those expensive gems. And the glow on her face rivaled their beauty.

Tearle waited at the door to the library, dressed in his favorite dark blue superfine coat, gray pantaloons, a white shirt, and white silk waistcoat.

He watched her come slowly down the stairs, her hand lightly resting on her father's arm, but her sparkling gaze locked with his. His chest swelled with pride. This beautiful creature was his bride, and even more important, she loved him and had taught him how to love.

Galen paused at the library doorway, gave his daughter a kiss on the cheek and moved away.

"Ah, my exquisite butterfly." Tearle smiled and caught her hand in his.

"Thank you, sir, and I see I made the right choice, too." Her crystal gray eyes simmered with mischief, love, and passion as she looked up into his. "I find myself much renewed by my bath. Let us not dally, my lord."

Tearle's fingers closed over her arm, and he propelled her toward the vicar. "Only long enough for propriety, temptress," he whispered.

The vicar made the ceremony simple and as short as possible so the children would not fall asleep in the middle. Both Sloane and the earl spoke their vows in clear, strong tones, promising with every ounce of conviction to be faithful "until death us do part." When told to kiss his bride, Tearle did so with such sweet longing that he brought a tear to her eye.

Immediately after the ceremony, the servants passed around glasses of champagne, and all the adults joined in a toast to the bride and groom. Then, amidst hugs and kisses, Sloane's family left in a flurry of good wishes.

Jonny and Angela were hustled off to bed by the marchioness and Corine; the marquess, Jonathan, and Bailey retired to the study to sip their brandy; and Sloane and the earl suddenly found themselves alone in the library.

Tearle looked around in disbelief and smiled down at his wife. "If I didn't know better, I'd say they just came for the food."

"The past few days have been hard on all of them."

"Not as hard as on me." He pulled her close, drawing a ragged breath. "When I found Annie and knew you had been taken, I thought someone had cut out my heart."

"Thank God it's all over now." She slid her arms around him and rubbed her hair against his chin.

"Let's go upstairs," he murmured.

"Yes, my lord." Sloane raised her head and smiled at him seductively. "You once promised me I'd find pleasure in your arms."

"I never break a promise." He shifted, guiding her toward the door. They were half-way up the stairs, each with an arm around the other's waist, when they heard riders coming up the lane, so they turned around and walked back down to the hall.

Grimley opened the door to admit Viscount Remington. "Well, it appears I missed the wedding after all," he said, with a good-natured smile. "It took longer in Worcester than we anticipated, but I delivered your message to Carlisle and his sister. They were shrieking at each other when we left, but I have no doubt they will leave within a few days."

"Thank you, Ashley. I know you're tired, so we won't keep you." Tearle's wink went unseen by Sloane. "Father, Jonathan, and Bailey are in the study, if you care to join them."

"I think a toss of brandy would be nice before bed. Do you think your cook could scrape up a little supper? Doesn't need to be anything hot, a cold collation would be fine."

"Of course. I'll have Grimley bring it in to you." He glanced at the servant who stood nearby. The old man nodded and shuffled off toward the kitchen, still smiling from the day's events.

"Well, good night. My best to you both." The viscount stepped through the study door without a backward glance.

"Make haste, wife, before someone else arrives," Tearle murmured. They raced up the stairs, laughing and gasping for air as they dashed into the earl's bedroom. He shut the door and leaned against it, watching Sloane slowly walk around the room, looking at a drawing here, a painting there. She stopped in front of his dressing table.

Catching his gaze in the mirror, she unfastened the clasp on her necklace and laid it on the table. The earrings followed as she slipped them from her earlobes and placed them beside the necklace. Still holding his gaze with hers, Sloane slowly reached up and, one by one, removed the pins from her hair and dropped them on the table.

Tearle pulled his cravat from his neck in a quick, decisive move, tossing it onto a nearby chair. He removed his coat and threw it in the same direction, ignoring it when it fell on the floor. Gradually crossing the room, he worked the buttons on his waistcoat and shed that garment also, flinging it over his shoulder to land in a heap near the coat.

Tearle stopped behind her and buried his face in her hair. Lavender surrounded him. He lifted his head and brought his hands up to comb out the silky strands with his fingers.

"You have the most beautiful hair," he whispered, nuzzling her ear. "The moment I met you, I wanted to touch it, to feel its softness beneath my fingers. And that evening at dinner, all I could think about was how much I wanted to make love to you. Every move you made, every word you spoke drew me into your seduction."

She looked at him in the mirror. "I wasn't trying to seduce you."

"I know, love." He pushed her hair over one shoulder and unbuttoned the five tiny buttons on the back of her gown. He smiled wryly at his trembling fingers. "I knew it even then. Somehow, it made the temptation irresistible." Gently brushing aside the satin, he replaced its coolness with burning kisses down her backbone.

Sloane gasped with pleasure, then chuckled sensuously. "I'm glad you yielded."

"Hmmmm?"

"To temptation."

He grinned and gathered her skirt in his hands, pulling the gown up over her head. Tearle started to throw it with the clothing scattered in the corner, but decided against it. Stretching away from her, he carefully laid it on a nearby settee. When he straightened, she had turned around to face him, still clad in her shift, hose, and slippers.

"You're wearing too many clothes, my lord." The earl stood still as she slowly unfastened his shirt, pausing with the release of each button to plant a kiss on his golden furred chest. She tugged the garment from his pantaloons and helped him shrug out of the sleeves. With an impish smile, Sloane tossed it carelessly toward his jacket, giggling when it landed only a few feet away from them.

Tearle laughed and caught her to him. How he loved the way she made him laugh! Her hands caressed him, slowly traveling up around his neck. She pressed her willing, yearning body against his, and he decided he loved the way she made him feel even more.

He touched her lips gently with his, giving and taking, teaching and learning. They drank from the cup of their love for several long minutes until Sloane finally eased back.

"You're still wearing too many clothes, my lord."

"So are you, my lady."

With silent agreement, they stepped apart and undressed, watching each other all the while. Tearle knew she wasn't perfectly made, no woman was, but if she had any visible flaw, his eyes could not see it. Her beautiful body was an exquisite compliment to her lovely face. He raised his gaze back to her face and encountered the same expression he had seen the night she professed to being little more than a servant. This time, her open appreciation was mixed with possession and satisfaction.

He asked the same question he had asked then, knowing his face was a reflection of hers. "Do I meet with your approval, madam?"

"Yes, my lord." She moved across the thick, Turkish carpet into his embrace. He held her close for a moment, then took her hand and led her to the bed, drawing her down with him.

They were weary from the past days' trials, yet the need to seal their vows was stronger than the need for rest. Slowly, they savored each kiss, each caress; warm hands and hungry lips learned hollows and curves, softness and strength, giving pleasure and seeking it. Murmured words of love mingled with soft exclamations of delight until patience was no more and they were united at last.

Their loving was not the wild passionate adventure they would share many times in their lives, but a gentle, sweet fulfillment of hopes and dreams, needs and hearts' desires. Complete, they dropped into an exhausted sleep, wrapped in each other's arms.

Early the next morning, Sloane raised her hands over her head and stretched contentedly. Her gaze roamed around the master bedchamber before coming to rest on the earl's smiling face. He ran his finger gently across her shoulder and leaned over to kiss her tenderly. When he lifted his head, she looked over at the marriage license unfurled on the bedside table.

"I'm certainly glad you picked up the special license. I like a man who thinks ahead."

"I have another surprise for you."

Her gaze skimmed over him. "Well, it can't be in your pocket," she said, with a laugh.

"How astute you are, and so early in the morning, too." He grinned and kissed the tip of her nose. "I talked to your parents last night before you *finally* came downstairs for your wedding—"

"I wasn't late; you were just impatient."

"True." His seductive smile and roaming hand indicated a certain impatience once again. "Now quiet, madam, and let me finish a sentence. Your parents have invited Jonny and Angela to visit them for a few days. My parents are accompanying Corrie and Bailey to Cheltenham, but they will return here in time to see us off to Italy and take over the care of the children. I want you to myself for a few days before we spend a little time as a family."

"What do the children think of the idea?"

"Well, they were reluctant, until I bribed them."

"Bribed?" She wiggled a little closer.

"Yes, I promised them they could have a small pony and cart. Your father will provide the pony. I'll supply the cart, and one of the stableboys to drive it. It should keep them occupied for a little while."

"What about Viscount Remington?"

"Oh, I'll drop a hint that he should go visit his Aunt Gertrude or something. He's a smart man. When he discovers everyone else leaving, he won't stay."

She yawned and snuggled next to her new husband, closing the tiny gap between them. "Jonathan will still be around."

"Only to sleep. In case you haven't noticed, he's pressing his suit with Roseanne. He plans to buy the Billington estate if she likes it. He knows she'll want to live near her family."

"How thoughtful. Tearle—"

"Yes, love?"

"My I use your plunge bath this morning?" She curled a sprig of golden chest hair around her finger.

"You may, but it is no longer mine alone. It's yours, too."

"Will you join me there?"

"Of course." He raised his head, propping it up with his hand and bent elbow. His smile spoke volumes.

"Oh, good; with Annie still recuperating, I don't have anyone to wash my back."

The earl laughed softly, letting his head drop on the pillow. "Your servant, madam—for the rest of my life."

ACKNOWLEDGEMENT:

My thanks to Gill Taylor of Beckford, England, for her tidbits about the Vale of Evesham and the excellent book on Cheltenham. I would also like to thank Roger Beacham, Local Studies Assistant, and Graham Baker, Assistant Divisional Librarian at Cheltenham Library for supplying those hard to find details on the horse races and life in Regency Cheltenham. It wouldn't have been the same without you!